Praise for Lisa Hall

'Breathlessly fast-paced and cleverly unsettling, this thriller about a couple trying to escape their past is the very definition of unputdownable.'
Heat

'An uneasy creeping feeling followed me through the book – I was never quite sure who I should be trusting – I read this book in one sitting because I had to know what was going to happen next. An excellent thriller that had me hooked from the start.'
Katerina Diamond

'A paranoia-inducing plot that makes you question everyone! Lisa Hall's new novel is one to get under your skin and has an ending that'll leave you reeling.'
Sam Carrington

'Gripping and unforgettable... and will leave you wondering who you should really trust...'
Inside Soap

'What a page turner! Compelling, chilling and an incredibly impressive debut.'
Alex Brown

Lisa Hall is the bestselling author of *Between You and Me* and *Tell Me No Lies*. She has dreamed of being a writer since she was a little girl and, after years of talking about it, was finally brave enough to put pen to paper (and let people actually read it). Lisa lives in a small village in Kent, surrounded by her towering TBR pile, a rather large brood of children, dogs, chickens and ponies and her long-suffering husband. She is also rather partial to eating cheese and drinking wine.

Readers can follow Lisa on Twitter @LisaHallAuthor

The Party

Lisa Hall

ONE PLACE. MANY STORIES

HQ
An imprint of HarperCollins*Publishers* Ltd
1 London Bridge Street
London SE1 9GF

This paperback edition 2018
1
First published in Great Britain by HQ,
an imprint of HarperCollins*Publishers* Ltd 2018

ISBN: 978-0-00-821499-9

MIX
Paper from
responsible sources
FSC
www.fsc.org
FSC™ C007454

This book is produced from independently certified FSC™ paper
to ensure responsible forest management.
For more information visit: www.harpercollins.co.uk/green

Printed and bound in Great Britain by
CPI Group, Croydon CR0 4YY

To the real life Katie and Amy

In memory of Frank Moylett – some stars burn brighter than others

Don't you ever wonder what would have happened if you hadn't made that particular decision? If you had decided to go right, instead of left? If you had said no, instead of yes? It's strange how one, tiny, sometimes seemingly insignificant decision can have a knock-on effect on life … like a cleverly constructed domino chain, crashing down into a broken and ruined pile of rubble. Maybe if I had been a little bit stronger, if I hadn't had that one moment of weakness, where I threw caution to the wind and just did what I *wanted* to do, as opposed to what I *should* have done, maybe then, none of this would ever have happened. Life would have gone on as usual, with no tears and recriminations. Nobody would have been hurt. Nobody's life would have been ruined. There wouldn't have been any lies, or betrayal, and we all would have carried on living our lives, completely unaware that everybody has two sides to them, completely oblivious to the fact that the people surrounding us carry their own secrets, locked deep inside them. It's easy to look back and say none of this is my fault, that I am exempt from blame, but deep down, I know that's not true. All of this — everything that has happened — all of it starts with me. And so now, I have to do what needs to be done. I have to finish it, once and for all.

1

NEW YEAR'S DAY – THE MORNING
AFTER THE PARTY

Something happened. Something bad. That's the first thought that swims vaguely through my mind as I struggle my way into full consciousness. Followed by the realization that, *I don't know what, but I know it's not good.* My head hurts. I try to open my eyes, the feeble wash of winter sunshine that tries to force its way through the lining of the curtains making me squint in pain. My head hurts and I feel really, really sick. I close my eyes again, willing the thud at my temples to die down and let me go back to sleep, before I crack one eye open again, a vague sense of uneasiness making me reluctant to keep them closed.

Where am I? Peering out from under the duvet cover, the room is unfamiliar to me and I swallow down the nausea that roils in my stomach. In the dim light, I can make out a large chest of drawers pushed against the wall, the top of it free of any clutter, and a mirror hanging above it. A generic picture hangs on the opposite wall, and there is no sign of anything personal – no photos, no make-up, no clutter that tells me that this is someone's bedroom. A spare room, then, and I seem to be alone, which is good, I think.

The same thought drifts through my mind as when I woke, that something happened last night, something that makes me feel somehow dirty and indecent. Scratching at my arms, I roll on to my back before pushing the duvet away from my clammy face, sweat making my hair stick to my forehead. The touch of fabric against my skin makes me stop for a moment, pausing in my quest to get comfortable, that and the fact that every muscle in my body seems to hurt. Sliding a hand under the covers I feel around – yes, my top is still on. No bottoms though, the fabric against my bare legs is that of the cotton sheets I'm lying on, not my trousers, or pyjama bottoms.

Something bad happened. My heart starts to hammer in my chest as I run my hand over my thighs, wincing at the sharp pain that lances me. Frowning, I push the duvet down, exposing my lower half to the warm air emitted from a large radiator under the window, and struggle my way into a sitting position. *Slowly, Rachel, go slowly.* As I push up on my elbows to shove my way up the pillows behind me, a surge of saliva spurts into my mouth and I swallow hard, desperate not to be sick. The thumping in my head accelerates and black dots dance at the corners of my eyes.

Closing my eyes again I wait a moment, drawing in a ragged deep breath and letting it out slowly. *I've never had a hangover like this before.* The nausea fades, and I run my hands over my lower half again, the skin on the inside of my thighs feeling bruised and sore. I slide my hands between my legs, and my heart beat doubles as I realize the bruised, raw feeling extends to there too. *Oh, God.*

I lean back against the cool of the pillow, eyes closed again against the watery light, trying my hardest to remember what happened last night. There's nothing, not a single thing that I can hook my memory on, just that uncertain feeling that something happened to me last night. It's like there's a gaping hole in my memory, a black bottomless pit that has sucked away any recollection of the previous evening. *Gareth*. What about Gareth? Where is he? I have to get home. I have to see Gareth; he'll be worried (*angry?*) that I didn't come home last night.

Steeling myself, I swing my legs round and out from underneath the duvet, pressing my feet to the floor as dizziness washes over me. My mouth is dry, so dry it hurts to swallow. Spying a plastic water bottle on the floor, half-hidden under the bed, I lean over, another wave of nausea making my mouth water, and take a sip. It tastes stale and dusty, as though it has been there for a long time, but it relieves the scratchiness of my throat, squashing down the bile that sits at the back of it. Placing the bottle back down on the floor, the sleeve of my top rides up to reveal a thick, purple bruise on the underside of my bicep. I poke at it, hissing as the tender skin shrieks out at my touch, the muscle sore and delicate. I wrap my fingers around my arm and see that the bruise is a perfect thumbprint, as though someone has grabbed me roughly. *Remember, Rachel.*

I slide my body slowly down the bed frame until I have sunk onto the immaculate carpet, the thick pile tickling the undersides of my bare thighs, my head pounding in time to a rhythm that no one else can hear. Scrubbing my hands over my eyes, I take a deep breath and look up – I am naked from the waist down, and that needs to be rectified before

I can go anywhere. *I need to get out of here.* Something flutters in my stomach at the thought of the door opening and someone walking in, finding me like this, half naked and vulnerable. Getting to my knees, and squashing down the horrid, shameful thoughts that lurk at the outskirts of my mind at the soreness in my thighs, I crawl towards a tangled mass of black, bunched into the corner of the room, against the mahogany of the chest of drawers. Reaching out a hand, I pull the bundle towards me, unravelling it to reveal my black wet-look leggings. *Thank God.* Relief floods my veins as I recognize the snarl of black fabric as my own clothing, but that fades as I shake them out, searching for my underwear. It's not there. I turn the leggings inside out and back again, hoping that I've pulled everything off in a drunken state last night, but my underwear is definitely missing.

And are you sure that YOU took them off, Rachel? A stern voice whispers at the back of my mind, *the bruising on your thighs … the fact that you can't remember anything … what does that tell you?* I hunch forward over the bundle of cloth in my arms, fighting back tears and the ever-present urge to throw up. *What the hell happened to me last night? What did I do? And who else was involved?*

On shaking legs, now clad in yesterday's leggings, the plasticky fabric clinging uncomfortably to my clammy skin, I gently push open the bedroom door and venture out into the hallway. The murmur of low voices wafts up the stairs towards me, uncertainty making me waver on the landing, not wanting to go and face whoever is down there. At least now though, I have some idea of who it will

6

be — a family portrait hangs at the top of the stairs, and I recognize the tiled hallway and stained-glass windows of the front door below. It's a house that I've only ever visited occasionally, and I've never ventured upstairs, which goes a long way towards explaining why I was confused when I woke up this morning. White Christmas lights glitter around the front door, and the scent of pine from the Christmas garland that circles the banister catches at the back of my throat. A tacky silver banner hangs drunkenly across the wall of the entrance hall, loudly proclaiming for all to have a 'Happy New Year'. The glitter of the lights makes me dizzy and I squeeze my eyes closed for a moment, gripped by vertigo, certain I am about to lose my footing and tumble down the stairs. The dizziness passes, and slowly I make my descent, one hand brushing the wall to keep my balance, as I still feel ridiculously hungover — more than I would ever have expected, the insistent throbbing in my temples making me long for my own bed, and the safe comfort of my own home. My silver sandals dangle from the other hand, found in the opposite corner of the bedroom much to my relief, although I think I would have walked barefoot if necessary.

As I reach the hallway, the tiles almost painfully cold beneath my bare feet, the chatter of voices gets louder, as though a door has been opened. I scoot across the cold tiles into the front room, where all the evidence of a party lies, scattered and ground into the carpet. A Christmas tree, looking worse for wear now, its needles dropping and littering the carpet, shines gaudily in the corner of the room, almost seeming out of place in the grim aftermath of what must have been a raucous party. Several empty wine bottles line the mantelpiece, and glasses litter the coffee table, some empty, some with the dregs of boozy Christmas drinks in the bottom. The table is usually polished to a shine, but now it is marred with glass rings on the wood, crumpled napkins, and several paper plates with the remains of buffet food smeared over them. I fight back the nausea that rises at the sight of left-over canapés, the faint smell of warm seafood hitting the back of my throat. A hefty splash of red wine scars the cream rug in front of the still smouldering open fire, and there are tiny shards of glass glinting on the hearth, where someone has made a drunken attempt to sweep away a broken wine glass. I breathe lightly through my mouth, as the scent of red wine and a hint of stale smoke rises up from the damaged rug. The curtains that line the wide front bay window have been left open, and wintry sunlight glints on a frost-covered garden, watery rays streaming in and highlighting the dust motes that dance in the air.

Turning away from the window, I catch sight of myself in the mirror that hangs above the fireplace, and double take; sure at first that someone else is in the room with me, my reflection looks so unfamiliar in that fleeting glimpse. Stepping closer, avoiding the still damp wine stain, I peer into the glass. I was obviously one of those partaking in the red wine last night – a faint purple stain marks my lips. I run my tongue over my teeth, cringing at the furry feel of them. My face is pale, my long, dark hair framing it in a tangled mess. I run my fingers through in an attempt to smooth it. My eyes look too big for my face, ringed as they are by dark circles. In short, if I thought I felt like shit, I look worse. My belly rolls over as the scent of frying bacon hits my nostrils, and I bend to slide my sandals on to my feet, intent on leaving and getting home before anyone realizes I'm still here.

'Rachel!' A deep, hearty voice behind me almost makes me overbalance, one sandal on, as I wobble precariously on the other foot.

'Neil.' I place my foot back down on the floor, the bruises twinging at the strain in my thigh, and inwardly sigh at not getting out before I was seen, unwilling to engage in conversation when I am so unsure of the events of the previous evening. 'Sorry, I was just …'

'I didn't know you were still here!' Jovial, and with no hint of a hangover, Neil grins at me, and gestures towards the kitchen. 'We wondered where you got to last night … end up in the spare room, did you? Come on through, Liz is in the kitchen, and I've got coffee and bacon on the go.'

My stomach gives another undulating roll at the thought of the greasy, salty meat. I give a small shake of my head and open my mouth to say, '*I'm sorry, I should go*,' but Neil holds out an arm and gestures for me to go first, and despite the ache in my head, the rolling nausea in my stomach, and the underlying fear that streaks through my nerve endings thanks to my black hole memory, I have no option other than to walk across the cold, tiled floor into the kitchen. I have obviously stayed here without my hosts knowing – *so who undressed me?* I remove the one silver sandal that I'm wearing and pad through into the open plan kitchen dining area, the bright sunshine pours in through the patio doors at the back of the room making me feel even more nauseous, if that's at all possible. My neighbour, Liz, sits at the kitchen table, sipping intermittently from a travel mug that sits on a coaster in front of her. She turns as I enter the room.

'Look who I found.' Neil pulls out a kitchen chair and motions to me to sit down, before walking over to the hob and flicking the gas on. He dumps more bacon in the pan and I have to swallow back the saliva that fills my mouth.

'Rachel!' Liz smiles and waggles her fingers in my direction. I slide into the chair next to her – she smells of bacon fat and stale coffee, and I have to hold my breath as she gets close to me. 'How are you feeling this morning? A little worse for wear?' She chuckles, but her face is pale and devoid of make-up, unusually for her. 'I think we all are. Some party, eh?'

'Yes. Some party.' I shift uncomfortably on the kitchen chair, the hard wood of the seat pressing against my bruises.

'Bacon sandwich?' Neil holds out a plate to me, and I try and fail to stop myself from recoiling. 'No New Year's diet actually starts on New Year's Day, does it?'

'No, thank you. Could I just have a glass of water, please?' I don't want to be rude, but I'm not sure I could keep the sandwich down if I ate it. My throat is still painfully dry, and I feel as though my entire body is craving a cold glass of icy water.

'Here.' Liz fills a glass from the water dispenser built into the fridge, her fingers leaving a trail in the condensation on the surface as she hands it to me, and as I reach out to take it from her, I get a flashback. Last night, Liz opening the door to me, a glass in her hand, the smile on her face much the same as it is now – slightly smug, a mildly boozy air about her. I feel the frosty air on my bare arms, as she opens the door and pulls me inside; warm, sweaty

10

air enveloping me, the beat of the music – something Christmassy? An old song, perhaps – thumping through the house. The smell of cloves and woodsmoke in the air – Liz has the open fire lit, even though the house is sweltering. I shake my head to clear the image, setting the bells clanging inside again, and sip at the water.

'Thank you … for letting me stay, I mean.' I sip again at the water, as Liz pulls a chair out across the table from me and sits back down. I try not to wince at the harsh scraping noise the chair makes as she drags it across the tiles. Neil hums under his breath as he slaps bacon between two slices of bread and drops the plate in front of Liz. 'I didn't mean to impose.'

'Oh, don't be silly, you're not imposing.' Liz takes a bite of her bacon sandwich, before dropping a Berocca tablet into her own glass of water. She offers the packet to me and I take one, gratefully, dropping it into my glass and watching the bubbles start to erupt. 'I didn't realize you'd stayed to be honest; I thought you must have left with Gareth.' *Oh shit. Gareth.* He's going to be furious, I should imagine.

'Well, thank you. For the hospitality, I mean. I don't really remember going to bed.' I watch her carefully, hoping that she'll tell me who it was that must have helped me upstairs. *Who bruised my arms, and my thighs, and … worse? And did I go willingly?* Liz gives nothing away, sipping at her travel mug and still munching on her sandwich, taking each bite with relish.

'God, I don't think many of us do.' She gives a huff of laughter through a mouthful of food, a stray crumb flying from her mouth and landing on her plate. It makes me feel sick. 'Never let it be said that the Greenes don't know how to throw a party.'

'Right.' I look away, wanting to ask her if she saw anything, but not wanting at the same time, afraid of what she might say. 'Was I ... was I bad? Like, drunk?'

'Oh darling, we were all tipsy. I don't remember you doing anything you shouldn't have, if that's what you mean. Gareth left early, and you wanted to stay for another drink, no harm in that. It was New Year's Eve, after all.' She pushes her plate to one side, and makes to take my hand but I pull away, grabbing at my glass of water. *No harm. Only, I think maybe there might have been.*

'It's bloody New Year! Gareth needs to lighten up,' Neil says, as he slides his own sandwich onto a plate. 'Rachel, it's lovely to see you, and if you're sure I can't tempt you with my fried pig slices, I'm going to slope off and watch last night's Hootenanny.'

I wait for Neil to leave the room, headed for Jools Holland and a mild food coma if the amount of food on his plate is anything to go by, before I speak again.

'Did we ... did we argue, do you know? Me and Gareth?' I pick at the skin around my nails as I ask, not wanting to make eye contact with Liz, as I feel as though I'm confessing to being absolutely hammered last night. *You're a disgrace.* The words float through my mind, spoken by someone else, an unseen, unknown someone, and I feel a hot flush of shame. 'I know he must have left without me, but I just wondered if we'd had a disagreement about things and that's why he left.' I raise my eyes to look at her, as she sips from her travel mug again, gripping it tightly in her hands as if afraid I might snatch it away.

'No, not that I'm aware of,' Liz says briskly, but her eyes slide away from mine, and I get the feeling that maybe she's not telling me something. 'He's probably at home wondering where you are.'

'Oh God, probably. I need to go. Thank you for … everything.' The urge to leave overwhelms me and I push back the chair roughly, slipping my sandals back onto my feet, the straps rubbing across the top of my foot. Startled, Liz gets to her feet but I hurry out of the front door before she can speak again, calling out a goodbye to Neil, and step out into the cold January air. Frost glitters on the front path, and I carefully make my way across the square to my own house, where I can make out the glow of the Christmas tree lights through the front window, calling me home. Home, to Gareth. Hoping that he can shed some light on what happened last night – why I can't remember anything … and why my body feels as though something, or someone has broken into the very core of my being.

2

As I walk up my own front path, the chill morning air making my exposed toes shriek with the cold, I realize that I don't have a door key. My heart sinks at the thought of having to ring the bell and not only face Gareth's wrath at not coming home, but also waking him up. Gently I press down on the door handle, sighing with relief when it gives under the pressure. I slide in through the door, closing it on a whisper behind me. Maybe if I can make it into the front room without being seen and get my shoes off, Gareth will just think I spent the night on the couch. I'm not sure why I feel like this is the best course of action, maybe because after everything that has happened between us over the past few months I doubt if he's likely to believe that I spent the night at Liz's, alone. I desperately want to avoid us having another row – I don't want to start the New Year with us fighting. And I don't know right now if he'll believe me when I tell him that I don't know what happened last night.

I blink back the hot tears that sting my eyes and pull off my shoes, before I push open the door to the living room. As I step into the room, Gareth stands from where he has obviously been sitting on the couch, waiting for me. He looks tired, the skin around his eyes grey and wrinkled,

15

worry pulling at the corners of his mouth. He still wears the shirt and jeans that he pulled on to wear to the party.

'You decided to come home then.' His voice is flat, his eyes cold. 'That's good of you.'

'Please, Gareth,' I force the words out, too tired and feeling far too fragile to be able to argue with him right now, not when I can barely stand up straight. 'Can we talk about this later?'

'Later? Are you kidding me?' As the level of his voice rises, so does the pounding at my temples, and once again I have to fight the urge to be sick. 'Rachel, you don't get to stay out all night, especially after what you've done, and then tell me we'll talk about it *later*.' He snorts in disgust. 'Look at the state of you, you're a disgrace.' His words sting, just as they are supposed to, and I close my eyes against the nausea that the words induce.

'Look, I didn't stay out on purpose, OK?' I rest a hand on the back of the couch, to steady myself, the heightened emotion making me feel dizzy. 'I was at Liz's, I swear. I … I stayed in the spare room. Please, Gareth, I don't want to argue.'

'Oh right, that's OK then, isn't it?' He steps towards me, a flash of anger in his eyes, and I feel ever so slightly afraid of him at that point, afraid that he's so angry he'll go one step further than just shouting at me. When he speaks again, his voice is low, the words catching in his throat, and it's as if all the rage has suddenly drained out of him. 'I'm not an idiot, Rachel.'

'You can ask her!' I take a step backwards, stumbling slightly as I pull my hand away from the couch, dizziness making me lose my footing. I close my eyes briefly, wanting the world to stop for just a second. 'I swear to you, Gareth, I stayed at Liz's. On my own.' I push away the thought of the soreness in my thighs, the bruise on my upper arms, the layer of fear that sits just under my skin, jangling my nerves and making me afraid to remember.

'You said you were going to stay for one more drink, Rachel. That was just after midnight, and now you're only just getting home, ten hours later.' Gareth raises his eyes to mine and I am shocked to see they are bloodshot and raw, as though he's been crying. 'What the hell am I supposed to think? My wife stays out all night, with no explanation, and I'm supposed to just be OK with it?' Before I can answer he speaks again, his voice hard once more, the flinty edges of his words scraping at my nerves. 'I saw Ted there, Rachel. Don't take me for a fool.'

'Ted?' Confused, I try to think, *did I see Ted? Was Ted there?* Nothing, I can't remember anything, just that gaping black void and a sense of vulnerability. 'What does Ted have to do with things, Gareth? I told you, anything between Ted and me is over, it's been over for weeks.' He huffs out a noise that sounds like laughter, but isn't, cut with a sharp, bitter edge, before pushing past me towards the kitchen. Angry, confused, and desperate to clear this up so I can just go and lie down and try to get things straight in my head, I follow him as he stalks over to the work surface and snatches up his phone.

'Gareth, please. Why would I lie to you? I told you it was over with Ted, we agreed that we'd try and make this work, so why would I jeopardize it? I chose *you*, Gareth.' I want to reach out to him, but he bristles with animosity, so instead I tug my sleeves down over my hands. 'I'm sorry

17

I didn't come home, I slept in the spare room at Liz and Neil's house, I swear.'

'Then why didn't you answer your phone?' Gareth throws his phone across the kitchen table at me and I fumble to make the catch, almost dropping it. Swiping across the screen I see the unanswered calls and text messages that he's sent to my phone over the course of the previous evening.

'I …' I lay his phone down and run my hands over my hips, even though I know the cheap, tacky leggings don't have any pockets, and my phone isn't in there. It hasn't even crossed my mind to think about my phone, so intent was I on getting home to Gareth. 'I don't have my phone; I don't know where it is. I must have lost it.' I picture the room I woke up in, Liz's spare room, but I don't recall seeing my phone anywhere – definitely not in the jumble of my clothes that I found on the bedroom floor.

'You had it last night. I asked you, before I left, if you had your phone and you waved it at me. So, if you had it then, where is it now?' He folds his arms across his chest and waits for me to answer.

'I told you, I don't know. I must have dropped it somewhere at the party. I'll call Liz and ask her if she's seen it.' I move towards the landline phone that hangs on the kitchen wall, before I remember that I don't know Liz's number, not off by heart. It's stored in my mobile, like everybody else's.

'Leave it, Rachel. I don't want to hear any more, OK?' Gareth sighs, and scrubs his hands over his face, wearily. 'You can tell me whatever you like, stories about staying at Liz's or whatever, but I don't want to hear it. Not now.

Did you even stop to think about Robbie? About what he might think about you staying out all night?'

'Where is he?' Guilt creeps over me in a hot wash, as I realize that Robbie, my boy, the one thing that has kept me going through all of this with Gareth and Ted, will know that I didn't come home last night. My cheeks burn with shame. 'Is he home?' I don't want him to hear us arguing — he might be eighteen, but he's had to listen to us rowing for long enough, no matter how hard I've tried to protect him from it. When Gareth and I agreed to make this work between us, I swore to Robbie that the rows were over.

'No, he's not home. He stayed at Sean's last night, if you remember.' Gareth turns away and busies himself by putting the kettle on and I realize this is also eating away at him. Not only did I not come home, but also Robbie stayed at Sean's last night — at Ted's, if you want to get technical about it.

'Sean's been his best friend since primary school, Gareth, you can't begrudge him spending time with him just because of what happened.'

'Oh, you mean when you decided your best course of action was a rampant affair with Sean's father, you mean?' Gareth slams a mug down on the counter and whirls round to face me, a deep red flush burning its way up his neck. 'Just fuck off, Rachel. You can't tell me how to feel, or how to act when you prance around doing whatever you want, not caring if you make me look stupid, not giving a damn if people think you're a whore.' On that last, spiteful word, one that scorches and burns, he slams his hand down on the table and I flinch.

'I can't talk to you right now,' I whisper, my whole body aching as though I have the flu, my head thumping and the fear and disgust that I first felt upon waking beginning to flood through my veins again. I don't wait to hear if he answers, just run from the room and upstairs to the bathroom, where I lock myself in and let the tears come.

Hot water thunders into the bathtub, and I move slowly and cautiously, aware of the muscles that twinge and pull with every movement I make as I pour in my own blend of aromatherapy oils and reach for a clean towel. I pull the leggings from my body, peeling them away from my skin, leaving my exposed legs feeling clammy and sweaty, before throwing them towards the laundry basket that sits next to the shower. They miss, landing in a heap on the bathroom floor, looking much the same as they did screwed up on the bedroom floor at Liz's. Sighing, I bend to pick them up, the sudden movement jarring my head and making bile rise in the back of my throat. Shoving the leggings deep down into the basket I have to move quickly to reach the toilet, before the vomit that has been threatening all morning rises up, quickly, urgently, scorching the back of my throat as I throw up the glass of water and anything else that was in my stomach, until finally, I crawl into the bathtub, exhausted and weeping.

I *know* that something happened last night at Liz's party … I rotate my arm, brushing away the bubbles that cling to it, in order to inspect the bruise on my bicep. It's a deep, angry purple colour, sore and tender, clearly the result of someone holding me far too tightly, but who? And what did I do? Did I upset someone? *No.* I shake my head; despite the way it seems to make my brain roll around inside my skull.

My fingers slide into the warm water, smoothing over the skin on my inner thighs. I clear a hole in the bubbles, raising my leg up and out of the water, flinching at the chill air that hits my skin. Peering closely, I can see now that there is more bruising to the inside of my thigh, round greenish-purple dabs, almost like fingerprints, that hurt when I press lightly on them. *Jesus.*

Sliding my legs back into the water, hiding the bruises from sight, I lay my head back against the cold enamel of the bath, hot tears stinging my eyes. *Think, Rachel, you have to remember.* Taking a deep breath, I sniff away the tears and try to pull myself together. The only way to deal with this is to try and remember what happened yesterday – then I can decide how best to move forward. Closing my eyes, I let out the breath I've been holding and try to concentrate. I remember getting ready…Gareth was in the shower, and I was drying my hair in front of the bedroom mirror, Radio X playing loudly in the background, and I remember feeling annoyed by one flick of a curl that I couldn't get to lie flat. Gareth came in from the shower, towel wrapped tightly about his waist, smelling of Hugo Boss aftershave and the fresh scent of shaving gel. He had tutted at my singing, as I wailed along to 'Boys Don't Cry' by The Cure, and I remember feeling secretly relieved that he was in a good mood, seeing as he'd spent most of the afternoon complaining that he didn't want to go to the party.

'Why are you tutting?' I had grinned at him in the mirror, while putting the finishing touches to my hair. 'Don't you like my singing?'

'Ha.' Gareth looked up from buttoning his shirt. 'Let's just say … I didn't marry you for your voice. You have far better talents than that.'

The unexpected compliment had brought tears to my eyes, and I had blinked them away quickly before my mascara could run.

'I could say the same for you,' I stood up, pushing the chair away from the mirror, to find Gareth had crossed the room and was standing directly behind me.

'You look lovely ... really beautiful.' He had looked down at me, brushing that stubborn curl that just wouldn't lie properly away from my forehead, before giving me a soft kiss on the lips, not even minding my pink lip gloss. 'Just, please ... and I'm begging you, now ... don't sing any more.'

I had swatted him on the arm, laughing, feeling buoyant and as though maybe, just maybe, we could put things behind us. I remember shivering as we crossed the green, on our way to the party, too stubborn to wear a coat, or a jacket, as it would have ruined my outfit and Gareth pulling me into him to keep warm, the huff of his breath on my hair as he laughed at me for being so ridiculous.

So, we were OK, at least when we set off for the party. Tears sting my eyes again, at the difference in Gareth's tone this morning when I arrived home. Another memory swims into view – the one that came to mind earlier this morning – Liz, pulling the door open and smiling at me, the faint scent of booze on her breath as she leaned in to kiss me on the cheek, Neil's raucous laugh in the background. That's all I remember. The rest of the night is just a blank, a darkness so thick and dense that I don't feel as though I'll ever see through it. My head feels packed full of cotton wool, fuzzy and blurry, as I wash myself slowly and deliberately, scrubbing every inch of my exposed skin, until I feel raw and sensitive, my usually pale skin shining a vivid pink as I roughly towel myself dry. My fingers skim over my inner thighs again, and I wince, unable to stop myself from pressing down on the bruising that mars the otherwise unblemished skin.

Pulling on clean pyjamas, I climb into bed, embracing the cool of the cotton and the darkness provided by the black-out blinds, trying to think rationally through what I do know. *What happened? Did I go upstairs willingly with someone and let them do this to me?* No, surely not. *Was I angry with Gareth – did we fight?* Not that I can remember – I remember feeling happy, as we walked over to the party. I didn't have that feeling this morning, the one that I've woken up to so many times lately – that prickly, miserable feeling that tells me Gareth and I went to bed on an argument. *And even if we had argued, I wouldn't have slept with someone else at the party to get back at him. I wouldn't have slept with someone else willingly, not after what happened with Ted, and the hurt and upset that caused.*

As I try to fall over the edge into sleep I fail miserably, as I attempt to force away the only other answer I can come up with as to what happened at the party last night. The idea clings stubbornly, like a stain that'll never wash out, which is appropriate really, and every time the words cross my mind I feel that same wave of nausea. *Something bad happened. Someone did this to me – someone hurt me, and did things to me against my will. Someone raped me.*

23

3

AUGUST – FOUR MONTHS BEFORE THE PARTY

I catch sight of Gareth's scowling face in the mirror as I lean in to smack my lips together, evening out the pink lipstick that stains them. He is frowning as he buttons up his shirt, his displeasure written across his face, and I sigh.

'Please, Gareth, I know you're not keen, but will you try and enjoy today? It's a barbecue, for heaven's sake, it's supposed to be fun.' Flicking my hair over my shoulders and smoothing the flyaway ends down, I stand, ready to head downstairs and put the finishing touches to the food. It's our turn to host the cul-de-sac's annual summer barbecue, much to Gareth's horror.

'I've got things to sort out – work to finish – this is the last thing I want to do this afternoon. You could have spoken to me before you agreed to it,' Gareth grumbles, shoving his feet into deck shoes, before marching over to the bedroom door and shouting for Robbie to get a move on.

'He's nearly ready.' I lay a hand gently on his shoulder, wanting to soothe him a little, or at least make him a little less fractious. If we're going to spend the afternoon and into the evening with the rest of our friends and neighbours on the street, then I want to him to at least be civil, even if he can't completely shake off the tension that seems to surround him lately. 'Look, I know it's not ideal, us hosting the barbecue when you're so busy with work, but look at it this way – at least it won't be our turn to host it for a few years after today.' I give him a smile, but he just rolls his eyes.

'OK. Let's get on with it. Hopefully the sooner people get here, the sooner they'll leave.' Gareth shrugs my hand off his shoulder and thunders down the stairs, leaving me with a familiar feeling of rejection, one that seems to be all too common at the moment.

The afternoon is warm, the sky a perfect, deep blue, and I've made a huge pitcher of sangria that is going down a little too well. I am hot and exhausted by mid-afternoon, having spent much of my time dashing backwards and forwards between the barbecue area and the kitchen, and topping up everybody's drinks. Gareth has spent the afternoon hunched over the grill, flipping burgers and shouting instructions to me every five minutes, somehow managing to avoid too much interaction with our guests. I'm pretty sure that none of them have picked up on the tension between us, but Lord knows I could do with a drink. Satisfied that everyone is happy for a moment, I double check Gareth has a drink before sliding into the garden chair next to Amy, my best friend. She smiles as she looks up and holds her glass out for me to top up from the jug I've brought out from the kitchen.

'Hey. How's things?' She glances over to where Gareth now stands with Neil at the barbecue, beer in hand and seemingly in a better mood, and raises her eyebrows at me.

'Hmmm. Could be better.' I take a large sip of the sangria, wincing slightly at the burn of the brandy on my tongue, still feeling raw and ever so slightly hurt by the way Gareth spoke to me before people arrived. We haven't had an opportunity to speak at all since people got here, apart from his barking instructions at me, and last time I looked he'd still got that frown on his face. 'He's got the arse because he doesn't want to be hosting today.'

'He seemed OK when I arrived? Well, not miserable anyway.' Amy looks at me quizzically and I sigh inwardly. Gareth has this knack of turning on the charm when it suits him. No one would believe that he doesn't actually want any of them to be here, or that we'd had a disagreement before they arrived, he hides it so well, coming across as good old Gareth, so friendly and charming. What a guy.

'Believe me, he doesn't want the neighbours to be here. He said he's got things he should be doing – work, you know,' I roll my eyes, 'but it's our turn. We argued about it before everyone arrived – he said that I shouldn't have agreed to host, not without discussing it with him first, but what was I supposed to say? We couldn't very well just say we weren't doing it, not after everyone else has hosted.'

'So things are still a bit difficult?'

'*So* fucking difficult at times. It's like a rollercoaster – sometimes he's just … brilliant. The Gareth I married – funny, kind, the old Gareth, you know? He'll do something unexpected, something that makes me think, *oh, that's why I love you.* And then other times …' I resist the urge to lay

my head on Amy's shoulder and cry. 'Other times he's just …
impossible. Constantly in a foul temper, but when I ask him
he tells me it's none of my business, or that nothing is wrong.
Either that or he just completely ignores me – literally, he just
blanks me when I speak to him, just carries on staring at his
phone. And then when he does speak to me, all we do is row.
It's awful for me – it must be hell for Robbie.' I look over to
where Robbie stands with his primary school best friend,
Sean, and his father. There's no sign of Angela, Sean's mother.
The West Marsham rumour mill has it that Ted and Angela
are on the verge of splitting up – apparently, she's been getting
friendly with her yoga teacher – and the fact that she doesn't
seem to be spending much time with Ted at the moment is
only fuelling the gossip. Robbie says something and they all
laugh, Ted – Sean's father – clapping Robbie on the arm. Ted
obviously doesn't seem to be too bothered by the rumours.
Either that, or he has utter faith in Angela's fidelity. Across from
them, Gareth stands alone at the grill, his mouth set in a grim
line. I incline my head towards him and Amy follows my gaze.

'Ahhh. I see what you mean. I don't know what to
suggest – if he won't talk to you properly, have you tried
suggesting counselling?'

I drain my glass, letting out a bark of laughter.

'Are you kidding? If he won't talk to me, there's no way
he'll even consider counselling. To be honest, Amy, Rob's old
enough now … sometimes I think it would be easier to leave
him and just start again.' Abruptly I get to my feet, under the
pretence of finding a fresh pitcher of sangria, but in reality, it's
so Amy doesn't see the tears that spring to my eyes.

'Rachel!' Gareth's voice cuts through my thoughts. 'Little
help here, please!'

I walk over, trying to keep a smile on my face as our guests look on, the empty pitcher dangling from one hand.

'Can you get rid of these things, please?' Gareth forces a smile, but you could cut the tension between us with a knife. He leans in close. 'You did say you'd take the empty trays in to leave me some space.'

'I was busy,' I hiss, anxious not to let our guests overhear, 'I've been trying to keep people entertained.' I snatch up the trays, trying to balance them and the empty glass jug without anything crashing to the floor. Walking away, I don't wait for Gareth to reply, knowing that whatever I say today won't help things.

'Here, let me.' A voice stops me, and a warm hand lands on my wrist. I look up to see Ted. 'You look like you're about to overbalance.'

'Thank you.' I smile up at him, letting him take the top two trays and the jug. He walks away, towards the kitchen and I glance over to see if Gareth has noticed. He hasn't.

I manage to relax a little after that, the tautness of my nerves loosening as the drink flows and the afternoon cools into early evening. Gareth also seems to be more like his old self, putting away the scowl that's permanently fixed to his face lately and actually engaging with people, now that the food is cooked and he doesn't have the excuse of the barbecue to hide behind. He still doesn't speak to me, though, and before long I stop worrying about what he is doing and whether he is making an effort, and try to enjoy the party.

Robbie disappears after a little while, telling me he's going to meet Courtney, a girl I know he has his eye on.

I wish him luck and tell him to make sure he has a door key, before settling back in to conversation with Liz, Amy and Natalie, all of us gossiping and swapping stories. It is dusk when Jonno and Melody, the neighbours from two doors down arrive, Melody greeting me with a hug and Jonno greeting Gareth with a hearty clap on the back, a fug of alcohol already surrounding them as they squeeze into the circle of friends and neighbours that sit around the small bonfire Robbie lit before he left.

Staggering slightly as I get to my feet, the sangria I've been steadily drinking hitting me as I stand, I wander towards the kitchen intent on getting drinks for the new arrivals, as Liz greets them with boozy kisses and Neil forages under the cover of the grill to find them a leftover burger. I am humming slightly under my breath as I peer into the wine rack for another bottle of red, the alcohol firing a warm buzz through my veins, when someone grips me tightly by the arm. Shocked, I drop the glass I'm holding and it shatters across the kitchen floor.

'Shit.' I pull away, rubbing at my arm as Gareth appears beside me. 'What the hell did you grab me for?' Scowling, I open the cupboard under the sink and start rummaging around for a dustpan and brush.

'Party's over.' Gareth pulls at my arm again as I stand, dustpan in hand. 'Come on, it's time to wrap it up. You've had enough to drink.'

'What? No, the party isn't over – Mel and Jonno have only just arrived! I need to clean this mess up. And I'm not drunk.' I bend and start to sweep clumsily at the glass on the floor, but Gareth shifts so that he blocks my way. 'Gareth, move, please. Someone could cut themselves.'

'I said *leave it*. The party is over. You need to come out and help me tell everyone it's time to go. *Now*.' He leans down and pulls me upright, almost knocking me off balance into the broken glass, as I put out a hand to steady myself.

'And I said *no*. Everyone is out there having a good time — everyone apart from you! I don't know what the problem is Gareth, but I've just about had enough — do you realize that?' My voice is raised, my throat thickening with tears of anger. 'You're unbearable at the moment, I don't know what's going on but ...'

'Keep your bloody voice down. There's nothing going on. These people have had our hospitality all day — I said the party is finished, so let's go out there and wrap it up.' He grips my upper arm again and I tug away violently, alcohol and the slight buzz of fear making my stomach clench.

'No. No, I'm not telling people to leave, it's far too early.' My palm throbs, and I look down to see a thin line of blood welling up.

'Fine. If what these people think is more important to you than I am, that's fine. You do what you want.' With that he storms towards the front door, leaving me shocked and confused by his outburst, with no idea what has brought all of this on, before shouting after him.

'Fuck you, Gareth!'

There is a light tap on the bathroom door as I lean over the sink, splashing cold water over my puffy, tear-stained face. I've picked a shard of glass out of my hand and managed to stop the bleeding, before dissolving into tears

31

at the thought of Gareth storming out and having to deal with his bad mood when he decides to come back. Thinking it's Amy checking up on me, I call out a soft, 'Come in,' before burying my wet face in a towel.

'Are you OK?' The voice isn't the one I'm expecting to hear, and as I lower the towel I see Ted's face peering round the doorframe at me, concern in his eyes.

'I'm fine, thank you.' Hanging the towel over the edge of the bath I turn back to the mirror, avoiding Ted's gaze as I fuss at my fringe.

'I didn't mean to … barge in on you or anything. I just, well I overheard you and Gareth in the kitchen and I wanted to make sure you were OK. It looked like you'd cut yourself.' Ted steps fully into the bathroom and gently pushes the door closed.

'I did. I mean, it's fine, just a scratch. Oh God, I'm sorry.' Covering my face with my hands I swipe quickly at the tears that spring easily to my eyes, the way they do when you've been on a crying jag, made worse by Ted's kindness and concern. 'I'm so embarrassed, I didn't realize anyone overheard us.'

'Hey, shhh,' Ted crosses the room in one easy stride and yanks a length of tissue paper from the holder, handing it to me as I start to sob.

'I'm sorry,' I hiccup again, scrubbing at my face with the tissue, but Ted pulls my hand away, his fingers closing easily around my wrist as he pulls me towards him. 'Oh, God, I have to go out there and tell everyone they need to leave.'

'I can do that. I'll tell them that you've got a migraine and Gareth is looking after you. Don't worry.'

I let out another hiccup-y sob at his kindness. 'Thank you. I'm sorry, I can't seem to …'

'It's OK, Rachel, you can cry if you want to.' I bury my face in his shirt, inhaling the cool, fresh scent of his aftershave, something sharp and citrusy that makes me think of Italy, and a holiday we spent staying on a lemon grove. I stay there for a long moment, feeling the thud of my heart against his chest, as he breathes in and out, before I look up to see him staring down at me. Without thinking, without even trying to stop myself, I reach up on my tiptoes, planting my lips firmly against his. Holding my breath, I wait for him to pull away but he doesn't, instead just moves his mouth against mine. I feel light-headed, the booze and the intoxicating smell of Ted's aftershave making the room spin lightly and I hold tight to his shirt in a wave of dizziness.

'What about Angela?' I breathe, pulling back, my heart pounding in my chest. *What about Gareth?* Yes, I know it's wrong, and I know that I am probably going to regret this in the morning when I wake up with a raging hangover, my head thumping and my mouth sour, but it's been so long since Gareth has been anywhere near me that my skin is aflame by Ted's touch, and I'm not sure what I'll do if he stops.

'She's left. Angela and I aren't together any more.' Ted mutters, pulling me back towards him. Our mouths crush together and I can taste beer and cigarettes on his breath. It was just a kiss – at least, that's what I try to tell myself after, when I wake the next morning feeling sick with shame. One drunken, unexpected kiss when I was feeling low, that eventually leads to so much more. That's how it starts. That's how I end up tangled in a dirty, sordid – and if I'm brutally honest – intoxicating, exciting, *enjoyable* affair with Ted Durand.

4

JANUARY – NEW YEAR'S DAY

A dip in the mattress as somebody's weight leans against the back of my leg pulls me from the uneasy doze I've fallen into. I've slept for a while – the light is almost gone, the bedroom swathed in darkness with just a faint orange glow from the streetlights outside – but it's not been a restful sleep; dark images and shadowy thoughts exaggerated in my dreams. Turning from where I lay on my side, I roll over to see Robbie perched on the side of the bed. He leans over to switch on the bedside lamp and I squint slightly as the yellow warmth chases the last of the shadows from the room.

'How are you feeling?' He hands me a glass of water and a packet of paracetamol as I struggle my way into a sitting position, the duvet tangled around my legs.

'Better,' I lie, swallowing the pills with two huge gulps of water. The insistent thumping in my head starts up again as my brain protests at being upright, but the nausea seems to have subsided a little, so I'm not completely lying. 'Where's Dad?'

There is only silence from downstairs.

'He's gone out. He said you were up here sleeping it off, but when you didn't come down for dinner I thought I'd just better check that you were OK.'

'Dinner?' I look at the clock on the bedside table, squinting at the numbers in the dim light. 'Oh Rob, I'm sorry, I didn't realize it was so late. Did you eat? I can get up now and make you something.'

'No, Mum, it's fine, honestly. Dad made a curry earlier – he said you always like a curry when you're hungover. We saved you some.' I give him a grateful smile, even though the thought of food makes my stomach roll.

'And now Dad's gone out?' I frown, the chalky aftertaste of the pills thick on my tongue. 'Did he take Thor for a walk?' Thor, our ancient beagle, and possibly the most inappropriately named dog in England. A splatter of rain hits the bedroom window and I frown again, knowing how Thor hates to go out in the rain, and hates to go out in the dark even more.

'No, I don't think so. He just said he was going out. Look, Mum, are you OK? You look really pale.'

'I'm fine, honestly. Just a little bit hungover, like Dad said.' I can't tell him the truth – not yet, anyway – that deep-seated maternal urge to protect my child from knowledge that will hurt him is in full swing. I smile to make the lie seem more like the truth, but my mind is whirring away in overdrive.

It's New Year's Day – where on earth would Gareth have gone? Surely everything is closed, it's not like he's got shopping to do. There is a little tickle at the back of my mind, a familiar one from the summer – the voice that whispered to me that maybe the reason why Gareth was so unbearable – snappy, irritable and secretive – was because he was having an affair. Then that makes me think about Ted, and the party, and what could have happened last night – no, not what *could have*, what *did*. My stomach turns over, and I have to swallow down the saliva that spurts into my mouth.

'I could make you some tea?' Robbie says tentatively, looking like a small boy again, and I wonder exactly what Gareth has told him about last night. Judging by Rob's reaction to me, he thinks I've just overdone it on the wine and I've got a raging hangover.

'That would be lovely. I'll be down in a minute.' Robbie leaves the room, thundering down the stairs like a baby elephant and I lie back on the cool pillows for a moment, before I force myself from the safety of the bed, the comfort of the bedroom, downstairs.

It's almost midnight before Gareth comes home. Our roles are reversed, and this time it's me sitting in the dark, nursing a lukewarm cup of tea, with Thor snoring at my feet. Robbie asked me if I minded him spending the night at Sean's again tonight, and I told him to go, secretly relieved that he wouldn't be home when Gareth came in, wouldn't be there to hear what I have to say. My head feels less foggy now after my sleep, and the more I think about things the more I am convinced that whatever happened to me last night happened against my will. I wouldn't have done that to Gareth – not after Ted, despite what people may think about me now, the thought of an affair never crossed my mind before Ted – and the fact that I can't remember anything past the start of the evening fills me with terror, especially as I don't think I drank that much. I hear the front door close, the lock engaging with a *snick*, and a few seconds later Gareth stealthily creeps into the living room, where I sit, waiting. He gasps as I flick the lamp on, clearly expecting me to be upstairs sleeping.

'Shit, Rachel, you scared me.' He holds one hand to his chest and I can imagine that, yes, I did scare him, sitting here in silence, in the dark. 'Jesus, you look awful.'

'Thanks.' I am fully aware that I look dreadful – a glance in the hallway mirror as I made my way downstairs confirmed that for me. My hair is wild and frizzy, thanks to my falling asleep with it still wet after my bath, and my eyes are ringed with dark circles despite my nap. Now, I am sure, they are red-rimmed and puffy, as I've tried and failed to stop the tears that seem to leak in a constant stream, every time my thoughts turn to the previous evening. 'Where have you been?'

'I went for a drink. With Neil.' He shuffles past Thor's sleeping body and slips onto to the couch beside me. 'I needed to get out for a bit ... I had a lot to think about, you know?' He takes a deep breath in, before he speaks again. 'I'm sorry for how I reacted earlier.'

I lean down to stroke the dog, using him as the perfect excuse not to look at Gareth, just for a moment. I don't know what to say in response, so I don't say anything, not yet. Gareth fumbles for my hand, pulling it away from Thor and tucking it into his lap.

'I spoke to Neil ... asked him about last night. He told me that you stayed in their spare room. On your own.' *So, he can believe Neil, but not me.* I squash the thought down, pushing it away to deal with it later. 'So ... I'm sorry. It's just hard, you know? After everything that's happened this year.' He huffs a tiny puff of laughter, and I think I see a tear shining in the corner of his eye. 'Last year. You know what I mean. After all the stuff with Ted, and us ... I'm just finding it hard to trust you, and when you didn't come home ...'

'Gareth, I need to tell you something.' I talk over his words, not wanting to hear how he doesn't believe me, not when I am about to tell him something that I desperately need him to believe, that I desperately need him to listen to, without questioning whether I'm being honest or not. 'It's important, I need you to listen to me.'

He stops talking and frowns at me, his hand tightening on mine, a warm comfortable squeeze that reminds me of the way he used to hold my hand, before we were married.

'Gareth, last night ... something happened. I think ...' I pause, my throat thickening so much that for a moment I struggle to get a breath and the sharp, bitter taste of panic floods my mouth. 'I think someone raped me.'

As soon as I say the words hysteria washes over me, and I want to laugh at Gareth's reaction. His mouth drops open and the blood drains from his face, leaving his skin pale and washed out.

'What?' He manages to force the words out, and as the hysteria leaves me I find that I am crying again. 'Rachel ... what do you mean? Someone ... Jesus. Are you sure?' Dropping my hand, he gets to his feet and starts pacing the living room floor, shoving his hand repeatedly through his hair. Thor squeaks indignantly as Gareth trips over his back half, before scuttling over to his basket to stay out of the way. I stand, drawing my dressing gown tightly around me until it digs into my waist, and step into the middle of the rug, hoping to stop Gareth's frantic pacing. As he reaches me, I grab both of his hands in mine, pressing my palms against his skin.

'No, I'm not sure. I think so. I don't ... Gareth, please listen to me.'

'What happened, Rachel? Is this why you didn't come home? Who did this to you?'

I shake my head, trying to deflect the torrent of questions. 'I don't know.'

'You don't know? Oh, Rach.' Gareth pulls me towards him, wrapping his arms around me and I wince, aware that my wrists are sore too, I just didn't realize earlier thanks to the heavier bruising on my upper arms. Tired, I rest my cheek against his chest for a moment, letting him hold me, before I look up at him. He smooths the hair away from my face. 'What do you mean you don't know? How can you not know? I don't understand.'

I pull away, rubbing at my wrists and sit back down on the couch, my legs feeling strangely jelly-like.

'I just ... don't know. I don't remember. I remember getting to the party, Liz opening the door. Maybe having a glass of red wine?' I look up at him and he gives a small nod, his face pale and his mouth pinched into a tight line. 'Then I woke up in the spare room at the Greenes' house, feeling like shit. Like, the worst hangover I've ever had. I don't even know how I got home this morning, I felt so awful.' I choke back a sob at the memory of coming to in Liz's spare room.

'But you think someone raped you?' He kneels in front of me, the scent of stale beer on his breath wafting up as he speaks, making me feel sick. I smell a faint whiff of smoke on him, and know that he's smoked a sneaky cigar with Neil.

'Yes. My ... I hurt. My thighs, at the top and ... inside.' Taking a deep breath, I slide the dressing gown off my shoulders to reveal the bruising at the top of my arms, the delicate skin underneath so purple, it's almost black. 'And I wouldn't have done that to you, Gareth, not willingly, not after all we've been through.'

40

'Fucking hell, Rachel.' His gaze sliding away from my bruises, Gareth breathes out hard through his nose and I see the skin across his knuckles whiten as he clenches his fists. 'And you have no idea who did this? No memory of it at all?'

I shake my head, fat drops hitting my knees and leaving wide, dark patches on the fabric of the dressing gown.

'Nothing. It's just black, like it's been wiped from my brain. A black hole. I've tried and tried to think, to remember anything about the party, anyone that might have done this but I don't know. I don't know anything.' I can barely swallow, my throat is so thick with tears and I am powerless to stop them from pouring down my cheeks, scalding as they drip from the end of my chin.

'Oh God, Rachel, come here.' Gareth pulls me to my feet and into his chest again, his arms tightening around me. The crush of his chest against mine takes my breath away, and for a moment I enjoy the sensation of not being able to draw breath. 'I'm sorry,' he whispers, 'I'm so fucking sorry that I left you there alone, I'm sorry that I wasn't there to protect you. I should have stayed. I shouldn't have left you there on your own. I should have made you leave with me.'

'It's not your fault,' I mutter into his chest, despite feeling that maybe, just maybe, it wouldn't have happened if he hadn't left me there, if I hadn't been so stubborn, apparently, about staying. 'I don't know what to do, Gareth. I don't know how to deal with this.' Fear rises up and I pull away slightly, fighting to catch my breath, black spots dancing at the corner of my vision, panic making my heart beat frantically in my chest like a caged bird.

'We're going to the police,' his voice is firm, 'and we're going to let them catch the bastard that did this.'

5

I stare blankly out of the car window, as the rain that hasn't stopped since yesterday evening lashes against the glass. Every now and again Gareth reaches over from the driving seat to pat my knee or squeeze my hand but I don't give him any response. I feel numb, unable to return his gestures, just wanting to get the whole thing over and done with. Last night, when he said he wanted to call the police, I felt my breath freeze in my lungs, the thought of having to tell people – people who aren't Gareth, people who have no idea who I really am – what actually happened, making panic swarm in my belly like a thousand angry bees.

'No, I can't,' I'd said, backing away from him and tying the dressing gown cord so tightly that I felt it cut into my waist.

'Rachel, you have to, you can't let whoever did this get away with it.' He'd reached for me, but I had flinched from him and he'd stared at me, hurt and confused. 'I'm going to call them, they need to know.'

'No, Gareth, please, I don't want them to know … I can't …' The words died in my throat as he reached for the phone and I shoved past him, headed for the safety of the bedroom. He hadn't phoned them, not then, but this morning when I woke up from a fitful sleep he was standing over me, phone in hand, ready to make the call. Now, I find myself sullen and angry, slumped in the passenger seat on the way to meet a police officer at the Kingsnorth rape suite.

'We're here.' Gareth rests his hand gently on mine, before switching the ignition off and I ignore him, still gazing out of the window as the rain makes the puddles leap and dance with splashes. 'Rachel? Come on, I'll be with you the whole time. I won't let you do this on your own, I promise.'

I turn to face him, exhaustion making my movements slow and clumsy, but I don't have the words to say how I'm feeling. Instead, I silently turn back and fumble for the door handle, pretending that I don't hear his little exhalation of relief that I am finally doing as I am told.

The building that houses the police station is a sprawling, double storey structure masked from the outside world by a short driveway lined with trees, quaint compared to the usual expectation of a police station. As I step out of the car and look towards the road, I realize I have driven past it hundreds of times on my way to drop Robbie off at school, without ever considering what goes on inside. I wait, scuffing the gravel with the toe of my shoe as the rain soaks my hair, for Gareth to lock the car unwilling to move even a step towards the building on my own.

'OK?' Gareth's eyes search my face, as he tucks the slip of paper he wrote the police station address on into his back pocket, before reaching for my hand. I give a small nod, lying again, as I don't think I'll ever feel ready for this. We walk slowly up the path together towards the door over which hangs a sign for reception. I stumble at the threshold, almost as though my feet don't want to carry me over, but I force myself onwards, following Gareth to the front desk.

He speaks in a low voice to the woman there, her eyes drifting towards me as he talks, and I turn away, not wanting to see pity on her face. It's not long before a slightly built blonde woman appears in my eye line, a small smile on her face showing off the gap between her two front teeth.

'Rachel?' She asks, and I nod. 'I'm Carrie – do you want to follow me?' I get slowly to my feet, casting a panicked look back at Gareth. 'Oh, your husband can come too, if that's what you'd like?' I nod again and take Gareth's hand gratefully, his palm warm against my cold skin, as he stands to follow Carrie though a set of double doors and along the corridor to a small room with a low couch either side of a coffee table with a fake vase of flowers standing on it. It feels homely and it throws me for a second – I somehow thought I would have to give a statement, be questioned or whatever, in an interview room.

'Have a seat.' Carrie sinks down onto one couch and Gareth and I follow suit, leaning in to one another on the opposite couch. 'Now, Rachel, I'm what they call a SOLO – sexual offence liaison officer – I'm specially trained to help you with what you've experienced, OK? I know you're frightened, but I'm here to do the very best that I can to help you.'

'OK.' I let out a shaky breath that I didn't realize I was holding and wiggle my toes in the ends of my shoes, pressing them into the beige carpet tiles.

'I'll take a statement from you, and if it's OK we'll do a medical examination. Trust me, Rachel, we will do everything we can to make this as less stressful as we can for you.' Carrie reaches over and pats my hand and I find I am already fighting back tears before I even begin to make

45

the statement. 'Can you take me through that evening – the evening of December thirty-first?'

'I don't remember very much. Only arriving at the party, maybe having a drink or two? It was hot in there. Busy.' I glance at Gareth who is chewing on the inside of his lip.

'Would you rather do this on your own, Rachel?' Carrie sees my glance and follows my gaze over to Gareth.

'No,' I say hastily, not wanting to be alone with her, afraid of the questions that she might ask me. 'It's fine. I just can't remember anything about that night. Not past the first hour or so of the party.'

'Do you think there's a possibility that something could have been put into your drink?' Carrie asks, her pen scratching away at the notepad in front of her.

'I … maybe. I don't know.'

'How did you feel when you woke up?' Carrie asks me gently, and Gareth gives my knee a tiny squeeze, letting me know he's still there.

'Rough. Really, really poorly. Like the worst hangover I'd ever had. Everything was a bit foggy … I was sick and dizzy, a bit unsteady on my feet.'

'And when did you first start to think that perhaps you had been raped?' Carrie's voice is kind, her tone soft and it makes tears jump to my eyes. I was so frightened that they wouldn't believe me, that they'd think that I was just a woman who'd drunk too much and stayed out all night and needed to concoct a story for her husband, that the fact Carrie seems to believe what I'm saying makes me feel almost faint with gratitude.

'Not until last night, not properly. It's not the kind of thing that you think will happen to you, you know? When I woke up the morning after the party … my whole body was sore, and there was bruising to my thighs and my upper arms. Also, I was sore, you know …' I gesture downwards towards my lap. 'I was trying to think of a reason why I would feel like that, but I know I wouldn't have … not, you know. I wouldn't have wanted to.'

'Is there anybody who you think might have … had something to do with this?' Carrie asks gently.

'What? I don't …' The words won't come and I grip Gareth's hand tightly, my whole body starting to shake.

'It's OK, Rachel, I don't mean to upset or confuse you,' Carrie says, with an anxious glance at Gareth, 'what I meant is, is there anyone who has upset you lately, anyone who might have a grudge against you? Have you fallen out with anyone? Friends or colleagues? Basically, anyone you might think would have a reason to want to hurt you. The reason I ask, Rachel, is that acquaintance or date rape is much more common than stranger rape, do you understand what I mean?'

'No … not that I can think of. I don't have any colleagues – I'm an aromatherapist. I work from home.' I say, my voice barely above a whisper. My brain is foggy and I can't think straight.

'There's nobody that would want to hurt Rachel,' Gareth's voice is strained and he runs his hand through his hair again, like some sort of nervous tic, 'she gets on with everybody. There were lots of people at that party – every room was crowded. There were lots of people that we knew there, but also lots of people that we didn't know. Presumably friends and acquaintances of Liz and Neil.'

'Rachel?' Carrie gives a brief nod to Gareth, but clearly wants to hear it from me. 'Nobody at all?'

47

'No.' I shake my head. 'There isn't anyone that I can think of who would ever do something as awful as this.'

The interview, the statement, whatever you want to call it goes on and on, Carrie asking me questions about every little aspect of the party. Who else was there? I have to tell her that I don't know, I only remember seeing Neil and Liz, although I know other people were there. What time did I think the party finished? I don't know, I can't remember anything past the first hour. Did anyone see me spending time with anyone in particular? At this I utter the same words for the hundredth time, *I don't know*, tears of frustration streaming down my cheeks. If only I could just remember something, *anything*, that could give Carrie a lead. Eventually I manage to stop the tears, my eyes feeling raw, and Carrie apologizes for causing me any distress. As she leaves the room to fetch tea, I turn to Gareth.

'Please, can we just go now?' Exhaustion is tugging at my bones and all I want to do is go to sleep. 'I've done what you wanted, I've reported it.'

'Not quite done yet, sorry, Rachel.' Carrie appears in the doorway, obviously overhearing, and replies before Gareth gets the chance to. 'I'd really like to get the doctor to give you a quick medical examination, and to take some photos of that nasty bruising, if that's OK with you. We'll also do some tests for STDs and a pregnancy test.'

God, I want to weep, the thought of someone pulling at me, inspecting the deepest parts of me, makes me want to throw up. I can't even entertain the thought that whoever he is might have given me something else as well.

'Rachel, please,' desperation leaches into Gareth's voice, 'you've been really brave. Please just do this one thing; whoever did this needs to be caught.' Fighting back the panic that seems to have been simmering under my skin since the night of the party I agree to the medical, despite feeling as though I might faint at the touch of someone I don't know. Gareth is right – whoever did this needs to be caught, and if it means I need to do this, then I need to do it. Gareth kisses my temple, and then I follow Carrie along a corridor towards the back of the police station, and realize that this must be the rape suite – a block of three rooms, one for examination, another room similar to the one I have spent the morning in, and a bathroom, complete with shower. Carrie explains that after the medical, I can have a shower and she'll give me clean clothes to wear home, if I want them.

'Where are the clothes you wore that night, Rachel?' she asks, as another officer photographs the bruises that stain the skin on my arms.

'At home,' I whisper, 'in the laundry basket. I haven't washed them yet.' Carrie tells me she'll come and collect them, that I don't need to worry, just put them in a bag and she'll drive over tomorrow to pick them up. She leads me into the examination room and I start to slowly slide my clothes off behind the paper screen, my heart thumping double time in my chest. Even the realization that the doctor examining me is a woman doesn't stop the fear from clogging my throat, and I lie on the examination table, my muscles so tense they hurt. Finally, endlessly, it is over and I slide from the table, wrapping the paper gown Carrie has left out tightly around my body and dress in my own comfortable, familiar clothes, ignoring the jogging pants and sweatshirt provided by the staff. Back in the room, Carrie perches on the end of the coffee table, talking to Gareth, both of them looking up startled when I appear in the doorway.

'All done?' Carrie smiles and gets to her feet, moving towards the door. 'Rachel, you've been fantastic – really helpful. I'll be over tomorrow to collect the clothing, and as soon as I have any further information for you I'll be in touch. Here's my number, you can call me any time, OK?' She presses a business card into my hand and I whisper my thanks. I don't want her to come over tomorrow. I don't want to have to call her. I just want this to never have happened.

We drive home in silence, the claustrophobic kind that you could cut with a knife. I have no words left to say, and after a few feeble attempts at starting a conversation, it seems that Gareth has run out of sympathetic phrases, something that I'm more than a little relieved about. Once back home indoors, he offers to take Thor for a walk, somehow sensing that I don't want to leave the house, and he grabs the lead from where it hangs by the back door.

'Will you be OK if I take the dog out? I won't be long.' He doesn't look at me as he fusses with the lead, not quite managing to clip it in even though Thor isn't moving.

'What were you talking to Carrie about when I was in the examination room?' I didn't want to ask, but the look on his face when I re-entered the room puzzled me, and I want to know what was said. He sighs and ruffles a hand through his hair before he answers.

'I asked her if it made a difference, the fact that you'd had a bath as soon as you got home that morning.'

'And what did she say?' My heart starts hammering in my chest and my mouth goes dry. I twist my fingers together to hide their shaking, but I already know what the answer will be, I knew straight away when I saw her face when I answered the question.

'She said it probably did. That it will have massively reduced the chances of them recovering any useable DNA.' He stands and clicking his tongue at Thor strides towards the back door, slamming it closed behind him. I stare after him, my breath coming in frantic huffs as I fight back tears, at the realization that despite seeming so supportive on the surface, perhaps my husband doesn't really believe me.

6

LATE AUGUST – THREE AND A HALF
MONTHS BEFORE THE PARTY

Ted slides a warm hand up my thigh under the table and I push him away half-heartedly, feeling guilty at the little thrill that runs through my veins at his touch.

'Don't, Ted. What if someone sees?' I look over my shoulder but the people at the other occupied tables are engrossed in their own lives, no one is paying any attention to us. We are sitting in the beer garden of a pub twenty miles outside of West Marsham, chosen for its tucked away location. Over the past two weeks things have escalated between Ted and myself, starting when he called me two days after the barbecue, seemingly to check how my hand was. We've met for coffee twice, just to chat, and now … now, we're sitting in a pub, tucked away from prying eyes, and Ted's hand is on my thigh. I have cancelled this afternoon's clients, a risk in itself, in order to be able to meet Ted and I have butterflies in my stomach at the idea that something more might happen, alongside shredded nerves.

'That's why we picked this place, isn't it? Because it's little known and secluded, so no one would see us?' Ted turns his blue-eyed gaze on me and stares intently. I look away, feeling suddenly shy. Feeling *noticed*. My stomach flips as I breathe in the scent of his aftershave and for a brief second, I long to feel his mouth on mine again, before I pull away, reaching for my wine glass.

'We can never be too careful.' Smiling, I tip my glass towards him before taking a sip of the cold, crisp white wine, perfect for the warm summer afternoon. Despite the buzz of spending time with Ted, there is always the niggle of fear that someone will spot us at the back of my mind. 'Where is Angela today?'

'Apparently she's at work. But she took her yoga mat and she was wearing her leggings, so I strongly doubt that that's the case, unless she's going in after her "class".' A shadow crosses his face briefly, as Ted makes air quotes around the word, convinced as he is that Angela isn't going to yoga so often to work on her flexibility. Despite the rumours, and what Ted told me that day in the bathroom, Angela is still living at the family home. 'What about Gareth?'

I shrug and bury my face in my glass to buy myself a few seconds. Who knows where Gareth is today? He's stopped telling me anything about the business, dealing with all the properties himself, and now that he's taken on an actual, proper secretary he doesn't even need me to do his paperwork any more, all under the guise of leaving me 'more time for your aromatherapy'.

'I don't know where he is,' I confess, draining the last of my wine. 'He's always either out somewhere, or closeted away in his office at home.' Even when he's only in his office, the emotional barrier he's put up between us means he might as well be a million miles away.

'So, things haven't improved much between you recently?' Ted asks, his hand moving from my thigh to rest lightly on the table, a respectable distance away from my fingers.

'Not really. They're worse, if anything. I mean, we've barely spoken since the night of the barbecue.' I flush a hot red at the thought of that night, the night this ... thing between Ted and I started. 'Every time I try to talk to him he tells me he's too busy and he'll speak to me later.' Of course, later never comes. I quite often have clients come to me after they finish work, meaning that I spend most of the evening in the log cabin at the end of the garden that serves as my treatment room, and then I'm usually asleep by the time he comes up to bed, if he even comes to bed at all, and he's gone by the time I wake up in the morning.

'You don't have to put up with it, you know, Rachel.'

'The same way you don't have to put up with Angela sleeping with her yoga teacher?' Immediately the words leave my mouth I feel like a bitch, even more so at the way Ted's face crumples slightly. He pulls it back quickly though, I'll give him that, and the look is gone before I'm even really sure I saw it in the first place.

'Rachel, I know that my marriage with Angela is over. I wouldn't be here if I didn't think that. I wouldn't have let anything happen at the barbecue if I wasn't sure that Angela was about to leave me.' Ted's voice is quiet, and deadly serious. His forehead creases in a deep frown as he speaks, as if it hurts him to say the words out loud. I wish I had another drink that I could nurse, a barrier that I could hold between us, so things don't feel quite so intense. 'Angela is sleeping with

Devon, or Cornwall, or whatever the bloody hell his name is. I've found the evidence – she's not exactly tried to hide it – and much as it pains me to admit it, she's going to leave me … the signs are all there.' I want to ask him what the signs are, what should I be looking for in Gareth, but he carries on speaking, his voice breaking slightly. 'That's the reason why I put up with it all – because when she does leave, when I am left behind, telling Sean that life as he knows it is changing, then I can't be blamed. It won't be me that my son can't stand to be around. I might not have Angela, but I'll still have Sean. Do you see?' His eyes search mine and my heart flutters under his intense gaze.

'Yes, I do see.' I look away, my right hand moving to fiddle with my wedding ring. It sits fast on my finger, metal snug against skin. 'It's different for me though, Ted – do *you* see? I do love Gareth – I want things to work with him, but I am so sick of being pushed aside, ignored … treated like I'm nothing.' I raise my eyes to meet his. 'I'm lonely, Ted, but when I'm with you, I'm not. I feel like you notice me. Gareth … he doesn't even know I'm alive sometimes, but he's my husband, and deep down he is still that man I married. I love him and I want us to get back to the way things were, but I also want this, here, with you. For now, anyway. Does that make me a bitch?'

'Some would say so,' Ted laughs, before reaching over and brushing his hand through my hair, in that way that makes me forget about Gareth and his cold, brittle demeanour, and I force away the feeling of self-loathing that bubbles under my skin.

I should leave, I know that. But sitting in the sunshine with Ted, enjoying the alcohol, the sun beating down on my bare shoulders, the feeling of actually being listened to for the first time in I don't know how long, I can't resist staying for one more drink before I head back to real life.

'Another beer?' I get to my feet, swinging one leg over the seat of the picnic bench, and picking up my empty wine glass.

'Wouldn't say no … but don't you have to get back?' Ted flicks his wrist to glance at his watch. Another thing I like about him – he's just as aware of where I need to be and when I need to leave as I am, although that might be fear of being found out that makes him so conscious.

'One more drink can't hurt, can it?' I smile down at him. 'And it's like you said, it's not as if there's anyone we know here.' Stepping my other foot over the seat of the bench Ted brushes his fingers across my ankle, sending a shot of desire straight through me. I'm not sure I'll be able to go straight home after this drink.

The inside of the pub is dark after the bright sunshine of the beer garden, and I squint slightly as I enter, willing my eyes to adjust. It's busier in here now, and glancing at the clock behind the bar I see it's almost six o'clock. Not that I have anything to rush back for, Gareth won't be home until goodness knows when, and Robbie will be out with Sean. I jostle next to a couple of men in suits at the bar as I wait to be served; the speedy service of this afternoon gone now as people stop in on their way home from work to enjoy a drink in the evening sunshine. Definitely best to make this the last drink before I get Ted to drop me somewhere close enough to the house to walk the rest of the way, but far enough out that we don't get spotted.

As I wait, the pub getting busier and busier, I feel less and less confident about staying. *What are you doing,*

Rachel? Are you really going to risk everything with Gareth for a fling with Ted? Just as the guilty feeling that sits heavy in my stomach becomes unbearable and I finally make the decision to leave it, to go home to Gareth and forget about seeing Ted again, I catch the bartender's attention and he mouths, 'Same again?' I waver for too long, and then it's too late – he pours a beer for Ted and another glass of wine for me. Turning, my hands full, I am startled by a man standing right behind me, almost too close. Beer slops over my hand and I yelp, holding the glass away from me to avoid it spilling down my skirt.

'Shit, I'm sorry …' He raises a hand to steady me before he squints at me over the top of his glasses, recognition dawning on his face. 'Rachel? What are you doing here?'

Fuuuuck. This is the last thing I need. I knew we should have left while it was still quiet, less chance of being spotted. Now it seems like I've blown everything. *Keep cool, Rachel, he doesn't know anything.*

'Aaron.' I keep my tone deliberately on the icy side, hoping that he doesn't want to stop and chat. 'I haven't seen you for years.'

'It's been a while,' he smiles, crinkling his eyes at me, 'so, is Gareth here? It would be good to catch up over a drink, if you guys have time.' He looks pointedly at my full hands, both carrying fresh drinks, and my heart sinks down to my sandals.

'Ermmm, no.' I manage to force the words out through my dry mouth. The urge to sip at the wine in my hands is overwhelming. 'Gareth isn't here, I'm just … having a quick drink with a friend, that's all.'

'Ah. Shame.' Aaron looks me up and down, and I remember how he used to make my skin crawl when he first started working for Gareth. Aaron and I had been at the same university together but had never really been friends, he'd just known some of the people that I had hung around with. I hadn't seen him since graduation, not until his CV landed on Gareth's desk. I didn't remember him being creepy at uni, but when he started working for us he had this … unsettling air about him. Intense – to the point of making me feel quite uncomfortable.

'We'll have to catch up though, really soon,' he's saying, 'I've just moved back over this way. I split up with Harriet, so I'm renting a place over in West Marsham, not far from you guys actually.' *Oh Jesus, I'm not sure things could get any worse.*

'Yes. Yes, of course. We'll arrange something. If you'll excuse me?' Heart thundering so hard I swear Aaron can see my pulse jumping in my throat, I lift the full glasses and nod towards the door into the garden.

'Nice to see you.' Aaron stands to one side and I walk as casually as I can towards the beer garden, feeling his eyes on my back until I'm out of his sight.

'Here.' I thrust the not quite full pint at Ted and take a healthy slug of the rapidly warming white wine in my glass.

'Easy tiger, what's the rush?' Ted looks at me in amusement as I swallow, not even waiting to sit back down on the bench. 'I thought we said one more drink would be OK.'

'That was before.'

'Before what?' Ted pats the bench next to him, but I shake my head and move to the opposite side, sitting to face him.

'Before I saw someone I know. Someone who knows Gareth.' I scan my eyes quickly over the garden, but I don't see Aaron anywhere yet. Hopefully he's decided that it's too hot outside and taken a seat at the bar.

'Shit,' Ted swears, but still doesn't seem fazed – he's certainly not as worried as I am. 'Don't panic, Rachel.'

'*Don't panic*? Ted, we have to go – I don't want us to be seen together!' I start collecting up my cardigan and bag, tucking the strap under my arm, but Ted lays a hand over it.

'Wait. If we rush off together it looks like we're up to something ...'

'We *are*!'

'... but if we just have a drink, talk and don't panic, we look innocent, OK? Plenty of people go out for a drink completely innocently.' He holds my gaze in a calm, steady look and I let myself take a deep breath. 'Now, who is this person?'

'Aaron. He used to work for Gareth, God ... it must be five or six years ago now.' Calmer now, I take another sip of wine. 'He's moved back here after he split up with his girlfriend apparently. He's a creep.' I suppress a shudder and peep over my shoulder, still anxious that he'll come out into the garden at any moment and spot us.

'Is he likely to tell Gareth that he saw you?'

'I don't know ... maybe. I don't know why he's back, or what his plans are. I don't know if he's made any plans to see Gareth, although he did say it would be good to catch up. I was so rattled to see him that I forgot to ask.'

'OK. If anyone asks ... or more importantly, if Gareth asks, we were meeting to discuss a job opportunity.'

'A job opportunity?' I'm not quite sure where Ted is going with this, or how he's going to make this convincing. 'Ted, you're a salesman. I don't even know what it is that you sell. What job could you possibly have for me?'

'I don't know ... part-time admin assistant at our offices? You used to do Gareth's paperwork so I asked you to meet with me to discuss it. You turned me down. Too busy with your aromatherapy business. Honestly, Rachel, keep it simple and it'll work, that's if we even need it to.' Ted's hand covers mine, and I pull my hand away, too unnerved by Aaron's appearance to even think of letting Ted near me.

'OK. Oh God, what was I thinking, Ted? This is all wrong, I shouldn't be here.' Panic makes my heart stutter in my chest, and the burden of guilt sits heavily on my shoulders. 'Please Ted, can you just take me home?'

Ted drops me a couple of streets away, behind the High Street that will still be busy even though it's past seven o'clock. Digging in my bag for my key as I approach the front door my phone bleeps in my bag, but I ignore it, intent on getting indoors and into my usual slouchy outfit, one that I wear around the house, before Gareth gets home. Thankfully, there is an undisturbed air as I let myself in, telling me that I've beaten both Gareth and Robbie home.

Breathing a sigh of relief, I head upstairs, kicking my sandals to the back of the wardrobe and brushing my teeth to rid my mouth of the sour taste of the wine I've drunk. I tell myself that's the reason – but deep down I know it's so that Gareth doesn't smell it on me and then question why I've been drinking in the afternoon. As I brush, I berate myself for being so stupid – *how could I have let myself stay so long? Someone was bound to see us. And if Gareth finds out … well, it's not just the two of us who will be affected. Am I really ready to jeopardize my marriage, to potentially lose Robbie who will no doubt take his father's side, all for a quick fling?* I spit out the toothpaste, eyeing myself critically in the mirror as I wipe my mouth. *Stupid. Stupid and reckless, that's what today was.*

Comfortable now in yoga pants (I think of adulterous Angela when I pull them on) and an old Suede T-shirt I grab a glass of water and slump on the couch in front of the TV, wishing I'd just worked as originally planned. Tired from the stress of the afternoon and with a mild headache starting behind my eyes thanks to the wine, I huff in irritation as my phone bleeps again in my bag, before I get back up and grab it. A text from Gareth telling me not to wait up (no surprises there – my guilt lessens slightly as I read it), and a notification from Facebook telling me I have a friend request. Sighing, I text Gareth back, before opening the Facebook app and tapping the requests button. My heart sinks as I read the words on the screen.

'*Aaron Power has sent you a Friend Request.*'

7

JANUARY – TWO DAYS AFTER THE PARTY

'Are you sure you'll be OK?' Gareth pauses from where he's stuffing paperwork into his laptop bag, running his eyes over me. He looks pale, washed-out, with dark circles like bruises under his eyes. I can only imagine how I must look – better than I feel, hopefully.

'I'll be fine. I know you're busy.' *Too busy.* The words hang in the thick silence between us. It's the first proper working day back after the Christmas holidays and I know that Gareth is itching to get back to the office. In a way, I'm happy that he's going for the day. I can't shake the feeling that he doesn't quite believe my story about what happened at the party; something about the way he looked at me when he told me Carrie said I had probably destroyed all the evidence. *Almost as though he thought I'd done it on purpose.* It's hard enough trying to process it all, without feeling as though I have to convince him to believe me.

'If you need me I can come home. You know that.' I nod as he crosses the small gap between us, pulling me close for a quick hug before he lets me go again. 'Or I can stay –

if you want me to, I'll cancel the meetings.' He pulls the laptop bag over his shoulder and reaches for his travel mug of coffee, saying the words, but not really meaning them.

I shake my head, playing my part to perfection. 'It's fine, honestly. I'm sure Robbie will be home before too long, and I have Carrie's number.' Not that I'll call her. 'I'll take the dog for some fresh air and then maybe I'll … I don't know. I'll find something to do.' I force out a smile, shooing him towards the door and he scurries off down the drive, giving me a brief wave as he reverses the car out and heads towards West Marsham.

I sit at the kitchen table, hugging my mug of tea for warmth. I don't seem to have been able to get warm since I woke up in that stifling, stuffy room in Liz's house, the morning after the party. Closing my eyes, I tilt my head back and try my hardest to remember something, *anything*, about that night. I'm tired of not knowing what happened, tired of the fear that hovers every time I try to fill in the blanks. *Music.* That's something that floats into my mind as I try and think – I remember as we walked in there was Christmas music playing, something old, maybe from the 80s, playing loudly, the bass line thudding in my chest. I remember Gareth rolling his eyes, laughing at me, as I started to dance my way into the house, grabbing at his hand to pull him along behind me. I still thought that I could jolly him into having a good time, that once he'd had a beer or two he'd loosen up and start enjoying himself. *Did he, though*? I can't remember. Liz said she didn't think we argued, but who knows? I should maybe start to think about talking to some of the others at the party, maybe they would know?

The shrill ring of the doorbell startles me, and I jump, slopping cold tea down the front of my dressing gown.

Shit. I dab at it pathetically as the doorbell rings again, before giving in and getting to my feet.

'Rachel. Hi. How are you doing?' I open the front door to find Carrie on the doorstep. True to her word she is here, just as she said she would be. She looks me up and down quickly, as if she's trying to assess me without me noticing. I notice.

'I thought you would have called first. I've just got up.' I feel as though I have to justify why it's nearly ten o'clock in the morning and I'm still in a scruffy dressing gown.

'I'm sorry, I was passing and I thought I'd pop in now, instead of having to drop back later. Is it OK to come in?' She already has one foot on the threshold so I pull the door fully open to allow her to come in. She moves aside to let me lead the way and I take her through to the living room, aware that I haven't tidied the kitchen after last night's dinner.

'Here,' I gesture towards the couch for her to take a seat. 'Would you like tea?'

'No, thank you.' Carrie sits, and digs in her bag for her notebook and pen. 'I'm going to be your dedicated officer, Rachel. That means that I'll be the one keeping you informed of everything that takes place during our investigation. I know you gave us a statement yesterday, but do you think I could ask you a couple more questions?'

'Yes, of course.' I draw in a shaky breath. 'Sorry. It's difficult to keep talking about it, you know?' Picking at the threads on my dressing gown, my stomach flips with nerves at the thought of having to talk it all through again.

'I know, I do understand and I'm sorry that I need to ask you more. I just want to check and make sure that you haven't remembered anything else, anything that might be significant.'

I shake my head, fighting back the wave of frustration that rises up in me at the thought of the black hole in my memory.

'Just that there was music. There was music playing really loudly when we walked in. That's it, there's nothing else. What have you done so far?' The question blurts out before I think. 'I mean … how are you investigating this? What are you doing to find out who did this to me?' The words tumble out and I raise my hand to my mouth to try to stop them. 'Sorry, I'm sorry … I just …'

Carrie leans forward and lays her hand on mine, squeezing in some gesture of reassurance.

'Rachel, I promise we're doing everything we can to get as much information as possible. We've spoken to the party host and asked for a complete list of guests. We'll be talking to every guest individually, asking them questions to see what they can tell us. Sometimes people see things that they don't even realize are relevant. Any information can be useful.'

'OK,' I nod, already feeling a little calmer, now I know that even if Gareth doesn't necessarily believe me, Carrie does. 'And you'll speak to everybody that is on the list?'

'Of course, we will.' Carrie makes a point of writing in her notebook, almost as if to prove to me that she'll do what she says she will. 'Once we have the results of your medical examination I'll be able to give you more information, but the truth is …' Carrie breaks off for a moment and I feel a swell of horror, as I know what she's going to say. She swallows hard, as if finding it difficult to speak. 'The fact that you had a bath won't have helped … it might make it difficult for us to pick up any DNA.'

'I had to! I had to have a bath … I felt …' the words stick in my throat, 'I felt filthy. And anyway … I didn't know, not at first.

I thought … I don't know what I thought; I just didn't think it was that. Everything was so … confused, blurry. Things like that don't happen to people like me.' I break off, the words unable to force their way out past the lump in my throat.

'I do understand, Rachel, I promise, and we will do as much as we possibly can to find whoever did this.' Carrie's voice is gentle and I take a deep breath, knowing that I need to trust her to get this right, if I'm going to find out who did this to me. 'Have you still got the clothes you wore that night?'

'They're in the laundry basket, upstairs in the main bathroom. Gareth uses the one in the en-suite so there shouldn't be any other laundry in there. Do you want me to show you?'

Carrie shakes her head. 'Would you mind going upstairs to fetch them for me? I'll wait down here, shall I … maybe put the kettle on? No need to show me through, I'll find everything.' She heads out into the hallway and turns right towards the kitchen. I pause at the foot of the stairs, one foot on the bottom step, and I hear the sounds of running water as she fills the kettle, followed by the clink of the mugs. Taking a deep breath, I head up the stairs to the bathroom and yank open the lid of the laundry hamper. I pull the clothes out, holding them gingerly between finger and thumb, just the sight of them enough to make my heart thump harder in my chest. I am back in the kitchen before the kettle even has a chance to boil, and I lay the clothes on the edge of the table.

'OK?' Carrie looks at me with a concerned smile, a paper bag in one hand. I nod. 'I'm just going to pop these in this bag, and I'll have a quick look and make sure we have everything, all right?' I nod again, and clear my throat.

'Yes. OK.'

'Right, so I've got a pair of black wet-look leggings, a black off the shoulder top and a strapless black bra.' She pokes into the bag with the end of a biro. 'There's no underwear in there though, Rachel?'

'No.' The kettle flicks off and I use it as an excuse to turn away from her as I take over the tea-making, pouring the water into the two cups she has set out. 'I couldn't find it. I mean, when I woke up I was looking for my clothes. I was only wearing my bra and top, my bottom half was naked. I found my leggings scrunched up on the floor with my sandals but I couldn't find my knickers.' Hot shame floods my cheeks staining them red, and I pull the dressing gown away from my neck in an attempt to cool down.

'Right, OK.' Carrie frowns but doesn't get a chance to say any more as the back door crashes open, and Robbie appears, letting in the cold morning air.

'Hi, Mum,' he steps in, sliding his feet out of his muddy trainers. His hair is ruffled and his cheeks are flushed red with the cold. He looks as though he's been playing football, or running, there is a healthy air about him. 'Who's this?' His eyes flick interestedly over Carrie's figure.

'I should go,' she says, picking up the paper bag. 'I have everything I need for the minute; I'll be in touch, Rachel, OK? I'll see myself out.' I nod, wordlessly and she hurries out to the front door. I hear it slam closed, and then the sound of a car starting up.

'Mum? Who was that?' Robbie peers out towards the front window, watching as Carrie's car heads off towards Kingsnorth.

'Errm … that was Carrie,' I falter, not sure what to say or how to phrase it. 'She's a …'

'Mum, you won't believe what happened,' Robbie cuts in, 'at Liz's party. Some bad shit went down. The police came by Sean's and spoke to us. They wanted to speak to Ted but he's away at the moment – some sales conference thing. They were asking if we went to the party – apparently a woman got attacked there, that's what they're saying.' He opens the fridge door and leans in, looking for something to eat. He closes the door, sausage roll in his hand and takes in my face.

'Mum?'

I am frozen, mug clenched tightly in my fist as I battle to find the right words to say to my son. I know I have to tell him, but this is possibly the hardest thing I've ever had to say to my child.

'That was Carrie. She's a police officer … a sexual offence liaison officer.' Tears spill down my cheeks as I watch Robbie's face change, comprehension dawning slowly, and I almost feel my heart break at the realization that I couldn't protect him from this. 'She came to take my clothes away … the ones I wore to the party … for forensic examination.'

'Forensic examination?' He sucks in a breath as it hits him, what I am saying. 'It was you? The woman they were talking about … the one who was raped? It was you?'

It takes me a while to calm Robbie down as he paces the kitchen floor, alternately shouting that he'll kill whoever did this, to asking me questions on repeat, unable to comprehend the idea that I have literally no memory of that night. Finally, he calms down and I manage to talk to him sensibly.

'What did you tell the police?' I ask him, as he finally takes a seat at the kitchen table.

'Nothing.' His gaze slides away from mine and I get the sense that he's hiding something, he looks much like he did when he was little and he didn't want to confess to some tiny misdemeanour. 'Just that Sean and I were at his house all evening, which we were.' He looks a bit shifty round the eyes and I deduce that probably wasn't the entire truth. I don't doubt that he spent the evening with Sean, but they probably had a sneaky cider in the park, or a joint at worst, and he doesn't want to 'fess up to it. In light of what has happened Robbie sneaking a cider or having a smoke is the least of my worries.

'Did they ask you about anyone else at the party?' I am burning to know who else might have been there – who else might have seen something, anything that could fill in the gaps in my memory.

'Just about Ted. They knew Angela didn't go, but they wanted to know if Ted went. Obviously, they can't speak to him yet as he left for that convention thing this morning.'

'Right. Did Ted go to the party?'

Robbie frowns at me, finally realizing that I'm not exaggerating, I really don't remember.

'Yeah. Well, he said he was going, and he wasn't at their house all evening so he must have gone.'

'Of course.' I give him a small smile and squeeze his hand. 'I'm fine, Rob, OK? I know this is easier said than done but please try not to worry about things. The police will find him and it'll all be sorted.' He nods, before pushing back his chair and putting his arms around me.

'I love you, Mum. Are you sure you're going to be OK?' he asks, and I manage to hide the tears that spring to my eyes, as he's so much taller than me.

70

'Love you too, Robster.' His childhood nickname slips out without thinking. 'I'm fine, I promise.' He kisses me on the head, and I sink into his vacated chair, swallowing hard to hide the bitter taste of lies on my tongue, the lies that say, *yes, I'm OK*.

Later on, I text Amy, asking her to meet me outside the gates to the park. I need to walk Thor, but on top of that I need to get out of here, to clear my head. I bundle up warm, pulling a hat low down over my forehead, in the hope that if I do meet anyone who attended the party they don't realize that it's me. I get to the front door, Thor straining at the lead, and panic threatens. I don't know if I can do this. What if he's out there, just waiting to get me on my own? I force the thought away, desperate for fresh air and someone to talk to, pushing my feet over the threshold and down the path. My nerves jangle the entire way to the park, and I find myself peering out from under my hat at people as they pass by. *Were they there? Do they know anything? What about that guy over there – was he somehow involved?* By the time I reach the park gates, Amy is waiting, hopping from foot to foot in an attempt to keep warm, and I am a nervous wreck.

'Hey,' Amy leans in to kiss me on the cheek, the damp, misty drizzle that hangs in the air leaving droplets in her hair. 'Are you OK? Did you hear about what happened at the party? Did the police speak to you yet?' I realize that in the whirlwind that has been the past two days, not only did I not tell Robbie about it, I also haven't told Amy. *You can do this, Rachel.* I suck in a deep breath, wrapping Thor's lead so tightly around my hand that it hurts.

'It was me, Amy. I'm the woman.'

'What?' Amy's hand flies to her mouth in horror, before she pulls me towards her in a tight embrace. 'Oh my god, oh my god,' she whispers over and over as her arms wrap tightly around me, so tight I can barely breathe. 'Fuck, Rachel, are you OK?' She draws back, holding me by the shoulders so she can look at me properly. 'Scrap that, you can't be OK. Shit. I don't know what to say?' Her eyes fill with tears and I lead her over to an empty bench, tucked away at the end of the path, where no one will disturb us.

'I'm OK,' I reassure her, lying again. I'm good at that now, you get that way once you've had plenty of practice.

'What happened?' Mascara leaves a black stain under her eyes and I hand her a tissue to wipe at it.

'I don't know, that's just it. I woke up and I knew, I just *knew* something had happened. You know, you can tell?' Amy nods, but doesn't speak, her fingers shredding the soggy tissue into tiny pieces. 'But I can't remember a thing past coming in to the party. I guess the police came and spoke to you?'

Amy nods again and leans down to stroke Thor, where he bumps his head gently against her legs.

'They came late yesterday evening. They said there had been a report of a serious assault on a woman at the party and did I see anything. Obviously, I told them no, because I didn't. I mean, I didn't even see you after a certain point in the evening, but I'd been drinking too so I couldn't even tell them much about that. Oh God … I didn't see you – does that mean?' Amy covers her mouth again and I shake my head.

'I don't know. I don't know what that means, Amy. But it's not your fault, OK? That you can't remember seeing me – you didn't know.'

'But maybe if I'd paid more attention ...' *Exactly my thoughts. Maybe if I had paid more attention that night then it would never have happened.*

'Please don't, Amy.' The words come out perhaps a little harsher than I mean them to. 'It's bad enough me blaming myself, don't you do it as well. Look, can you remember who else was at the party? My memory is a total blank, and I need to know who else was there. I wanted to ask the police if they could tell me but I'm not sure that they would.'

'I can try.' Amy gets to her feet. 'Let's walk while we talk.' She casts a glance over her shoulder towards the park gates, frowning slightly, but when I look there is no one there. 'There was us, and Gareth, obviously. Ted.' She raises her eyebrows.

'It's OK; I know he was there. Robbie mentioned it.' Amy looks at me quizzically, but I motion for her to go on.

'Liz and Neil, obviously. Oh God, Rach, I don't know – there were loads of people there! It was like Liz had invited the whole village. I know there were a few people from the gym ... but there were tons of people I didn't recognize; every room was heaving with bodies.' She puffs out a long breath as she thinks. 'Katie and Brett – they came a little later on in the evening, I think, I don't remember them being there at the start. Melody and Jonno definitely came late, as usual, they turned up right before Gareth left.'

'Was Gareth OK when he left?' I ask, still uncertain if we argued that night.

'Yeah, I think so. Who can tell with Gareth?' She gives a little half-laugh, conscious that while he might be an arsehole sometimes, Gareth is still my husband. 'I can't remember who else, I'm sorry, there were just too many people milling around. I drank too much and it's all a bit of a blur if I'm honest.'

I thank her, and once we've taken Thor on a lap round the park I kiss her goodbye.

'Just call me if you need me, even if it's the middle of the night.' She frowns, her eyebrows meeting a sharp V under her hat. 'Are you sure you'll be OK?'

My mind on other things, I nod and smile and pulling my hat down further over my forehead, I prepare to face the walk along the main road back towards my house.

Clearly, I need to go and see Liz myself, to find out who exactly was at the party. She was the host, after all, so she must have a reasonable idea of who came. Time to take things into my own hands – I can't sit around and wait for the police. It might be difficult for me to talk about it, but every minute that passes feels like a minute wasted. I need to be doing something, to feel as though I am doing something myself. I don't want to be a victim, even though the thought of remembering what happened leaves me paralyzed with fear.

As I reach my front door, hands trembling slightly as I try and get the key in the lock, I catch a glimpse of someone turning into our street. Jiggling the key impatiently, my fingers shaking as adrenaline spikes, I get in and close the door, breath coming in sharp pants. I unclip Thor's leash, trying to get myself back under control, when I see him, strolling casually past the living room window. He raises a hand to me as I duck behind the curtain, not wanting to see him. *Aaron.* Why won't he leave me alone?

8

Hands. Hands pushing at me, forcing me backwards. Then over my mouth as I try to scream, crushing down over the bottom half of my face. There is a sharp, tangy scent in the air and I am unsure if it is the smell of him, or the scent of my own fear tainting the air. I want to struggle, to push him off, but I can't, my limbs are like lead.

Gasping, I sit up, thrown from sleep and a vivid, toxic dream. Sweat cools on my skin where I have pushed away the duvet in my nocturnal struggle, and I shiver slightly in the chilly air, twisting round to look at the clock. One o'clock in the morning. The other half of the bed is cool and empty, Gareth clearly not having made it up. Not that that is unusual in any way, not lately.

Lying back on the pillows I take a minute to get my breath back, tucking the duvet under my chin and pushing away the terrifying images that haunted the little sleep I have managed to get tonight. *Was that a dream? Or a memory? Forcing its way out of the black hole left by that night?* I push the covers back down, shivering again, before swinging my legs out of bed and grabbing my dressing gown.

As I tiptoe along the landing a strip of light shows under Robbie's door. I push the door open gently and see him curled up asleep on his bed, headphones clamped to his ears as the overhead light still burns. I sneak in and kiss his forehead, like I used to when he was little, before switching off the light and pulling the door closed again, careful not to wake him.

I make my way downstairs, intent on warming some milk, maybe with a splash of brandy to help me back into a – hopefully – dreamless sleep. Moonlight streams in through the glass panel in the front door, lighting the hallway, and as I creep along the cold tiles I notice that Gareth's office door is ajar, a warm yellow glow seeping out into the shadows that the moonlight can't reach. Without thinking I reach out and push the door open, as Gareth sits slumped at his desk with his head in his hands.

'Gareth? Are you OK?' At the sound of my voice he starts and sits up straight, shuffling the papers on the desk in front of him.

'What? Yes, I'm fine. What are you doing up? It's late.' His eyes are bloodshot and there is a faint fug of alcohol in the air. I sniff, delicately. Whisky, I think.

'I couldn't sleep.' I am reluctant to tell him about my nightmare, although I'm not sure why. 'I thought I'd come down and get some warm milk. What about you? You're still up.'

'Just finishing up some paperwork.' He rearranges the papers again, sliding them under an A4 diary stuffed with drawings and loose sheets of paper.

'Carrie came to see me today. The police spoke to Robbie while he was at Sean's house. I don't think they realized who he is.' There is a tissue in the pocket of my dressing gown, and I ball my fist around it, feeling my nails dig into my palm as I squeeze it tightly. 'So, he knows what happened.'

'Shit.' Gareth exhales, his stubble rasping as he rubs a hand over his chin. 'How is he?'

'Angry. Shocked. A bit disbelieving at first, then he wanted to kill someone, but I calmed him down. He was more worried about whether I was OK or not.'

'They came to my office today, too.' Gareth reaches behind him for the crystal decanter that his parents gave us on our wedding day, and pours himself a measure of good Scotch. He lifts the decanter in my direction and I nod, sliding into the armchair opposite his desk. 'They wanted to ask me about that night ... the party.'

'Oh.' I sip at the Scotch, relishing the way it burns as it slides down my throat. I don't know what to say, I just assumed that they didn't need to speak to Gareth, that they would have asked him anything they wanted to know while I was in the examination room. It never even occurred to me that they might want to speak to him separately about it. I take another sip of Scotch and wonder what he's told them.

'They asked me what happened ... what time I left, who was there, that kind of thing. What I thought when you didn't come home.'

'What did you tell them?' I twist in the chair, the seat pressing into the bruises on my thighs.

'The truth ... what else?' Gareth sips at his drink, his eyes never leaving my face. 'I told them that everything was fine; everyone was having a good time. I left just after midnight, maybe quarter past twelve; you were dancing in the living room.' There is a muscle twitching under his eye, like a tiny pulse, and I am mesmerized by it, unable to look away.

'What about what you thought when I didn't come home?'

77

'I told them that I thought you had gone home with Ted Durand. That you'd had an affair with him back in the summer, and I thought that my leaving and Angela's absence provided the pair of you with the perfect time to rekindle it. I told them that I waited up for you all night.'

Tears fill my eyes, spilling over as I shake my head. Gareth slugs back the rest of the whisky in his glass and refills it messily, slopping it over the desk. The whisky leaves an amber stain, glinting under the light of the lamp and I have to drag my eyes away. A question burns at the back of my mind, has done since we left the police station, and reluctantly I force my lips to shape the words. I have to ask him.

'Gareth, do you believe me? Do you believe that I was … raped?' The word is so ugly, so full of fear and anger that I struggle to force it past my lips every time I have to say it. 'Do you believe that I don't remember what happened that night?' My breath hitches in my chest and I let the tears fall, not caring if Gareth thinks I'm losing control. As I wait for him to reply the time spins out, the silence between us feeling endless, and I think, *our entire marriage depends on what he says next.* He sighs, running a hand through his hair before getting to his feet and coming round to where I sit. He takes my hands in his, the difference in temperature overwhelming. His hands are warm, clammy and slightly sweaty, while mine still carry that icy feel, as if frozen from my core.

'Yes,' he says quietly, after a pause, 'I do believe you. But that's not what I thought at the time, you understand? I thought you were in love with Ted, I thought you wanted to be with him, not me. I love you, Rachel, you know that?' His voice cracks on my name.

'Yes.' I do know that now – at least, I think I do – but I didn't last summer. 'I told you; it's over with Ted. I want to make things right here, but I need to know that you believe me.' I pull the tissue out of my pocket and blow my nose noisily, the taste of whisky at the back of my throat. 'Did the police say anything else to you? Has anyone said they saw anything?' I am desperate to know what others may have seen that night, but nothing seems to be forthcoming. 'Carrie didn't tell me anything, only that they would be speaking to the people that attended the party.'

'They just said the same thing to me.' Gareth pulls me to my feet and kisses the top of my head. 'Listen, I'm sure as soon as they have any information they'll let us know. Try not to worry, OK? They'll find whoever did this.' I nod, my cheek rubbing against his shirt. Closing my eyes, I try not to think about my dream, the sensation of hands pressing me down. Trapping me.

Panic flutters at the pit of my stomach as I press hard on the doorbell, hearing the familiar tone ring out somewhere towards the back of the house. A few seconds pass and then the door is thrown open to reveal Liz, immaculately made up and dressed to impress as ever, even if she doesn't have anywhere to be.

'Rachel!' Her tone is one of surprise, and I nearly take a step backwards, the déjà vu that washes over me leaving me panicky and breathless. It could almost be the night of the party, the way Liz threw open the door. 'What are you doing here?' She's pasted a smile on to her perfectly made-up face but the tiny line between her eyebrows, and the underlying air of tension that surrounds her, tells me that I'm not necessarily welcome.

'I just wanted to chat … about the other night, you know … the party? Is it OK to come in?' I sound pathetic, vulnerable, and I pull my shoulders back in an attempt to seem more confident. I can't let her refuse to speak to me, not when it's taken me half the morning to get my courage up to come here. Liz flounders for a moment, her mouth opening and closing in a way that would be comical if it were under any other circumstances, but she can't think of an excuse in time. Instead, she forces out another smile and opens the door, gesturing for me to come in.

'Of course. Come in.'

I follow her over the expensive Italian tiles into the kitchen, batting away the memories of the morning after the party as I do. Liz heads straight for the kitchen counter, filling a stainless steel pot with ground coffee.

'Coffee?' She raises an eyebrow at me and I nod. She leans across the table to pass me a mug and I see she's not quite so perfectly made up as I first thought. Her eyeliner is smudged at one end, one wing not quite perfect, and a tiny dot of something orange stains her blouse just below the collar, as though something has splashed up or spilled.

'So,' she settles into the chair across from me, her red travel mug next to her. She takes a sip, running her tongue over her lips, an action that makes me feel slightly sick. 'How are you? I mean, are you …?'

'I'm OK, I think. Thank you.' Cautiously I take a sip of my coffee, the scalding liquid burning the tip of my tongue. 'I just wanted to …'

'I'm so very sorry, Rachel,' she blurts out, cutting me off mid-sentence. Fat, wet tears fill Liz's eyes and she sniffs dramatically, tugging a clean tissue out from her sleeve and dabbing at her face. 'I feel awful that something like this could have happened – to one of our friends, and in our house, of all places.'

'Not your fault,' I say. Liz carries on sniffing into her tissue, before swigging from the travel mug again, and I can't help but feel as though she's secretly enjoying the drama.

'Did they find out who did it yet?' She asks, tears miraculously drying up, tucking the tissue back into her sleeve. 'I mean, I just can't believe that someone we know, someone we let into our home, could do something as awful as this.'

'That's actually what I wanted to talk to you about,' I shift in my seat, curling my toes up inside my boots, 'the police came to see you – about a list of guests for the party?'

'Yes. They came a couple of days after the party, quite late in the afternoon. I told them the names of everyone that I could remember seeing, but you know we'd all had quite a lot to drink, and there were a lot of people there. I don't think anyone turned down the invitation.' A defensive tone has crept into her voice, as a flush makes its way slowly up over her collarbone, leaving a pink stain across her neck. Unprompted, she carries on and begins reciting a list of party attendees. 'There was us, obviously, Amy, Katie and that funny little man that she lives with, I can never remember his name.' The travel mug goes to her mouth again, and she looks up at the ceiling as she tries to recall the other names on the list. 'Ted – no Angela, obviously, as she's gone off with that yoga chap. I didn't think it was appropriate to invite her, seeing as she doesn't live in the close any more.' I resist the urge to roll my eyes and hurry her along; Liz just can't help herself, it seems.

The residents of The Vines are destined to be her gossip fodder, and I've just provided her with the juiciest gossip of all time. She reels off a few more names.

'Anyone else?' I prod gently. She's already given me a couple of people that I wasn't sure about, I just want to make sure that she tells me as many as she can remember.

'A few people from Neil's gym, some of his colleagues, I can't remember *all* of their names but I'm sure Neil gave them to the police … oh, and the new guy. What's his name? Quite dishy, he moved here back at the end of the summer?' My heart starts to thunder in my chest, as I realize who she is talking about. 'Aaron. That's his name. He was there too.'

'Aaron? He was definitely at the party?' I ask, tucking my shaking hands under my thighs, as heat prickles along the back of my neck, the very definition of a cold sweat making me feel clammy. I definitely don't remember seeing him there. I would have left immediately if I had.

'Oh, not for long – you might not have seen him. He only arrived towards the end of the party; he wasn't even sure whether he'd be back in time to make it at all, at first. He might have arrived after you went … to bed.' Waving her hand, her eyes looking anywhere but mine, Liz trails off, a look of horror on her face as she realizes what she's said. 'Oh God, Rachel, I'm so sorry. I'm such an oaf. It never even occurred to me.' Her eyes fill with tears again and I find it's me reaching for her hand, to comfort her.

'I know you didn't mean anything by it, really. But I do need to know if there is anyone else you can remember being at the party. The police weren't really that forthcoming about it, and I just think that if I knew for sure who was there maybe it'll jog my memory.'

'Can you really not remember anything?' Liz asks, her wet lashes spidery with mascara. 'The police asked about drugs … whether anyone was seen with any illegal substances, whether someone could have put something in your drink. Do you think that's what happened?'

'I honestly don't know, Liz. I think maybe it's likely that someone spiked my drink. I can't remember anything past coming into the house − I remember the music, dancing as we came in, you asking me if I wanted a drink. That's it.' *Hands. Hands pushing me backwards, limbs like lead.* I blink, and scrub my hands over my trousers.

'Oh, gosh, you poor thing. I feel awful for you − I'm so sorry I can't be more help.' Clearly much more together now, Liz gets to her feet and carries her travel mug over to the work surface. Her gaze flicks towards the fridge before her eyes come to rest on my face again, as she leans up against the worktop. 'I don't remember a lot about the evening, if I'm honest, and that's exactly what I told the police. Neil was pretty much in the same boat. We'd all had rather a lot to drink by the end of the night and while I saw Gareth leave, I didn't see you. Not for the rest of the evening. I assumed you must have left with Gareth and then when you appeared the next morning in the kitchen I guessed you must have just had too much to drink and slept in the spare room. I never dreamed that anything like this would have happened.' She bites her lip and looks as though she might start to cry again.

'Look, none of this is your fault; I'm not blaming you, or Neil, for what happened. I'm sorry if I've upset you this morning, I'm just desperately trying to get things straight in my head, you know? But you've been great. Thank you.'

I stand, and tug my cardigan more tightly around my body, eager to get home, to get back to where I know that I'm safe. The atmosphere in this house feels unstable, volatile in some way, but maybe that's just because of what happened to me here.

'I should go. You've been really helpful.' More helpful than perhaps she realizes. Liz walks to me to the front door, and as she says goodbye she leans in to kiss me on the cheek. She smells of Opium perfume, a scent that makes me think of my mum, with a strange, spicy smell underneath, one that I can't quite put my finger on. I promise to call her if I need her, and turn to walk down the front path.

As I walk, a movement catches my eye and I pause, my breath catching in my throat. Seemingly oblivious to the cold Jason, Liz's gardener, stands in the far corner of her expansive front garden, clippers in one hand, rose in the other, tattoos winding their way down his forearm from the bottom of his T-shirt sleeve. Hearing the sound of my footsteps on the path, he turns to face me, his features blank and expressionless, and I tug my cardigan closer about my body wishing I'd put my winter coat on, as his gaze makes my skin prickle under my clothes. I look away, unnerved by the bland look on his face, and hurry down the path towards home. When I look back he is engrossed in his gardening, with no sign that he even noticed me at all.

9

JANUARY – ONE WEEK AFTER THE PARTY

While my nerves jangle every time I think about leaving the house, the urge to run is even more overwhelming, until I can't ignore it any longer. I wait until Gareth has left for the office before I quickly shower and pull on my running gear, eager to get out and feel the pounding of the pavement beneath my feet. At the front door I pause, that same panicky feeling washing over me, the thought that whoever did this to me is out there, possibly watching me, making my breath catch in my throat. Anxiously fingering the rape alarm strapped to my wrist (so ironic, it turns out rape alarms are more useful at parties, than out running alone through the West Marsham woods), I force my feet over the threshold holding my breath steady in my chest.

By the time I have reached the end of the High Street I have settled into a rhythm, my feet thumping against the concrete, the stretch of the muscles in my thighs feeling familiar and welcome. The cold snap that started off the New Year continues – this morning the sun hangs low in the sky, frost glittering on the pavements and swirling icy patterns on to car windscreens, and my breath streaks out ahead of me in huge, smoky plumes.

For me, running is a form of meditation – all the time I'm out there my mind is full of the rhythm of my feet on the pavement, the strain of the muscles in my thighs and the regular in and out of my breath, leaving no room for me to think about anything else. It's just what I need right now to give me some time to get my head together. This morning I let the comforting familiarity of it all overtake everything else and let my mind become blissfully blank.

After letting my feet take me where they want to go, I look up, realizing where I am. Coming to a stop, for a moment I pause at the edge of West Marsham woods, my heart beating double time in my chest, unsure as to whether I want to follow my usual route, but my feet itch to press on, so I do, reasoning that I have my rape alarm, and it's eight o'clock in the morning – people are on their way to work on the other side of the trees ... and surely, *surely* something couldn't happen to me twice, could it?

My first few steps into the woods are cautious and my breath loses rhythm in my throat, making me gasp and giving me a stitch in my side. I push on, breathing through it, fingers pressed against my ribs to ease the sharp pain. By the time I reach the tiny wooden bridge that spans the small stream running through the forest floor, I can see the motorway bridge in the distance, and people scurrying over it on their way to work, school, wherever they need to be. I stop, checking the time on my watch – my best time yet, it seems as though fear works for me in terms of personal bests – and lean over the handrail of the bridge, sucking in gulps of fresh, so-cold-it-hurts early morning air. I am so intent on drinking in the fresh air, watching the swirling eddies in the no doubt icy water, that I shriek as I feel a hand land on my arm. I whirl around, one arm raised to strike, fumbling for the button on the rape alarm with the other.

'Wait, Rachel, please.' A familiar voice tries to calm me, 'It's me. It's only me.'

I lower my arms, heart racing and breath coming in gasps as fear pumps obscene amounts of adrenaline around my body.

'Jesus, Ted. You scared me.' I wipe surreptitiously at my top lip, where tiny beads of sweat have gathered and try to regulate my breathing. 'What the hell were you doing, sneaking up on me like that?'

'I wasn't sneaking, honestly – I'm sorry if I scared you. I was just walking Flora and I saw you ...' He lifts one hand, dog lead wrapped around it, Flora, his Doberman, attached to the other end. She sniffs at the edge of the bridge, before pacing backwards and forwards, letting out a little whine of frustration. 'I just wanted to make sure you're OK.'

I look at him, taking in his familiar features, the smile on his face that could make my heart race and my knickers fall off. Once. Not any more. He's been away at a conference, or so Robbie said, so I have no idea whether he knows what happened at the party or not.

'I don't need to be in the office until later today. Can we get a coffee?' he asks awkwardly, his cheeks rosy from either the cold or a blush, I'm not sure which. 'I mean, if you want to? Just to chat ... catch up, you know.' He gives another awkward smile. I think for a moment, worry that Gareth will hear about it, sparking a niggle of anxiety; I don't want to make things any worse between us. But then I think of Gareth's face when he said I had washed away all the evidence, and how I felt, despite his reassurances, as though he didn't believe me about what had happened. It's just a coffee. And Ted is a friend, no matter what went on between us before.

'Yes,' I say.

The coffee shop on West Marsham High Street is busy, heaving with customers grabbing their latte, or cappuccino, or whatever 'to go' on their way to work. While Ted ties Flora's lead to the post outside, I push my way through the busy café, headed towards the back of the room where I spy an empty table tucked away from prying eyes. The last thing I need is someone reporting back to Gareth that I was having coffee with Ted. I think for a moment about leaving, about saving myself the bother that this coffee could potentially cause and just walking out and heading home, but when I turn Ted is at the counter, gesturing to me about muffins. I shake my head and sit down at the table, no chance of escape now. At least I can use this opportunity to find out what Ted remembers of the party, to see if he can tell me anything that Liz couldn't. I watch as he winds his way through the now thinning crowd, a coffee in each hand. He hands one to me and I take a cautious sip, the scorching liquid puffing fragrant steam into my face. *Hazelnut latte.* Ted remembers my coffee order, even if Gareth doesn't.

'Thanks.'

'Rachel, I wanted to speak to you … about the party.' Ted leans forward across the table and I get a hint of his citrusy aftershave. The smell makes me feel slightly sick, and I shake my head, pulling back slightly, unsure as to why I would feel that way.

'What about it?' I whisper, holding my coffee cup to my mouth in order to hide behind it.

'People are saying …' He breaks off, taking a deep breath before he goes on, 'people are saying that something happened to you there. That you were attacked. Is that true?'

'Yes.' I don't know how else to say it. 'At least, I think so.'

'You *think* so?' Ted frowns, his brow crumpling. 'What do you mean? You don't know?'

'I *do* know. I know that something happened to me, I just don't know what. I can't remember anything clearly past the first half an hour or so of the party. I think my drink was spiked.' The air in here is cloying and humid, thick with the scent of coffee and buttery pastry, and my stomach rolls over as I breathe it in. I push my fringe off my forehead and wish that I hadn't put running skins on after all.

'Oh God, Rachel, I'm so sorry.' Ted leans over and grasps both my hands in his. I squirm uncomfortably, sliding my hands out from under his. I don't want it getting back to Gareth that I was holding hands with Ted in the coffee house. 'You really don't remember anything?'

'Not much. Although I remember more now than I did when I woke up the next morning.'

Ted leans back, running his hand over the whiskery stubble on his chin, a frown dipping his eyebrows down in to a deep V.

'God, Rachel, I don't know what to say. I'd ask if you're all right, but it seems to be a bit of a stupid question.'

He looks devastated, and I almost feel sorry for him, before I remember that it's me that I should be feeling sorry for, me who was hurt. 'What can you remember?'

'Bits and pieces, that's all. I remember arriving, hearing music. Not much more than that at the moment.' I don't want to talk about the sensation of hands pushing me down, sure that if I do mention it there's a chance I'll go to pieces and I can't, not in here. 'Listen, Ted ...' It's my turn to lean across the table towards him now, my words hushed to avoid the woman on the table next to us, whose ears are practically out on stalks trying to hear our conversation. 'Can I pick your brains about the party? The police are apparently speaking to everyone who was there, but I just ... I have this huge gap – a big, black hole in my memory – and I'm trying to connect the dots. See what other people can remember in the hope that it'll jog something in my own mind, something that will help me remember.'

'Of course,' Ted still has that look of concern etched into his face, 'anything I can do to help. Although, I've already told the police everything I know.'

'They've seen you?' I don't know why but for some reason I thought I was speaking to Ted before they had. Stupid, I should have known.

'I came back from the conference to a message to contact them urgently. I went into the station on my way home from work last night and told them what I knew.'

'What do you know, Ted?' My words are clipped, and I give a small smile of apology. I just want to know what Ted remembers from that night.

'Not a lot really.' He puffs out a long breath as he thinks. 'I got to the party a little later than everyone else; it was already busy by the time I got there. Angela called just as I was about to walk out the door, something she wanted to discuss about Sean. She wants him to go out to the US, to stay with her and Devon, a gap year, she called it, but I'm pretty sure she'll spend her time trying to convince him to stay there.' Ted shreds the napkin in front of him, littering the table with tiny scraps of tissue. I stay silent, waiting for him to go on.

'You were there when I arrived ... talking in the kitchen, I'm sure. I said hello but I didn't hang around because I knew Gareth was there, somewhere.'

'He wasn't in the kitchen with me?' I ask, anxiety bubbling up in my stomach once more.

'Not that I saw. You were talking to Melody, laughing about something. You both had a glass in your hands – red wine, I think? I went through into the living room and then I saw Neil and we started talking about the football.'

'What about Gareth? Did you see him leave?' I still have that underlying feeling that something wasn't quite right when he left – that we maybe *weren't* OK by the time he wanted to leave the party.

'No, I didn't see him, but then I didn't actively look out for him. I didn't see him all night, I don't think. But then maybe he was avoiding me. I mean, it would be pretty awkward, wouldn't it? The two of us making small talk at a party.' Ted gives a rueful huff of laughter, but I say nothing. 'Do you really not remember me leaving, Rachel?'

He looks at me strangely, and I get that twist of fear low down in my belly again, my heart beat stuttering in my chest.

'Did I see you leave?' My mouth is dry as I ask the question; pretty sure I know what his answer will be.

'You were with me,' he says, and I feel sick again, my stomach rolling. 'You were quite drunk – I was a bit worried about you. You were slurring your words and staggering a bit, and there was no sign of Gareth, so it must have been after he left. I was going to help you home – just walk you across the green, make sure you got back safely – because you weren't in a fit state to get there on your own. My phone rang just as we were about to leave, and it was Angela ... I had to take it, we'd rowed earlier, and she was a bit hysterical.'

'So why didn't you end up walking me home?'

'I left you in the kitchen, sat at the table – I did tell you I'd be right back once I'd spoken to Angela – but when I came back in the kitchen, you were gone. I checked all over downstairs to see if I could find you, but ... obviously I couldn't. I checked with Liz to see if she'd seen you, but she seemed to think that you'd left when Gareth did.' Ted looks down at the mass of shredded paper all over the table. 'I'm sorry, Rachel, I should have gone upstairs, I should have looked for you.'

I can't speak for a minute, trying hard as I am to see the scene he just described. I imagine myself slumped against Ted's shoulder, the weight of him sturdy beneath me. The rolling floor, trying to upend me as I walk – no, stagger towards the front door, but I have no idea if this is a memory, or just my own twisted imagination.

'It's OK,' I say, but it's not, not really, why didn't Ted look for me properly? Why did Gareth leave without me? How did I get in such a state that I could barely stand on my own? Anxious now to get home and think things through, I push the empty coffee cup away from me and get to my feet. 'I have to go, Ted. Thank you … for telling me what you know.'

'Wait, Rachel,' he stands and lays a hand firmly on my arm. I stare down at it, until he pulls back. 'Let me know what the police say, won't you? When they have anything new to tell you?' I nod and make my way through the now thankfully empty café. I just want to go home. I should never have gone running this morning.

Once home, I strip off my damp, clammy running clothes and head straight for the shower, my mind whirling with everything Ted has told me this morning. Standing under the powerful spray I let the hot, almost too hot, water thunder down over my face and hair, into the stiff, aching muscles that I failed to warm down properly. I toss over Ted's words in my mind – *you were quite drunk, slurring your words* – and I struggle to believe what he's said.

I would never have let myself get in such a state that I couldn't walk or talk properly on my own. *Gareth* would never have let me get like that, even if he was angry with me. Yes, there have been times in the past when I *have* drunk too much, and not remembered things in the morning – who hasn't been there? But not like this. Previously, I've always been able to remember the majority of the evening – who I spoke to, who else was there – but this time there is literally nothing beyond Liz opening the door, the thumping bass of the music thudding through the walls.

The other thing that strikes me as unusual is Ted saying I slurred – when I drink, I am a puker, much to Gareth's disgust. I am a lightweight, and I have never, ever reached a point where I slur my words, simply because I have usually been sick and gone to bed before I can reach that point. *And the smell of citrus aftershave,* that persistent little voice whispers at the back of my mind, *see how you reacted to the smell of Ted's aftershave? Why would that make you feel sick? You used to love the smell of Ted's aftershave.* I reach up and lather shampoo roughly into my hair, trying to force that thought from my mind. It terrifies me to think that Ted perhaps had more to do with things that night than he's told me.

An hour later, my hair still drying on my shoulders, I am seated on our living room couch, feet tucked up on the cushion next to me, listening to Carrie tell me the good news, and then the bad news.

'The good news is that all your tests came back clear.' *Thank God.* 'But I do have to tell you that things with the investigation have slowed down a bit since I last spoke to you.'

'What?' I slide my feet out from under me and place them firmly on the floor, as if to ground me. The world tilts slightly and I feel as though I am underwater, as though I might faint. 'What do you mean, things have slowed down? It's barely been more than a week!'

Carrie looks down at the floor, fiddling with her watchstrap, keen to avoid eye contact with me.

'I'm sorry, Rachel, I really am. If it were down to me I wouldn't … let you down like this.' She finally raises her eyes to mine, and I shake my head disbelievingly. 'We are still working on it; I can assure you. I'll still be on the case, but unfortunately the leads we've been following don't seem to be giving us much more information to go on at the moment.'

'Surely you can't just … give up like this?'

'We're not giving up on you, Rachel, I promise. There's just no evidence, no leads for us to go on right now, but that doesn't mean that we won't keep looking for things – we still need your underwear to turn up for starters.'

'And the information you already have hasn't helped?'

'Your medical examination showed that you had had intercourse, but there was no DNA, no tearing, nothing that could have been anything more than rough sex. You'd been drinking … and by the time you came in anything that might have been slipped into your drink didn't show on any blood tests. I'm sorry.'

'But what about the bruises on my arms, and on my thighs? Doesn't that prove anything?' My voice rises into nigh on a shriek, scratching the back of my throat. At the sound of raised voices Thor staggers from his basket, throwing himself down on the rug at my feet. Carrie shakes her head.

'It's not enough,' she says, and I hear the click of her throat as she swallows, 'sometimes we do hit a bit of a wall in cases like this. I wish I could tell you differently. But believe me, Rachel, this doesn't mean that I won't keep investigating.'

'What about the other people at the party?' I whisper, as I feel the anger that fired me up fading, 'surely someone saw something? One of them must have been able to give you something to go on – how could nobody have seen anything at all?'

'Apparently not. We've spoken to everyone we're aware of attending, and no one saw anything, apart from you seeming to be more drunk than usual. I'm sorry, Rachel, we've done as much as we can for the moment. Until we can find your underwear there's no evidence.' *You washed it all away.* The words stand in the thick atmosphere between us, as sure as if they were written in neon.

'Did you speak to a man named Aaron Power? Apparently, he was at the party,' I say, desperate to give Carrie *something* to go on. 'I had … some trouble with him before Christmas.'

'Yes, we did.' Carrie tucks her pen back inside her notebook. 'There were a lot of people at the party and there seems to be some slight confusion over who actually attended. He says he wasn't there, Rachel.'

Unable to speak, so furious am I, I show her to the front door, eager to see the back of her now, disappointed that she could just give up on me – because that's what it feels like, even though she says she's not – making me feel heavy and lethargic.

She tries to apologize again at the door, but I wave her away, closing the door on her before she can finish speaking. Resting my head against the cool of the door, I close my eyes, not even attempting to blink back the hot, angry tears that fall. *I'm on my own.* That much I do know now – the police aren't interested, despite Carrie saying they'll still be working on my case I know it'll just fall further and further down the list as more, even worse crimes come in, and despite Gareth saying he does believe me, I still have that creeping feeling that he doesn't, not really.

Before I can move away, the shrill ring of the doorbell makes me jump, and I think maybe Carrie has come back – maybe she's realized that *something* sinister happened that night and she's going to try and get a full team back on it. I pull the door open, only to see a stranger standing there, no Carrie.

'Yes?' I don't think it's too obvious that I've been crying, but I tug the door close to my body ready to slam it shut.

'Hiiiiii.' The woman in front of me draws the word out in an attempt to sound chummy. She is about my height, with a thick face of make-up, a line of orange foundation marring her bottom jaw, and bleached spiky blonde hair. I have no idea who she is. 'Rachel, right? Rachel Walker?'

'Yes,' I reply cautiously, peering past her to see if Carrie's car has left yet. There's no sign of the little blue Fiat she turned up in last time.

'Hiiiiii,' she says again, extending her hand to me. I don't shake it. 'My name is Helen Faulkner. I'm from the Marsham *Echo*.' A journalist.

'Oh no, no, thank you.' I go to push the door closed but it seems that she's somehow wedged her booted foot in the gap between the door and frame. 'Take your foot out of my door.'

'I just wanted to speak to you, Rachel. I can call you that, right?' she soothes, biro already in hand.

'No, you can't. Get off my doorstep.' I push the door harder on to her foot, relishing the tiny wince that crosses her features.

'I heard about what happened to you, at the party on New Year's Eve — don't you want to tell your side of the story, Rachel? Only, no one seems to know what really happened that night, so I thought you could put things straight ... tell us what you know and give us your version.' She staggers as I manage to dislodge her foot, slamming the door firmly in her face. 'Here's my card.' A small white square card rattles through the letterbox, Helen Faulkner's name, email and telephone number typed neatly across it. 'Call me when you're ready to talk, Rachel. Only, maybe don't leave it too long, the story is already out there. People are already talking.'

I stay silent, leaning against the door, the small white card on the mat the only thing marring my vision. I hear the tap-tap-tapping of her heels as she marches back down the path towards the main road, waiting until the sound dies away and I am sure she has left. I slide down the doorframe, sinking on to the doormat, in much the same position as I found myself that awful morning.

So, people are talking about what happened. The police have spoken to everyone at the party and found nothing. Aaron has told the police that he wasn't at the party – but Liz told me he was there. Ted says I was slurring and staggering, but I'm sure I wouldn't have let myself get in that state. I can reach only one conclusion from the things I've heard today. Someone is lying.

10

SEPTEMBER – THREE MONTHS BEFORE THE PARTY

I deleted Aaron's friend request as soon as it arrived on my phone the other night – but another now sits blinking at me on my laptop screen. Sighing, I take a sip of wine and angle the laptop to show Amy, where she sits across the kitchen table from me, Thor laid on her feet.

'Yikes. He's keen,' she says, as her eyes scan the screen. 'Some people just don't know when to take "no" for an answer.'

'Hmmm.' I turn the screen back to face me and click on to his name. 'He hasn't got many friends … or even many posts, it's like he only just set it up.' *Creepy. The guy is definitely creepy.*

'So just ignore it.' Amy shrugs, reaching down to pet Thor. The thin, silver bracelets that line her arms jangle as she moves. 'If you don't accept it, and just leave it on your account waiting to be dealt with, at least that way he can't send another one. Let's look at Ted's account instead.' She waggles her eyebrows at me suggestively.

'Oh, shhhhh,' I laugh, a little buzz of anticipation rippling through me as I type in his name. Angela moved out a month after the barbecue, moving straight in with Devon, the yoga instructor. It turns out Ted's instinct was right all along. I had told Amy about the row Gareth and I had in the kitchen on the day of the barbecue, and I had even told her about Ted coming to check on me in the bathroom. I told her he kissed me, but that's all. She doesn't know about the rest of it, all the other times we've been together since then and what we've done together. 'Here. Happy families, pre Devon.' Amy gets up and comes to sit next to me, peering at the screen, filled with photos of Ted, Angela and Sean together on various days out, faces squashed together as they all huddle in.

'Ugh,' Amy says, a sour tang of wine on her breath, 'the before pics … before Angela ran away with that stringy yoga dude. Imagine what *their* bedtime looks like.' Light-headed with wine, I snort with laughter at the thought of Angela and Devon tying themselves up in knots in bed, before Aaron sneaks into my thoughts again and I sober quickly.

'So, you reckon just ignore him then?' I ask, closing the lid of the laptop. I reach for the wine and top both of our glasses up, even though I already feel a little tipsy after that one glass.

'Yeah, I reckon.' Amy raises her glass to me before she takes a sip. 'He's a bit of a weirdo, but he's harmless, right? Just ignore it, and if by chance he does ask you why you haven't accepted, just tell him you don't really use that account. No harm done.'

We move out into the garden, carrying our wine and a few snacks. September has brought with it a cool breeze and sunshine, and I sigh with pleasure as the warm sun strokes its way across my bare arms. Amy's right – he's harmless.

My good mood fades when Gareth stomps into the house, two hours later than expected. The dinner I cooked is wizened and dry from being kept warm in the oven too long, but I slide on an oven glove and pull it out, ready to dish it up to him anyway.

'How was your day?' *Make an effort, Rachel, he's probably just tired.* I sit across the table from him and watch as he wrinkles his nose at the congealed mess on the plate, resisting the urge to tip the food over his ungrateful head. There is a permanent frown etched into his forehead recently, and I can tell today has been another tough day as his hair sticks up on end, as though he's been running his hand through it all day. A sure sign that something is wrong.

'Fine.' He takes a bite of dried-up chicken pie, ignoring his phone as it pings with a message alert on the table next to him.

'You're late back. Everything OK?' I watch him as he shovels the terrible, dried-up food into his mouth, a shrunken pea whizzing off his plate and disappearing somewhere underneath the kitchen unit. His phone buzzes on the table next to him again. 'Shouldn't you get that?'

'For fuck's sake, Rachel.' He slams down his knife and fork, leaving half of his meal uneaten, and scrapes his chair back, getting to his feet and grabbing the phone. 'Just leave it, OK? Just mind your own bloody business.' He marches from the room and a few seconds later I hear the door to his study slam shut.

Closing my eyes, I rest my head on my arms on the table, the thud of a tension headache starting to thump in my temples. *Is this it? Is this how it's going to be for the rest of our lives?* I have no idea what is making Gareth behave this way, but I know that he's driving me towards Ted more and more with every bad mood, every curt response, every time he swears at me. Getting to my feet wearily, I start to clear the table, my

101

mind turning Gareth's behaviour over and over in my mind, when a ping alerts me to a message on my own phone.

Thursday, 10 a.m.? West Marsham woods. I have the morning off.

I smile, my spirits lifting immediately. *Ted Durand wants to see me.* I haven't saved his number in my phone for fear of being caught, but by now his number is as familiar to me as my own, more so even.

'Yes,' I reply, careful not to put anything else that could incriminate us. If anyone (read, Gareth) sees the text I can pass it off as someone who isn't Ted, a running buddy maybe. My lips twitch with a tiny, secret smile and the weight of Gareth's … what? Anger? Disappointment? Whatever it is that I seem to have done to annoy him lessens slightly. I can make it to Thursday.

On my way to bed, I pause outside Gareth's study. There is a chink of light showing under the door and I tap lightly hoping he'll let me in. Maybe now he's had some time to himself he might be in the mood to talk. There is no response, so I press my ear tightly against the door, listening hard, feeling like a spy in my own house. I hear the low murmur of Gareth's voice and guess he's on the phone, maybe replying to whoever was so insistent at dinner.

Or maybe Gareth is having an affair? Maybe that's why he doesn't seem to want you around lately. Maybe he's saving all his good humour for someone who actually deserves it.

I shake my head, and press harder against the wood of the door, trying to hear what he is saying. It sounds as though Gareth is pacing, and I draw back slightly in case he throws open the door, making his words even more indistinct. After a moment, it goes silent and I start to tiptoe away towards the stairs, when the door flies open.

'Rachel!' Gareth looks startled to see me. 'Did you want me?'

'No …' I say, my heart thumping at almost being caught, 'I just wanted to see if you were OK, that's all. Sorry, I'll leave you — I know you're busy.' Turning away I take a step towards the stairs but Gareth lays a hand on my shoulder.

'Wait, before you go …' he hurries back into the office, returning with two slips of paper in his hand, 'can you give these to Robbie? I saw the email the school sent out about high ability pupils with his name on the list and I thought he might like these as a treat.' I look down to see two tickets to Robbie's favourite band — tickets that have been like gold dust.

'Wow — how did you get these? Rob will be thrilled.' I didn't even realize that Gareth knew which bands Robbie was in to.

'Don't ask,' Gareth gives a wan smile, 'look, Rach, I have to get on. I'll be up in a bit.'

'OK.' I nod, and he leaves me there in the dim light of the hallway, the two tickets burning a hole in my hand.

As I slide under the covers, my feet searching out the cool of the sheet, I wonder what it could all mean — one minute Gareth is stressed out, rude and abrupt, not caring if he hurts my feelings, and then the next he does something so completely unexpected, so sweet that makes me think, *there you are, the man I married*, and it's like an invisible cord draws me back to him again.

My phone buzzes on the nightstand next to me, and I almost don't check it, my head is so full of trying to decipher what Gareth could be so stressed about, and trying to unravel the guilt I'm feeling about Ted – every time Gareth does something thoughtful, the weight of my betrayal hits me like a wave of disgust, harder and harder each time – but then I think maybe it's Ted and perhaps I should just text him back and cancel our meeting. I roll over and grope in the dark for my mobile. A message request icon flashes up on the screen, illuminating the room with an eerie blue glow. Tapping on it, my breath sticks in my throat.

'*Aaron Power has sent you a message request. They will not see you have read this message until you accept it.*'

Fuck. I feel a bit queasy as I open the message, careful not to tap the accept button just yet.

'*Hey, Rachel. I sent you a friend request but you don't seem to have accepted it yet. Just wanted to say it was lovely seeing you the other day. Perhaps we could get together for a drink? For old time's sake. ;)*.' Winky face. A winky face, for fuck's sake. What are we, fifteen? I press the accept button and start to tap out a reply. Maybe if I'm just honest with him he'll get the hint.

'*Hi Aaron. Sorry, I don't really use this account.*' Thanks for the tip, Amy. '*I'm sorry, I can't accept your offer of a drink either.*' I pause for a moment, thinking how best to word what I want to say. '*I'm happily married, and I just don't think it would be appropriate, but thank you. Rachel.*' Happily married. I flick the phone on to silent and flip my pillow over to the cool side. Closing my eyes, I will sleep to come, trying to ignore the bitter taste of lies on my tongue.

Days later I am at the supermarket, meandering along the aisles, picking things up and putting them down again. I'm not in the right frame of mind for food shopping, occupied as I am with Gareth and his still erratic mood swings, but I have a rare afternoon free of clients, and we have nothing in — an eighteen-year-old boy eats a lot, even if his father isn't there for dinner every night. Gareth also decided to spring it on me this morning that he's arranged a works dinner party for tomorrow evening. I am leaning over the edge of a large freezer, trying to decide whether frozen prawns are a better bet than fresh, when a tap on my arm startles me and I nearly upend into the freezer fully. Straightening up, I turn to see the last person I wanted to bump in to.

'Aaron. Hello.' I realize I am clutching a sweaty packet of frozen prawns as though my life depends on it, before slinging them back into the freezer. Aaron looks far more together than I feel right now — I feel a bit discombobulated, caught on the hop, while Aaron looks fresh from a catalogue page in a crisp white shirt and chino style trousers.

'Rachel! Nice to see you.' He leans in to kiss me on the cheek and I have to resist the urge to pull away. His aftershave is strong and sickly, making my stomach flip and not in a good way.

'Yes.' I don't know what else to say.

'Doing your food shop?' Aaron peers into the trolley and I feel exposed and vulnerable by his prying eyes, even though all I have in there so far is a large bag of salad, a tube of Pringles and some wine.

'Looks that way,' I say brightly, inching the trolley forward slightly. 'Well, I should go,' I gesture towards the trolley, 'lots to do, you know?'

'I do.' He smiles, and I am reminded of a shark circling its prey. 'I'm just grabbing some lunch, on my way back to work.' He raises an eyebrow and I feel as though I'm missing something, like he knows something I don't.

'Well, see you then.' I place both hands firmly on the trolley and start to push it away from him, but his hand shoots out and he grabs the end, stopping me from going anywhere.

'Why don't you want to go for a drink with me, Rachel?'

I flounder for a moment, giving a little cough to buy myself some time.

'It's nothing personal, Aaron.'

'So why not then? We've got history together, Rachel, you know that.'

'History?' Surely, he can't think that a couple of pints in the student union bar over twenty years ago amounts to history? I barely spoke to him, he was just on the fringes of our friendship group. I know he worked for Gareth for a bit, but I had barely anything to do with him then either, not if I could help it.

'Yeah, history.' He smirks, small, white teeth showing through his fashionable hipster beard, and I shudder inwardly. 'Come on, it's just one drink. You don't even need to tell Gareth about it. Or, I could just book in to come and see you for a treatment.'

The thought of him laid out on my massage table makes me feel more than a little uncomfortable. 'Look, Aaron, I'm flattered, I really am, but I'm married … to Gareth, for goodness' sake. You know Gareth, your old boss? It's really not appropriate. Please, I need to go, I have things to do.' I glance anxiously over my shoulder, hoping that someone else is nearby, but the aisle is deserted, clearly no one is in great need of frozen food this afternoon. My fingers shake slightly, and I grip the handle of the trolley tight until my knuckles go white, my pulse starting to throb in my temples.

'Shopping for the dinner party?' He relaxes his grip on the trolley but still stands barring my way.

'Excuse me?' My mouth goes dry – how does he know what I'm shopping for? As far as I know Gareth only arranged it with the guests a couple of days ago.

'The dinner party. Tomorrow night. I'm guessing that's what you're shopping for.'

'How do you know about that?' I turn back towards the freezers, trying to disguise my anxiety from him by pretending to be engrossed in the frozen fish. I pick up the packet of prawns again.

'Well, Gareth invited me, of course.' A smug grin slides across his face as he realizes that I know nothing about his invitation. 'We're all invited. Well, two of our most important clients, plus the senior management from the office.' *Our* clients? Realization dawns and I have to swallow down the dread that washes over me.

'You ... Gareth gave you a job again? You're back at the office?' *Oh God, that's the last thing I need.* I was so relieved when he left the last time, so thankful that I wouldn't have to avoid his creepy gaze every time I went to the office, that it never even occurred to me that he would come back.

'That's right.' Aaron beams at me. 'So, I'll see you tomorrow, about eight o'clock? We can have a drink together then, although it's not quite the same, is it?' I say nothing, but my palms feel damp against the plastic of the trolley handle. Aaron steps closer to me, leaning down to whisper in my ear, that sickly aftershave filling my nostrils again. I swallow hard, fighting back nausea.

'You might want to throw those back in the freezer. To be honest, I'm not too keen on fish. Especially the cold kind.'

11

JANUARY – TWO WEEKS AFTER THE PARTY

'Are you sure you don't mind taking me? I'm happy to drive myself if you don't feel up to it.' Gareth hefts the suitcase into the boot of the car and walks round to the passenger side to let himself in.

'I said I didn't mind. It's fine.' I slide in to the driver's seat and fiddle about with the settings, attempting to inch forward so my feet can reach the pedals. I'm trying not to be anxious about the fact that Gareth is going away for a week to look at property in Croatia, leaving me alone in the house with Robbie. He offered to cancel the trip, but I told him not to. Having him gone gives me the space I need to carry on my own investigation, even if the thought of being alone does terrify me. The thought of letting people into the house terrifies me even more, and I still haven't booked any clients in for treatments since before the party. 'Have you got everything?'

'Yep. Will you be OK?' Gareth eyes me carefully as I reverse out of the drive on to the main road. 'If you need me just call and I'll try and come home.' *Try. Just that one little word changes the whole sentence structure and tells me that he didn't really*

109

mean it when he offered to cancel his trip. I should imagine he'd be relieved to get away from me, to get a break from it all.

'I'll be fine.' I bite the tip of my tongue in lieu of crossing my fingers. The truth is, I *am* anxious about being here alone. What will I do if he knows where I live? What will I do if he breaks into the house while I'm alone to do it all over again? I did try to voice my concerns to Gareth, but he just looked at me oddly and told me that wouldn't happen. So, I am settling for driving Gareth to the airport in his car, which I will then park on our drive thereby making people think that Gareth is home. It was the best idea I could think of, to make me feel safer.

'Maybe it's time to start thinking about going back to work?' Gareth says, breaking the silence that has accompanied us on the journey so far. I indicate to move across in to the left-hand lane, ready to turn on to the M23 towards Gatwick, my pulse fluttering at his words. 'You could always come in and give me a hand for a few days, if you don't fancy having clients at home just yet. Just to get you out of the house.'

'Back to the office?' I feel sick at the thought of it, especially as Aaron flits in and out of there all day from what I can gather. He's worked his way up over the past few months to become Gareth's right-hand man, the bond that has forged between them something I can't understand. Especially now. Now I know Liz saw Aaron at the party, even if he is denying it. 'I don't think … I mean, you have Aaron …' My mouth feels dry and gritty, my throat sticking as I swallow. I don't want to go back there and have to come face to face with Aaron every day. The very thought of it makes my ears ring, as though I am about to faint.

'It doesn't have to be the office,' Gareth replies, 'it doesn't even have to be your aromatherapy, not if you feel uncomfortable ... I was thinking something along the lines of counselling – remember you wanted to do that course? Maybe that would help.'

'Help? How will that help?' I keep my eyes fixed on the road. 'You don't just go on a course and what happened miraculously goes away, Gareth. You know that, right?'

'I didn't mean ... oh, for God's sake.' He swears under his breath and twists in his seat to face me, tugging the seatbelt away from his neck. 'All I meant was maybe you need something to help take your mind off ... all of this. That maybe being closeted away in a log cabin at the bottom of the garden, on your own with clients who you don't necessarily know, isn't the best thing for you right now.' He sighs. 'I found your notes, Rachel.'

My notes. Every scrap of information I've found about that night, like Ted trying to help me home, I've scribbled down in an old notepad that I hide under my pillow. Writing things down helps me keep things straight in my head, and I figure if the police are scaling down the investigation then it's up to me to find out who did this, and why.

'They're private,' is all I say to Gareth, still keeping my eyes on the road, prickly with irritation at him going through my things. A white van tries to cut me up at the roundabout and I hang back, letting him push in. 'They're just notes, that's all.'

'I'm worried you're getting obsessed. The police said things were slowing down for a reason, Rachel. Whatever happened that night, there just isn't enough evidence for them to go on. Please, I know this is hard for you but can't we ... maybe we can try to move on?'

Are you fucking kidding me? I bite back the words and yank on the handbrake as I pull into the dedicated drop-off zone, trying not to show Gareth how angry I am. *How can he want to move on without finding out the truth? At least the police have lack of evidence as their excuse – what's Gareth's?* I push away the other thought that rises to the surface, the one that says he doesn't believe anything really happened that night, at least, not the way I said it did.

'You'd better go, you'll miss your flight.' I pop the boot and stare out of the window, not wanting to see his traitorous, unsupportive face. He leans over and grasps my wrist, where my hand lies on the steering wheel, tugging it towards him.

'You've got the phone I got you?' Gareth asks, and I point towards the glove box. My mobile still hasn't turned up, so Gareth bought me a cheap supermarket phone until I can get a new one. He squeezes my wrist lightly. 'Please, Rachel. I know it's hard, but just think about it all, OK? I want …' he breaks off, sighing again, lacing his fingers through mine. 'I want everything between us to be all right. I know I haven't been … I know things have been difficult, but we can put all of this behind us, can't we? Please, maybe just think about the counselling course?'

He's obviously not going to leave until I agree, and much as I don't want him to go and leave me alone in the house (with Robbie, not that that makes much difference) I want him to miss his flight even less.

'OK, fine. Whatever. I'll drop it. Just go, you're going to miss your flight.' I let him kiss me on the cheek, and he gets out, only to lean back in again.

'Call me if you need me?'

I nod, and the minute he slams the boot shut I pull away, glancing in the rear-view mirror to see him standing watching me leave. I've told him what he wants to hear, but I have no intention of letting things go. I'll find out what happened to me that night, and who was involved, even if it kills me – there's no way I'm giving up.

Pulling on to the drive way an hour later, I have calmed down a little and resolve to be nothing but sweetness and light to Gareth tonight when he calls. I'll hide the notebook and tell him I've got rid of it, and I'll just have to be super careful about snooping around. What's one more lie among the mountain of them that exist between us already?

I get out of the car, relieved that I seem to have found a way to keep us both happy, and raise a hand in greeting to Mrs Gregory next door as she peers out between her net curtains. I am halfway up the path to the front door when I see it. A flash of silver caught by a weak ray of sun, a quick trick of the light that I could have so easily missed. Frowning, unsure if I even saw it at all, I crouch down in front of the driver's side of my car, a Mini Clubman, distinctive by the red stripes that race along the bonnet and the sides, clashing wildly with the black paint. There, etched carefully into the polished black exterior is the word 'SLUT'.

'Shit.' I press one hand to my mouth, the other to the cold concrete path to stop myself from falling. Taking a deep breath, my heart hammering hard enough in my chest to hurt, I press my fingertips lightly to the roughened edges of the metal. Someone has taken great care to make sure the word is not only legible, but it is scored so deeply into the car door that the only way I'll get rid of it is to replace the door completely.

'Are you OK down there, lovey?' Mrs Gregory is standing over me, wringing her hands together. 'Only I saw you crouch down there and you look a little bit upset.' She peers over my shoulder, at the ragged letters scratched into the door panel.

'Oooh,' she breathes, her breath whistling through her false teeth, as I stand upright, fighting back tears. 'That looks nasty.'

'It's fine, Mrs Gregory. I'm fine, I mean.' I angle my body against the car to try and hide the damage, even though I know it's too late, she's already seen it. 'Gareth will sort it out.' A thought strikes me – Mrs Gregory must spend ninety per cent of her day peering out of her front window. 'I don't suppose you saw anything, did you? Anybody on the drive, perhaps, while I was out?'

'Oh no, dear,' she says, shaking her head, grey curls immobile from the hairspray she uses. 'I just got back from the hairdresser's, only a few minutes before you, that's why I saw you from the front window.' A likely story – she can't help herself from spying on all of us that live in the close, we're her daily entertainment. Something I'm conscious of every time Gareth and I have a row.

'OK. Thank you anyway.' She makes no effort to leave, so I turn away on shaking legs and start to walk towards the front door, when she calls out to me.

'It's probably got something to do with that article on the Internet today.'

I stop, my mouth suddenly dry. 'What article on the Internet? Are you sure?'

'I might be old, dear, but I do know about the Facebook, you know,' Mrs Gregory sniffs indignantly, 'it's on the Marsham *Echo* website. There's an article all about you.'

'Thank you for coming over.' I usher Ted inside quickly before Mrs Gregory can spy him, although chances are it's already too late. 'Have you seen it? The article?' I haven't been able to bring myself to open up my laptop. Not yet. I feel too sick at the idea of the entire village talking about me.

'Yes, but … have you seen your car?' Bewildered, Ted is glancing over his shoulder as I pull him roughly inside.

'That's why I called you and asked you to come over. I came home and found that word scratched into the side of my car, and Mrs Gregory said it must have something to do with an article the *Echo* has posted online today. I have no idea what she's talking about, but it's all over social media apparently.' I am jittery, my words tumbling out over one another.

Too frightened to leave the house, and with Robbie nowhere to be seen, I called Amy to ask her to come over, to quite literally hold my hand as I read what has been written about me, but her mobile just rang out and went to voicemail. The only other person I could think to call was Ted, only now he's here I'm not sure I made the right decision – and I'm pretty sure Mrs Gregory will have seen him arriving and will report back to Gareth. Ted follows me through into the kitchen where I shove a mug of coffee at him and open up my laptop. I sign in and search for the Marsham *Echo* page. There it is, the most commented on article.

WOMAN ASSAULTED AT NEW YEAR'S EVE PARTY

I feel sick. The gist of the article is that a woman (namely me) claims to have been sexually assaulted after Liz's party, and that the police have no evidence to back up my claims. The article digresses into a long discussion on the failure of rape victims to be believed, and contrasts this with evidence of cases of men being falsely accused of rape. At the bottom of the article a 'source close to the victim' claims to have been at the party, and says that no one else there saw anything. The by-line is Helen Faulkner, and although she doesn't mention any names, my name is offered up repeatedly by people commenting on the post – people I don't even know, so God only knows how my name has got out there.

'Oh my God.' I cover my face with my hands. 'Why would she do this? Why would she write this crap? Surely, it's not allowed? Can't I sue them or something? And all those people giving my name in the comments! Can't I report them?'

Ted puts his arm around me, pulling me firmly into his shoulder.

'Look, I don't know if there's anything you can do but …' He stops as the slam of the front door makes us both jump and he quickly slides his arm away. Robbie and Sean tumble into the room, both shedding coats and scarves as the warmth of the central heating hits them. At the sight of us, me tear-stained and puffy, the smile slides from Sean's face and he frowns slightly as he sees his Dad next to me, as though not expecting him to be here. He looks at Robbie, who is headed towards me, concern etched on his face.

'Mum? Are you OK?'

'Yes, of course,' I sniff, wiping at the end of my nose with my sleeve, 'just this stupid newspaper article that's been posted online. It upset me a bit, that's all.'

'That, and the fact your mum's car has been vandalised,' Ted says. 'I don't suppose you two have seen anything, have you?'

'What newspaper article? Vandalised?' Robbie looks horrified. 'Vandalised how?'

Pushing the laptop towards him, I watch quietly as his eyes scan the page, his mouth a grim line across his face. When he's done reading, before he can speak, I tell him about the graffiti scored into the metal and his nostrils flare, his fists clenching at his sides, before he demands to see the damage. Ted lays a hand on my arm as I get to my feet, my legs still shaky.

'I'll go,' he says, and I watch with quiet relief as they head back outside leaving Sean and I alone together in the kitchen. I don't want to look at the ugly word carved into the metal, not if I don't have to.

'We didn't see anything when we went out earlier,' Sean says, his feet shuffling slightly on the tiles, looking as if he'd rather be anywhere else than alone in the room with me.

'No, whoever did it was clever and made sure no one else was around.' I try to smile, but it wobbles across my face and won't settle. 'It's only words, anyway.'

Maybe if I try and shrug it off it won't seem so threatening.

'I guess worse has happened,' Sean says, his face contorting in horror as he realizes what he's said. 'Oh I didn't mean … I'm sorry.' He blushes a bright red and this time I manage to paste the smile on properly.

'It's OK, Sean. Everyone knows what happened to me now, thanks to the *Echo* today. Whether they choose to believe it or not is another matter.'

'Have the police said anything else? Do they have any ideas about who did it?' he asks, as he fiddles with the rope bracelet around his thin wrist.

'No. I think they've pretty much given up, to be honest – no evidence, they've said. They've told me that they're still looking into it; they just haven't got a lot to go on, apparently.'

'Right.' Sean nods seriously, and before he can speak again Robbie and Ted clatter back into the kitchen, Robbie calmer now, thank goodness, and the two teenagers disappear upstairs. Moments later we hear the thud of music from above and Ted turns to me with a smile.

'Robbie is furious, but I think I've convinced him not to go off half-cocked at anybody.' His face grows serious. 'Listen, Rachel, I've remembered something else from the party.'

'Oh?' I frown, trying not to let my emotions show as I feel my nerves fray a little more around the edges. I am eager to hear what Ted has to say, and terrified of what Ted has to say, both in equal measure. Taking a deep breath in order to calm myself, I wait for Ted to speak.

'It's about Jason – the Greenes' gardener?' *The guy with the tattoos.* The memory of him staring at me as I left Liz's house that day, leaning on his shovel, his blank, dark eyes following my steps up the path. The unnerving feeling that accompanied me as I left. 'I saw him earlier, on the way here. I was turning into your street, and it looked as though his van was parked across the road from here. When he saw me coming he drove off. It reminded me that I saw him. That night, at the party.'

'Jason?' I blink rapidly, and the skin on the back of my neck prickles. 'He was at the party? But no one said anything about seeing him there. Why would he be there anyway? I can't see that Liz would have invited him – you know what she's like. She's funny about things like that – and saying that, I can't see that Jason would want to spend the evening with any of us.'

'Ideas above her station, eh? I did think it a bit odd to see him there, like you say, why would he want to spend time with Liz outside of working hours, especially on New Year's

Eve?' Ted pours me another mug of coffee and adds a heaped teaspoon of sugar. 'Here. Drink this. You look a bit pale.'

I sip at it gratefully, glad to hold on tight to the warm mug as I feel my hands starting to shake.

'I forgot I even saw him, to be honest,' Ted says, 'I'd had a few drinks, and I didn't really pay much attention to him. It was only when I saw him outside earlier that it jogged my memory. When I came outside to take the phone call from Angela he was in the garden, by the rose bushes. It didn't even register, the fact that he probably shouldn't have been there.'

I don't know what to think. 'Should I tell the police, do you think? No one else has said anything about him being there, so maybe you were the only one who saw him. And if Liz didn't invite him then he won't be on the guest list she gave to the police.' Fumbling in my cardigan pocket for my cheap, plasticky phone, I almost send the coffee mug flying, and Ted puts out a hand to still me.

'Wait, Rachel. It's probably better if I call them, don't you think? After all, I am the one who saw him.'

'Yes. Yes, that's probably for the best.' I feel as though the police already think I am some hysterical time-waster, so it probably is best coming from Ted.

'Look, I have to get going. Angela is skyping me to talk about the divorce in half an hour, so I'll call the police as soon as I finish speaking with her. Will you be OK?'

I tell him I'll be fine, and show him out, making him promise to tell me what the police say as soon as he's spoken to them. As I close the door, something catches my eye. Heart thumping, with the thought of 'please, not more, not today' ringing in my ears, I bend down to pick it up. The square, white corner of a card peeps out from underneath the doormat, possibly pushed under there in error by the postman. I didn't notice it earlier, the state I was in. There is a tiny love heart in the corner, and my name on the front. There is no stamp or postmark on it, meaning it must have been hand delivered, not left by the postman as I first thought. Frowning, I flip it over but there is nothing on the back, just blank white space.

'Mum? What's that?' Robbie bounds down the stairs to peer over my shoulder.

'I don't know. Some sort of card. Where's Sean?' Distracted, I turn the envelope back over and try to see if I can recognize the writing.

'Oh, he left a little while ago. His mum is going to Skype apparently and he wanted to talk to her for a bit before his dad does. Something about the summer. Maybe that's an early Valentine's card from Dad.' He gestures towards the envelope, before he squeezes past me into the kitchen, on the hunt for food, no doubt. I slide my finger under the flap and ease the card out. It's clearly homemade, a heart on the front made with pink wool, silver glitter showering the carpet. Frowning, I wait a moment before I open it up to read the message. Gareth wouldn't have time to make a Valentine's card – come to think of it; I'm lucky if I even get a bought card. A finger of cold ripples down my spine and there is a sour taste in my mouth as I open the card to reveal the message inside.

Roses are red
Violets are blue
Rest assured, Rachel
I'M WATCHING YOU

12

The night is long; feeling never-ending as I toss and turn in bed, convinced that every little noise I hear is my rapist, back to hurt me again. The darkness feels thick and invasive, not at all comforting, and an insistent tapping has me huddled up; shaking under the duvet, my heart racing and my eyes squeezed shut as I wait for the inevitable footsteps creeping up the stairs towards my bedroom door.

When they don't come, I force myself out of bed and down the stairs, only to find a bare, wintry branch tapping against the living-room window. I try to force out a laugh, but it won't come, sticking somewhere between my chest and my throat, as if it can't get past the lump of fear that sits heavy inside me, weighing me down. Wrapping my dressing gown tightly around me I give up trying to sleep and head towards the kitchen for a hot drink and my laptop, deciding to use this time to carry on my investigations.

After speaking to Gareth the previous evening, the lies tripping off my tongue easily as I told him that everything was fine, and that of course I would seriously look into the Open University counselling degree while he was away, I waited for Ted to contact me. He promised he'd call after he'd spoken to the police, but my phone has stayed silent all evening. And when I called his phone it went straight to voicemail.

I grab the laptop and mug of tea and carry them both upstairs, checking on the way up that the front door is double locked. Once upstairs, the branches of the bare tree outside tap against the window again making my heart leap into my throat, so I run back downstairs, this time double checking all the windows are locked and snatching up a bread knife from the block that sits on the kitchen counter. I can't be too careful.

Now, back under the duvet, laptop screen perched on my knees and illuminating the darkened room, I take a deep breath. I've updated my notebook with the events of yesterday and I've come to a conclusion. I can live in fear – waiting for him to come back, suspecting every man I come into contact with of having something to do with it, afraid of my own shadow – or I can properly look into this myself, find out exactly who did this and why, and actually do something about it. Only then do I think I'll be able to move on.

I remember Ted's words about how I was behaving that night, and without pausing to let myself think about it any more I type 'Rohypnol' into the search engine and wait for the results to load.

Two hours later, my eyes gritty and sore from lack of sleep and staring at the computer screen for so long, I look up as Robbie peeps his head round the door. Fingers of light are starting to creep in through the curtains as the sun starts to rise, and I hear the click of the central heating as it turns itself on. A quick glance at the clock on the nightstand tells me it's seven fifteen.

'You're up early, Mum.' Robbie grins at me, his face marked with pillow creases, hair standing on end.

'I could say the same about you.' I smile and lower the laptop lid, hoping he can't see how shaken I feel.

'College trip,' he explains, 'I'm a bit late actually. Do you want a cup of tea or anything before I go?'

I shake my head and wait for him to leave, straining my ears to hear the click of the latch as he locks the front door behind him, before I open the laptop again. There's no doubt about it. I am sure that Rohypnol – the date rape drug – was used to spike my drink at the party. The symptoms are shockingly similar to those I experienced – the loss of memory, and the way Ted says I was staggering and slurring are prime examples of how the drug takes effect. Plus, it didn't show in the tests carried out by the police, which fits, as according to the websites I've checked it only stays in your system for a short while.

Weirdly, this information is reassuring on one hand, as it tells me that I wasn't so drunk I could barely stand – someone *must* have spiked my drink. On the other hand though … I shudder as I allow the thought to form fully. This means that whoever did this planned it. They planned to do this to me at the party, and they made sure they came prepared.

An hour later I am out of bed, showered and dressed, despite the exhaustion that hangs over me like a thick, oppressive cloud. I force myself to smear concealer across my face, to hide the dark circles under my eyes and my grey pallor, but draw the line at mascara and lipstick. I don't want to feel pretty – just human. I've made a decision, and now I have to see it through, even though my palms are sweaty and my heart thunders in my chest at the thought of it. I get into my defaced car and take a deep breath, before reversing off the drive and heading in the direction of Gareth's offices.

'Rachel, hello.' Tina, Gareth's receptionist looks nervous as I stand in front of her desk. 'Errr … how are you? You do know Gareth isn't here?' Her words tumble out in a rush and her hands flutter around her collarbone before her fingers seize on the butterfly necklace she wears around her neck.

'I do know that, Tina, thank you.' Her nervousness is making me more jittery and I just want to do what I came here to do, no fuss. 'I'm here to see Aaron.'

'Oh. Aaron. Of course, I'll just …' She reaches for the telephone.

'No need,' I say, with a confidence that I'm not feeling. 'I'll let myself through.'

Aaron looks up with a sly grin as I push the door open to his office, with my best brave face on. I refuse to let him see how frightened I am by what has happened.

'Rachel.' He stands and comes around to the other side of the desk. 'What a pleasant surprise. What can I do for you?'

'I want to talk to you about Liz's party.' My voice shakes on the last word and I cough to try and disguise it.

'What about it? I heard a good time was had by all, some more than others.' He raises an eyebrow and I have to fight the urge to flee, fear beating at my breastbone.

'You know what happened to me. At the party. The police came and spoke to you.' It's a statement, not a question.

'Yes, they did.' He has a mildly amused air about him and I think for a moment how there is no one on this earth I despise more than Aaron right now.

'Stop fucking me about, Aaron.' This time the words come out steady and firm, and I draw strength from that. *You are not a victim, remember that, Rachel. In order to finish this, you have to remember – you have to KNOW.* 'Liz says you were there, but you told the police you weren't, so were you at the party or not? Did you see anything on New Year's Eve?'

'Oh, Rachel.' His eyes narrow as he looks at me, raking over my unwashed hair and tatty jeans. 'I saw lots of things on New Year's Eve.'

My skin prickles with discomfort under his gaze, and I know he's toying with me. Changing tactic, I pull out the card.

'What about this? What do you know about this?' I shove it under his nose, but instead of drawing back as I thought he would he leans in closer to me, so close I can see the tiny blackheads that dot his nose, the smell of his aftershave making my pulse pound in my temples and sending a rush of saliva to my cheeks.

'Pretty. It looks like you have an admirer.' He is so close I can feel his breath on my cheek. 'I don't know about the card. It's nothing to do with me. But you know what? Sometimes, Rachel, we reap what we sow.'

Shaking, almost faint with fright, I rush back to my car, desperate to get away from Aaron and the scent of threat and danger that filled my senses in that office. Afraid that Carrie won't answer her phone if I call her, I drive to the station, clutching the print out of all the information I could find on Rohypnol, and the card that was left under the door mat yesterday.

On arrival, I march into the reception area before I can change my mind. The reception area is busy, and I wait my turn to see the desk officer, the thin, antiseptic smell on the air making my stomach roll as I remember coming that morning for the examination. Finally, I am seen and I ask for Carrie by name, remembering at the last minute that she might not even be on duty today. I don't know what I'll do if she's not here. Thankfully, she is, and I only have to wait a short while before she comes striding towards me, her hair scraped back from her face into a short ponytail. She looks tired, and nowhere near as pleased to see me as I had hoped.

'Rachel.' She smiles wearily, not holding out a hand for me to shake. She gestures for me to follow her and for a moment my heart seizes in my chest as I think she's going to take me through to the room she took me to that morning. Instead she guides me through to a grey, bland interview room, taking the seat opposite me.

'What can I do for you?' she asks, folding her hands on the table in front of her. 'You know we still don't have any new information, don't you?'

I can smell her perfume on the air, something sweet and childish that a teenager would choose.

'I know,' I say, pulling the bundle of papers out and laying them on the table in front of her. 'I've been … looking into things for myself. I went to see Aaron Power at his office this morning.'

'Rachel, that isn't how these things work …'

'Did you really speak to him? Did you question him about the party? Because you said he wasn't there, only I think he's lying.'

'Lying? Rachel, please …' Carrie looks as though she wants to put her head in her hands, before she pulls herself upright and opens her notebook. 'OK. Why is he lying – did he say something that contradicts what he might have told us?'

'Well, no. He didn't say anything concrete, it was more a feeling … like he knows more than he's letting on.'

'Rachel, a feeling isn't evidence. I know you want to find him, I do too, but we can only move within the law. You can't go and do your own investigation.' She closes the notebook and I get the vibe that she thinks we're done here. We're not done. Not yet. I will never be done, not until whoever did this is caught and punished, stopped from ever hurting anyone again.

'But I found out something else … Jason, the gardener for the Greenes?' Panic that she's going to leave before I can tell her everything makes my words tumble over one another. 'He was at the party. I don't know why, I don't think he was invited, so Liz wouldn't have put him on her list … but Ted saw him there, he told me himself, and then he saw him again outside my house yesterday afternoon. He said he was going to call you, but I don't know if he did … and then there's this.'

Grabbing the card by its corner I pull it out and show it to her.

'What's this?' With the tip of her pen she opens the card and reads the sinister poem inside. 'Where did this come from?'

'It was pushed through the door, I think. It was under the doormat, so at first, I thought it was from Gareth,' a rueful laugh escapes me, 'maybe an early Valentine's Day card. But obviously it's not. I think it's from *him*.' I bite my bottom lip hard on the inside to try and stop the tears that threaten.

'And when did you find it?'

'Yesterday afternoon.'

'Could anyone else have put it there?' She turns the card over and runs her eyes over the front of it. 'You don't recognize the writing?'

'No.' The writing is all in neat, evenly spaced block capitals. There's no way anyone could identify it. 'I know it doesn't look like much ... but there's something else as well.' I tell her about the word carved into the side of my driver's door, and we head outside for her to see it for herself. Crouching on her heels, she runs her finger over it much the same as I did the first time I saw it, before sighing and standing up.

'Look, Rachel, I'm going to be really honest with you.'

My heart sinks and I know she's going to tell me she can't help.

'I saw the article on the *Echo*'s website and on their Facebook page this week – I think a lot of people have. And West Marsham is a tiny place, there's going to be some backlash. I don't mean to sound cruel ...' I must look devastated as she reaches for my hand and gives it a squeeze. 'I'm going to log this, the card and the vandalism, but it could be anyone who did this. You might want to think about having CCTV installed at home, if you feel unsafe it can be reassuring to know that cameras will pick up anything that does happen.'

'Right.' I give her a brief nod, disappointment clogging my throat and making it hard to speak. 'Thanks anyway, I guess.' Turning, I pull my hand away, but Carrie tightens her grip.

'Wait a minute.' She glances towards the building, as if making sure no one will come out and overhear us. 'I *do* believe you, Rachel. I know there isn't enough evidence for us to get any strong leads right now, but I want you to know that I won't let this go, OK? *I do believe you.*'

'You do? But I thought …'

'I do. You're not the only woman this has happened to, Rachel, and it's so difficult to make these accusations stick, especially when there isn't enough evidence – and in your case, you don't even know who was involved. But if you *can* bring me evidence – something solid – then I'll do anything I can to get the investigation back up and running at full capacity, understand?' Her eyes bore into mine and I get the distinct feeling that there's something personal in this for her.

'OK.' I offer up a watery smile, and she drops my hand, walking away towards the police station without a backwards glance. I can do this. I can totally do this.

Fired up by Carrie's words, I jump back into my graffitied Mini and turn towards The Vines and home. The first person on my list of people from the party to talk to is Melody, seeing as she arrived later and was probably (hopefully) more sober than anyone else by the time I was taken upstairs.

Hurtling along, traffic lights with me for a change, I see Amy walking up the High Street towards her flat, and I beep and wave. She turns, but I think she can't see me behind the wheel, as she doesn't wave back, instead putting her head down and hurrying off.

Anxious to reach Melody before I chicken out, I zoom along the High Street, adrenaline making my nerves hum and buzz before it fades as I pull up on the drive, leaving me feeling drained and empty. I slide out of the driver's seat and take a deep breath, before I make the short walk over to Melody's front door. *OK, Rachel, you can do this. Just go in there and ask her what she remembers.* Tentatively I knock on the slightly cheesy lion's head knocker, before banging it down properly. I don't have to wait long before Melody yanks the door open, clad in an expensive looking yoga outfit, blonde hair teased high on her head.

'Rachel! How are you?' She leans over to kiss me, and I smell the flowery, tacky scent of pressed face powder with a hint of cigarettes.

'I'm … fine. I just wondered if we could have a chat?' I resist the urge to stamp my feet – despite the feeble sunshine that fights through the clouds, the temperature has dropped and the adrenaline buzz has left me cold and tired.

'Of course, sweetheart. Come in, you look half frozen.' She shows me through to the living room, plushly carpeted and littered with photo frames, all depicting her and Jonno swooning over each other. 'What's the problem?'

I fidget in the large, squashy armchair I've found myself in, feeling the cushion suck me down into its depths, before I manage to squirm free to perch on the edge. The room is uncomfortably warm and as fast as my toes thaw out, beads of sweat start to prickle under my armpits.

'It's about the party … the New Year's Eve party, at Liz and Neil's house.' I watch as Melody's eyes slide away from mine and she finds a piece of lint on her sleeve more intriguing than necessary. 'You know what happened to me, don't you?'

'I did hear … and I'm so sorry, I've been meaning to call you …'

'I'm not worried about that,' I cut her off, so many have been 'meaning to call me' but haven't got around to it, it

130

seems. 'I wanted to ask you if you saw anything, noticed anything … did you see Gareth and me together at the party?'

'Oh.' She looks relieved, flicking the imaginary lint from her sleeve and meeting my eyes again. 'Yeah … I mean, yeah, I did see you two together, not that I saw anything. You know.' The hint of an Estuary accent peeps through as her enunciation slides.

'So, you didn't notice anybody acting strangely, everything was normal?'

'Yeah, just normal. You were dancing in the living room when we arrived, and you waved at me. You had a glass in your hand, but I don't know what you were drinking. You were fine, then at least anyway. You were quite … flirty, if you don't mind me saying.'

'Flirty? Flirty how?' This is the first mention of my behaviour before Ted found me and I feel nauseous at the thought of someone thinking that my having fun, dancing and drinking meant that I wanted something else entirely.

'Just dancing a bit close to some of the chaps, that's all, nothing serious. Gareth wasn't very happy when he left …' Melody jumps as a door slams, and Jonno's voice booms out. Instantly she is jittery, her knee starting to bounce up and down as she rubs her hands along her expensive yoga pants. 'Jonno! We're in here.'

Jonno's bald head appears round the doorframe, a scowl lifting from his face as he sees me sitting in the armchair.

'Rachel. How are you, love?'

'Rachel was just asking if we saw anything at the party,' Melody jumps in before I can speak. 'I told her we didn't see anything. She's just off now.' Melody gets to her feet, but I'm not done yet.

'Wait,' I say, 'you said Gareth wasn't very happy when he left? Why?'

'Maybe you should ask him that,' Jonno says, the welcoming tone gone now from his voice, a hard look on his face. 'There's probably a few things you want to be asking him about.'

I frown, confused by what is meant by his comment, but Melody butts in again before I can ask him what he means.

'He was a bit cross with you before he left, that's all Jonno means.' She looks nervously at him, her fingers picking at her cuticles.

'Why? Did we argue?' I knew there was *something* that night, some vibe that made me feel as though things between Gareth and me weren't one hundred per cent right.

'He … errr.' Melody flinches as Jonno disappears from the doorway, slamming the door behind him. 'He wanted you to leave. You were both in the kitchen, only a few minutes after we arrived, and he wanted to go. You refused; you said you wanted to stay for one more drink. He had hold of you by the arms, like this.' She comes towards me and grabs me by the upper arms. Dizziness washes over me, and I have to blink hard to get rid of the black spots that dance at the corners of my vision. She holds on to me tightly, her fingers matching the exact spots where the bruises marred my skin on the morning I woke up in Liz's spare bedroom.

'Gareth did?' I whisper, my mouth dry. 'It was Gareth who grabbed my arms?' I had just assumed that whoever did this to me was the one to bruise me there.

'Yes, sorry.' Melody lets me go, her blue eyes full of concern. 'You know you can talk to me any time, if you need to. You don't have to put up with that.' She peers out at me from under her lashes and I get the feeling it's more that she wants to talk to me. I shake my head impatiently.

'Did you actually see him leave the party, Melody? Actually see him walk out of the door?'

'Well, no. I saw him grab you and I … I felt uncomfortable, so I left the room. I was thinking that maybe I'd find Jonno or Neil and get one of them to have a word with him, you know, but then Liz stopped me and … by the time I came back you'd both disappeared. I'm so sorry, Rachel.'

'No, it's fine. You weren't to know what was going to happen.' I get to my feet, gathering up my bag and wrapping my scarf tightly around my throat. 'I have to go. Thank you, you've been really helpful.' I rush towards the front door, fumbling with the lock. Melody leans across to help, that powdery scent wafting up in my face again.

'I would have spoken to you sooner,' she says as she snaps the lock and moves aside to let me out, peering back over her shoulder to make sure she isn't overheard, 'only I was kind of … with … someone else at the party. Someone I shouldn't have been.' She looks at me, her fingers shaking on the lock. 'You won't tell Jonno, will you? Only, he'll kill me if he finds out.'

'I won't tell.' Anxious to get out of her overheated, stifling home, I push past her, bile swirling in my stomach. All I can think of is Gareth, his hands wrapped tightly around my arms. *Gareth gave me those bruises. And no one seems to have seen him leave the party.*

13

SEPTEMBER – THREE MONTHS
BEFORE THE PARTY

Gareth seems weirdly jittery tonight; as though he is nervous about the dinner party, getting under my feet and snapping irritably at me when I ask him to move out of the kitchen. Maybe it's because the clients he's invited are a big deal, but he seems oddly anxious, unusually for him. I am feeling the pressure already, attempting to prepare this last-minute dinner party and Gareth's agitation isn't making things any easier.

'Gareth, please,' I sigh, as I turn around with my hands full, to find him in front of the fridge, exactly where I need to be. 'They'll all be here really soon. You arranged this dinner party, so why are you so …' I break off, not sure how to word it – moody? Out of sorts? Just plain old miserable? To my surprise, he doesn't storm out or snap back; instead he just sinks into a dining chair and scruffs his hair with his hands, his skin looking grey under the harsh light of the kitchen spotlights.

'Rachel … do you ever think … what I'm trying to say is …' He sighs, his stubble making a scratching noise as he rubs his hand over his face, and swallows hard as if finding it difficult to locate the right words. In this unguarded moment, he looks vulnerable and my heart twists a little. 'I mean – if everything were to go wrong, would you …'

The shrill ring of the doorbell cuts him off and he gets to his feet, already headed towards the front door before I can stop him and urge him to go on. I am left alone in the kitchen, feeling unsettled and confused by what he was about to say – what does he mean, *if everything were to go wrong*? What exactly is it that he was trying to say? I try to shake away the feeling that creeps along my spine, the feeling that says maybe he knows about Ted and me.

Wiping my hands on a tea towel I head through to the lounge, hoping it's not our dinner guests arrived early – I still need to change – but it's Amy, with Pete, one of Gareth's major clients.

'Amy!' I lean in to give her a kiss, and peck Pete quickly on the cheek, aware that I probably stink of garlic. 'And Pete … when did this happen?'

'Just after the barbecue last month,' Amy blushes, 'Pete was there and after … your migraine came on,' she casts a nervous glance at Gareth, who is preoccupied, slapping Pete on the back before moving to the cabinet in the corner of the living room for drinks, 'he asked me to go for a drink with him and then … well, we've seen each other a few times. I like him.' Her cheeks are flushed, a smile playing at the corners of her mouth and I am thrilled that she finally seems to have found someone decent after her messy divorce three years ago.

Excusing myself, I go upstairs to change out of my jeans into something more dinner party appropriate. As I rifle through my wardrobe I keep an ear out for the doorbell – I'm still hoping that Aaron will, for some reason, not be able to make the dinner party, but if not, maybe he'll arrive while I'm still getting ready and Gareth can deal with him. I stretch out the time it takes to freshen up my make-up, lingering over the exact shade of lipstick to wear and dithering over what perfume to spray over my wrists, until I hear the doorbell ring twice more and Gareth shouts up the stairs at me that our guests are here.

I let out a long breath, check my hair once more in the mirror and head for the stairs. I feel nervous, my heart jumping in my chest as I make my way down to greet our guests, slightly worried that Aaron will spend the whole evening making me feel anxious and awkward. I pause outside the kitchen door and give myself a shake – Aaron can only make me feel anxious if I *let* him. Plastering on a smile I shove the door open, but when I enter the kitchen there is still one spare seat and no sign of Aaron.

My eyes flick to the clock. Twenty past eight. Gareth invited people for eight o'clock, so Aaron is either aiming for fashionably late, or – I cross my fingers behind my back for a second – he's decided not to come. I wave a 'hello' to everyone, skirting around the edge of the table to let Jonno kiss my cheek. Melody looks as over made-up and brittle as ever, and when I lean in to kiss her there is the faint smudge of a bruise on her collarbone, plastered over with foundation. I give her a smile and avert my eyes, not wanting to alert her to the fact that I've seen it, sure that she would be mortified if she realized it wasn't covered as well as she'd thought. Maybe I'll speak to her about it later, when we are alone – definitely not now, not with Jonno sitting next to her.

Gareth seems to have recovered his good humour, his nerves disappearing, and his voice booms out as he laughs with Pete about something, a bottle of champagne in his hand. The cork pops, and a cheer goes up, the table starting to buzz with chatter as people begin to talk. I force a smile, the beginnings of a tension headache nudging at my temples, and move into the kitchen in a search for champagne flutes.

'You look nice.' Gareth follows me into the kitchen, letting the door swing shut behind him. He wipes the neck of the bottle, smearing away the condensation, before pouring the bubbles into the glasses I've lined up on the kitchen worktop, carefully tilting each glass as he pours so they don't over run.

'Thanks.' I smile at him over my shoulder as I open the oven to check the beef. 'You seem … better. A bit happier, anyway.' Fragrant steam puffs into my face as I peer into the oven, before slamming the door closed and turning to face him.

'Hmmm.' He takes a sneaky sip from one of the glasses. 'I think Jonno has agreed to invest. I'm hoping to pin him down a bit later on tonight once he's got a belly full of your lovely meal.' Winking, he plants a kiss on my mouth, the taste of champagne sour on my lips.

'Gareth … what did you mean earlier? When you said what if everything were to go wrong?' I lay a hand flat on his chest, in order to stop him from turning away from me, but he does it anyway, reaching back to pick up two of the full champagne flutes, bubbles streaming up the sides of the glass in a race to the top.

'Hmmm? Nothing, it's fine.'

'But you've got me worried, saying that. Is everything OK?'

'Of course.' He drops another kiss on my cheek; two kisses more than I've had from him in a long while, before backing out of the kitchen, letting the door swing closed in my face.

The prawn cocktail starter is on the table (retro, I know), I'm on my second glass of champagne and I've finally started to relax when the doorbell rings again. Gareth has excused himself from the table and as everyone turns to look at me as the sound chimes through the house again I have no option but to get up and answer it. I should have known that things were too good to be true. At the front door, I steel myself for a moment, before throwing it open.

'Aaron. Hello.' A slight tinge of ice to my voice, I stand to one side to let him in, but he pauses on the doorstep, holding out a bunch of brightly coloured blooms towards me.

'Rachel – these are for you.' He smirks. 'I bet you thought I wasn't coming.' He is so close to me that I can feel the heat of his breath on my cheek. I turn my face to one side, taking the flowers from him even though I don't want to.

'Aaron! You made it!' Gareth's voice booms down the hallway and the tension is broken. Relieved not to be alone with him any more, I stand back, as far from Aaron as I can get without looking odd.

'Aaron was just saying he thought maybe we thought he wasn't coming,' I say pointedly, but Gareth just laughs good-naturedly. *Something has definitely changed for him to be so upbeat this evening.*

'Ha! I knew you wouldn't let me down.' Gareth grasps Aaron's hand in a tight handshake, before leading him towards the dining table. 'Come through,' I hear him saying, 'I want you to meet Jonno, seeing as you'll be dealing with a lot of his portfolio.' My heart sinks at these words, realizing that Gareth has no intention of getting rid of Aaron any time soon – he'll be referring to him as his 'right-hand man' before too long, if I'm not careful. Not bothering with a vase, I throw the flowers into the sink and take the spare prawn cocktail into the dining room, resisting the urge to slam it down on the table in front of Aaron.

'Prawn cocktail.' Smiling up at me he digs in with his fork, a smear of Marie Rose sauce running along the stainless steel prongs, making me feel slightly sick. 'My favourite. Sorry to have kept you all waiting, folks. Busy day at the office.' He winks at Gareth, then Jonno asks about a property on the other side of West Marsham and the table is suddenly full of talk about rising house prices, leaving me to sit quietly for a moment. Sitting back in my seat I fork the fish into my mouth, trying to look as though I'm enjoying myself, but the food tastes like ashes on my tongue and I have given up any pretence of trying to follow the conversation. Every time I raise my eyes from my plate Aaron is staring at me, but no one else seems to notice.

'... isn't that right, Rachel?' My name on Gareth's lips pulls me back into the conversation, and I nod enthusiastically, even though I have no idea what I am nodding in favour of.

'Well ...' Aaron lets his knife and fork drop to the plate with a slight clang, 'that was delicious, Rachel. There's just something I can't resist about cold fish ... always tempts me.' His eyes lock on to mine and I fumble with my napkin as I shove my chair backwards, eager to get into the kitchen for a moment's respite.

'All done, everyone?' I say brightly, smiling my thanks at Amy as she passes me her empty plate. My fingers are shaking, and the plates come together with a clatter as I stack them clumsily, drawing a frown from Gareth and an amused smile from Aaron. I look down, keen to avoid eye contact, snatching up the crockery and heading for the door. Once in the relative safety of the kitchen I lean my head against the refrigerator door and heave in a deep breath. Only a few more hours to get through. The sound

140

of the chatter from the table gets louder as the door swings open and I raise my head to see Amy slipping into the kitchen, clutching two empty plates.

'Thought you could do with a hand,' she says, placing them on the counter. 'Are you OK?' Her eyes are wide with concern and I realize I must look worse than I feel.

'Oh God, I was hoping Aaron wouldn't make it,' I blurt out, sloshing a giant, fizzy glug of champagne, slightly warm now, into a mug and grimace as I take a large mouthful.

'Oh, he's not so bad. He's quite good-looking actually, I didn't realize.' Amy takes the mug from me and has a sip herself. 'Is this still about the friend request thing?'

'The ... no, God no, I just ignored that. He stopped me in the supermarket – demanded to know why I wouldn't go for a drink with him. I was in the frozen fish aisle and he made some comment about "cold fish".' Amy claps her hand over her mouth as she snorts with laughter, her blonde curls bobbing.

'It's not funny,' I hiss, one eye on the kitchen door in case one of the others walks in, 'didn't you hear him say that just now? Another comment about "cold fish" and being tempted by it. That was aimed at me.' I blink back tears, and something in my voice must resonate with her because she stops laughing abruptly, the smile dropping quickly from her face. She grasps my hand in both of hers.

'Rachel, come on. Don't get upset. I think he's harmless – yes, I think maybe he does like you, probably in an inappropriate way, and yes I agree he is a little ... socially awkward, but I don't think he probably means anything by it.'

'He's a creep. He always used to make me feel uneasy, on edge, and now it's no different. Sending me message requests, demanding to know why I won't go out for a drink with him. It makes my skin crawl.' I shudder, goose pimples rippling up my arms. '*He* makes my skin crawl.'

'Look at it this way,' Amy says, 'he's just broken up with someone, just moved back to an area that holds good memories for him. He's probably a bit up in the air at the moment, emotionally. He might have latched on to you a bit because he knows you from before … he feels comfortable with you, or maybe you just remind him of when things were better for him. I think you're reading too much into it all – just keep him at a distance and I'm sure once he meets someone new he'll forget all about you.'

'Hmmm.' I'm not entirely convinced but maybe Amy is right – maybe I am reading too much into all of this. All I do know is that I don't want to be alone with Aaron under any circumstances.

Dinner goes without a hitch, and everyone raves about my dessert so I don't mention that I picked it up in a particularly upmarket supermarket this morning on my way home. Aaron doesn't make any further comments, and the weight on my shoulders feels as though it has lifted slightly by the time Gareth pours the port and sets up the cheese board. He has been in high spirits for the rest of the evening, and I can only assume that Jonno's agreement to invest has something to do with it. Finally, Amy murmurs about 'making a move' and people start to drift towards the front door. Gareth and I stand together in the light of the porch, as we wave people off. Aaron is the last to leave – I am feeling relaxed from the port and the warmth of Gareth against my side, so I don't even hear what he says at first.

'Let me grab you that file, the one we talked about. You can have a read through while you're out of the office tomorrow.' Before I can say anything, or offer to get it, Gareth has marched down the corridor to his office, leaving Aaron and me alone on the doorstep.

'Thank you for a lovely evening, Rachel. It was a pleasure spending time with you. And Gareth, of course.' Aaron gives a small smile, letting the tips of his canines show below his upper lip.

'You're welcome.' I say no more, reluctant as I am to engage in conversation with him.

'I'm sure I'll be seeing more of you, now Gareth and I are working so well together.'

'Maybe.' I wrap my arms around myself, as though cold, even though the night is still mild for September.

'I'm pretty sure I will.' Smile gone now, his face has lost any geniality, and in the glow of the streetlights his eyes look flat and cold. Unnerved, I take a step back, wanting to keep my distance as he leans towards me, as though he wants to whisper in my ear.

'Here you go, no rush.' Gareth appears next to me, and I lean gratefully against him, exhaling a quiet steady stream of air through my teeth as he hands Aaron the folder.

'Cheers, mate. And thanks again, Rachel, brilliant night.' Aaron turns and walks down the path, jacket slung over one shoulder, not looking back. I watch until I see him turn the corner on to the High Street, until I am satisfied that he is gone. *If Amy is right and I am reading too much into things, then why do I still feel so unsettled?*

14

JANUARY – TWO WEEKS AFTER THE PARTY

Amy is already sitting on the bench next to the small lake at the park, where we have agreed to meet. She has the last of a crust of bread in her hand, and as she sees me approach she tosses it into the water where it is immediately surrounded by ducks, all squabbling and fighting to reach it. She dusts her hands on her long, floaty skirt, entirely inappropriate for the damp, misty weather, and pulls me into a hug, Thor wrapping his lead around her legs.

'God, Rachel.' She pulls back, holding me at arm's length. Her hands grip my biceps and I resist the urge to wince, even though the bruises have faded to faint green smudges, ringed with yellow. 'You look dreadful.'

'Thanks.' I manage a weak smile as we sit, the damp wood of the bench seeping through my jeans, catching a glimpse of myself in the darkened window of the tea hut that sits on the bank of the lake. *God, Amy is right.* After too many sleepless nights to mention, I look like a walking zombie. My face is pale, my fringe frizzing into wayward curls where my hat doesn't quite cover it. Dark circles ring my eyes, and I am aware that my wedding ring spins on my finger, where once it sat snugly. The beginnings of a cold sore makes my upper lip tingle and I run my tongue over it, unable to stop myself.

'When was the last time you had a full night's sleep?' Amy takes my hand in hers, and I curl my fingers, not wanting her to see where I have picked off the skin around my nail beds, a nasty habit from childhood that rears its ugly head whenever I am stressed.

'I don't know,' I admit. I long for the nights when I used to fall into bed, struggle through one or two chapters of whatever book I was reading before falling deep into a dreamless sleep, oblivious to Gareth tossing and turning beside me. 'Probably the night before ... the night before the party.'

'Here.' Sliding her hand from mine, Amy leans down and rummages in her bag before handing me a tiny brown bottle. 'Try this. It's Rescue Remedy – all herbal, so don't freak out. It might calm you down a bit ... de-stress you.' I take the bottle, tucking it into my coat pocket, even though I'm not convinced by it – perhaps Valium would go down better.

'Amy, listen,' I say, before she can go off on a tangent – she loves anything herbal, any kind of alternative remedy and I don't want her to try and convince me that I should be seeing one of her therapists. 'I wanted to ask you ... did you actually see Gareth leave the party?'

'Well ...' she scrunches her nose up slightly, as she thinks, 'I saw you guys in the kitchen ... but you mean actually physically see him leave?'

'Yes,' I say, my heart starting to hammer in my chest. *Please, Amy, please have seen him go. Tell me he wasn't there till the end.* 'Actually saw him leave Liz's house.'

'No,' she says, frowning as she catches sight of the look on my face, 'I saw you both in the kitchen, and then that was it. I didn't see you, or him again. I did look for you both, when Pete and I were leaving but someone said both of you had left already.'

'Who?' Maybe they saw Gareth leave and just assumed that I was with him. 'Do you remember who it was who told you that?'

'No, sorry.' She shakes her head; blonde curls brushing her shoulders, and rubs her hands together, trying to warm them up. 'Why? You don't think ...' She stops, fingers in front of her mouth as she blows on them.

'Melody said she saw him in the kitchen – he was angry with me and he had me by the arms.' I swallow, feeling bile rise up and scorch my throat. 'The way she said he was holding me, that's exactly where the bruises were the next morning. He said he left just after midnight, but no one seems to have seen him leave the party.'

'Oh, Rachel ... no.' Amy's mouth twists into a grimace, and she reaches for my hand again. 'You really don't think *Gareth* did this to you?'

'I don't know,' I whisper, hot tears stinging my eyes, 'I don't know what to think any more. Why would he grab me like that? What did I do to make him so bloody cross, that he would grab me hard enough to leave bruises? He's never, ever been violent with me before.' *Apart from that one time,* a voice whispers at the back of my mind, *the night he found out about Ted.* 'And why is he so keen for me to "get over it"? That's what he said, that he thinks we need to "move on". Does he think maybe I deserved it?'

'No. *No.*' Amy puts a finger under my chin and forces me to meet her eyes. 'Whatever happened that night, whoever

147

did this, Gareth had nothing to do with it. He loves you, Rachel, he wouldn't have …' She breaks off and looks away.

'He wouldn't have what?'

'He … he wouldn't have stayed with you after the whole thing with Ted if he didn't love you. You and Robbie are everything to him. I know he can be a shit, I know he makes you miserable sometimes but come on, you don't seriously think he could be responsible for hurting you?'

'No.' Deep down, I don't, not really – at least, I don't want to. We've been married for almost twenty years, and Gareth has never shown any signs of being violent before. But I still don't know why he grabbed me like that, or what I did to make him lose it. 'I don't know what to think, if I'm honest. I just … I need to know, Amy.' The tears spill over, creating dark splotches on my jeans where they fall. 'I don't think I can ever sleep again, ever feel safe again until I know who did this.' Rage simmers low down in my belly. 'I don't want to be a victim, you know? I don't want people to look at me and think, "*oh, poor thing*," I want to find out who did this and make sure they get punished for it. I can either live in fear, scared in case he comes back, or I can make sure he doesn't ever get to hurt me, or anyone else, ever again.' Emotion makes my breath catch in my throat and I struggle for a moment to draw breath.

'Look, there was something else I wanted to tell you,' Amy says. She pauses for a moment as a woman pushing a baby in a pram walks slowly past, casting me a side-on glance as she passes. 'Have you spoken to Liz lately?'

'No. Not since I went to her house to ask her what she knew about that night.'

'Right.' Amy takes a deep breath. 'The thing is, she's had to fire Jason – you know, the guy who does her garden?'

My breath sticks in my throat and I get the same sensation in my belly as when you get in a lift and it descends too quickly. My stomach flips over and I have to fight to hear Amy over the roaring in my ears.

'Are you OK? Rachel, you look as though you're about to faint.'

Finally, I manage to suck in enough oxygen to speak, the rushing in my ear canal dying down.

'I'm fine. Tell me what happened. Why did she fire him?'

'OK.' Amy gives me another hard look before she speaks again. 'Apparently the police showed up at Liz's looking for him. They had a report that someone had seen him at the party – although I didn't, not that I remember anyway. And I really can't see Liz inviting her gardener, can you? You know how snobby she can be about things.' I shake my head, but say nothing. 'Anyway, they asked him if he was there, and he said yes.'

Tucking my fingers under my thighs so I resist the urge to start pulling at the skin around my nails, I suck back the little gasp that rises to my lips. Ted said he would call them, but he never let me know whether he did or not – I had the feeling that he wouldn't say anything. Perhaps he did after all … or maybe Carrie has taken my report seriously.

'He said he'd left some sort of gardening tool behind in the shed at the bottom of the garden, he needed it for another job early the next morning, that's why he came back to get it. He's denying anything else.' Amy carries on, her breath puffing out in little clouds as she speaks. 'He says he never saw you.'

'And the police believe him?' I feel sick at the memory of Jason watching me leave Liz's house the other day, then his van parked across the road from my house – the idea of him sitting outside, watching me, making my skin prickle with fear.

'Well, there's not a lot else they can do apparently. No one else saw him at the party, not that I know of anyway, and there's nothing to place him inside the house at any time during the evening.' Amy sighs. 'I know this probably hasn't helped in any way, but I just wanted to let you know. Liz has fired him, obviously. She says she doesn't trust him now.'

'He was outside my house. The other day. His van was parked across the street, and then when Ted arrived, he drove off.'

'Ted?' Amy frowns but I carry on talking, barely aware that she's even spoken.

'I thought it was strange, but even when Ted mentioned seeing him at the party I didn't think that he ... What if he was watching me? What if he realized someone saw him there and he was waiting to see if I realized ... what if it *was* him?'

'Rachel, listen. This doesn't necessarily mean anything. There is no evidence of his being inside the house that night, and absolutely nothing at all to say that he had anything to do with what happened ... God, look at you, you're so pale and you're shaking.' She looks across to the tea hut where a woman is raising the shutters. 'Let me get you a cup of tea, I think you need the sugar.' She reaches down into her bag and pulls out a handful of change, before walking briskly across the damp grass to the little tea hut, her shoes leaving dark footprints in the dew.

That's when I see it. Peeping out from the open zip of her bag is a white corner of card, a partial logo visible that seems vaguely familiar. Glancing up, I check to make sure that Amy is otherwise preoccupied – I see her standing at the hatch, gesturing to the woman at something behind the counter – before leaning down and snatching up the card. Dizziness washes over me as I run my eyes over the wording, before that tiny flicker of rage in my belly flares into life.

I am looking at Helen Faulkner's business card. The blood-sucking journalist who made sure to discredit me so thoroughly in her article, quoting a 'source close to the victim'. I stare blankly at the white background, trying to process why on earth Amy would have this in her bag.

'Here you go, I put two sugars in it but hopefully it won't be too horrific ...' Amy trails off as she sees what I'm holding in my hand. I look up, to see her face pale, her teeth biting down on her lower lip.

'It was you?' I get to my feet, wrapping Thor's lead tightly around my wrist. He lumbers to his feet, not at all happy to be on the move again so soon. I shake my head. 'Jesus, Amy, how could you?'

'Me? What ...?' Amy's eyes flick from my face to the card, 'Oh, Rachel, no, listen ...'

'Listen? To what? Bullshit?' I yank the zip of my coat up so hard it traps a piece of my sweater in it. 'I hope she paid you a lot of money, Amy. I really hope it was worth it – telling that bitch what happened so she could twist it and make me look like a liar. You were supposed to be my friend – I was supposed to be able to trust you. Obviously, I can't.'

Without thinking I knock the hot cup from her hand, tea spilling out across the tarmac path, steam rising, before I march away, towards the park gates. She shouts something after me, but I can't make out the words through the pounding of my feet on the pavement, the wind carrying her words away from me. My breath hitches in my throat and by the time I am through the gates and around the corner I can barely see, my eyes swimming with tears. I thought Amy was my friend – my best friend – and I've poured my heart out to her over everything. I thought I knew her, thought I was safe to tell her my innermost thoughts and darkest secrets, but it's looking more and more as though you can never really, truly know anyone.

15

Gasping, I pull back in shock as I collide with someone coming the opposite way. I'm blinded with tears and sick with anger and humiliation as I try to come to terms with the idea that Amy has completely sold me out.

'Shit, sorry.' A hand steadies me, keeping me upright. 'Rachel? Are you all right?'

I wipe my eyes, pushing my tangled, windswept fringe back under my damp hat, the mist that sat low on the ground when I left the house this morning finally lifting.

'Oh, Sean. Sorry, I wasn't looking where I was going.' Aware that my eyes are puffy and my face is blotchy, I keep my head down, intent on getting past him and heading home, away from the prying eyes of neighbours and villagers, and any other people who might have seen the online article about the party.

'You look like you've been crying. Is everything OK?' Dressed in jeans and Superdry hoody, he looks younger than Robbie, even though he's nearly a year older, the two of them only ending up in the same school year by the skin of their teeth. There is a large pimple on his chin and I feel my eyes being drawn to it, the pale pink bump almost exactly in my eye line. A faint aroma of smoke lies on his clothes and I recognize it as not your usual plain, old tobacco smoke.

'Yes, just …' I let out a breath that I didn't realize I was holding, 'a silly argument, that's all.' I smile to try and hide the hurt that Amy's betrayal has caused. 'Are you going to meet Robbie?'

'Yeah, he's at mine. I'm just nipping out for supplies … crisps and stuff, you know.' He scuffs his foot into the mulch of damp leaves that have fallen on the pavement from the tree above. I suppress a smile, remembering the days of suffering attacks of the munchies, before I remember Robbie and the smile drops from my lips. I'll be having a word with him later.

'Umm … did you hear about the gardener?' Sean asks, his voice tentative. 'The police have been to see him about being at the party.'

'Yes. Well, I heard something, I'm not sure how true it is.' A thought strikes me. 'Was it your dad who told the police he saw him there?'

'My dad?' Sean looks puzzled. 'No, not him. I don't know who told them. Josh told me.' *Josh, Liz and Neil's son. Of course, he would be the one to tell his friends.* My heart sinks – Ted has let me down too. If I hadn't gone to see Carrie then no one would ever have spoken to Jason about the party and it would have all been forgotten, the fact that he was there.

'It doesn't look as though what happened on the night of the party had anything to do with him anyway,' I say, feeling uncomfortable discussing this with Sean, a boy I've known since he was tiny. 'No one saw him in the house, and he said he just went back to the garden to fetch some tools.'

'So, you didn't hear the rest of it, then?' A look crosses Sean's features, one that I can't put a name to, and for a brief second I feel unnerved, a spark of adrenaline shooting through my veins.

'The rest of it? What do you mean, *the rest of it?*' My lip tingles and I run my tongue again over the cold sore festering there, anxiety bubbling up from somewhere deep in my chest.

'The reason that he had to leave Newcastle. I think this is the real reason why Mrs Greene got rid of him, nothing to do with him sneaking back on to the premises behind her back.'

'No, I didn't hear the rest of it.' Thor whines at my feet, as if he doesn't want to hear the reason either. Sean looks at me, a little apprehensively as though he doesn't really want to tell me. I nod at him briskly; for him to just tell me whatever it is he has to say.

'They're saying that the reason he had to leave Newcastle was because he was arrested. For rape.'

The world tilts around me and I have to reach out a hand to steady myself. I hear the thundering of my pulse in my ears and for a moment I think, *this is it, Rachel, you really are going to faint. You're going to hit the pavement any second now. Let's hope you don't crack your head open.* And then it passes, and I feel the sharp pain of a splinter in the palm of my hand where I've steadied myself against someone's garden fence.

'Rachel? Let me help you. Here, lean on me.' I feel a heavy weight, and the faint musty smell of marijuana as Sean puts his arm around me, taking Thor's lead from my hand and turning me in the direction of home. 'I didn't mean to shock you like that. I didn't know if anyone had spoken to you and well, I thought you should know.'

'Rape?' The word is like sour lemon, making my tongue pucker and saliva shoot into my mouth. I swallow it down, thankful that it is only saliva and not sharp bile. 'How ... how do you know?'

'Everyone seems to know, you know how people are in West Marsham – they love to have something to talk about.' *Oh yes, that's a lesson I've learned recently.* 'I'm not sure he'll get much work around here now. He'll probably move on.' Sean shrugs, dropping his hand to his side now that I'm steady on my feet again.

'What happened? I mean, does anyone know the full story?' My head is swimming with this new information and I feel the familiar thud of a headache pinching at my temples. I should have drunk that sugary tea, not knocked it out of Amy's hand.

'Not really – just the basics. Josh overheard the police talking to his mum when they came to speak to Jason. They asked her if she'd had any police checks done before hiring him, and she said no. Didn't think they needed it for a gardener. You wouldn't, would you?' Sean stops, reaching into his pocket to pull out a cigarette. He offers the pack to me and I take one, despite giving up smoking when Robbie was little. He lights my cigarette, and then his own, blowing out a long stream of smoke. 'Look, don't worry, Rachel. It doesn't mean that he had anything to do with the ... that night.'

'Right.' I suck on the cigarette, resisting the urge to cough. The ashy taste coats my tongue and I wish I could stub it out, but don't want to offend Sean. 'Sorry, it was just a shock to hear it. I had no idea.'

'I didn't mean to upset you. If you need anything, or if you're worried ...' Sean takes one last drag on his cigarette before grinding it out under his shoe, 'you can always call us. Even if you just want to talk about it, you know, how the police are getting on and stuff. I know Gareth is away at the moment and he wouldn't want you to feel frightened.'

We've reached the gate at the front of my garden and Thor is straining at his lead to get to the front door, home and inside away from the cold, damp weather.

'Thank you, Sean.' I'm touched that he's being so considerate. Ted and Angela have brought him up well, pot habit aside. 'And thanks for letting me know ... about Jason, I mean.'

'No worries.' Sean gives me a grin, shrugging, before heading off back in the direction we just came, no doubt to stock up on his snacks.

As I close the front door, I catch a glimpse of a van turning into the street, a white transit van with distinctive red writing on the side. If I were closer, I would be able to read the words that adorn the side panel – 'Hooper Gardening Services'. Fear beating a tattoo in my chest I slam the front door closed, double checking the lock and putting the chain on, just in case. I check the lock on the back door, and then test each of the windows in turn to make sure they too are secure. Still, I don't feel safe.

16

OCTOBER – TEN WEEKS BEFORE THE PARTY

Gareth's text is curt and to the point, as they usually are these days. He wants me to take the keys to the Kingsnorth property over to the house he's working on, on the other side of West Marsham. No *thank you*, no X to show any affection – I thought after the dinner party his much-improved good mood was here to stay. It did, for approximately three days, and now he seems to have withdrawn into himself even more, only communicating with me when he wants something. I've tried repeatedly to ask him what the problem is, but there are only so many times you can be faced with a closed office door before you give up. Despite the guilt and self-loathing I feel every time I leave Ted's bed, if I didn't have him I wouldn't have any human affection at all – I'd shrivel up and die like one of those Rhesus monkeys we learned about back in A-level Psychology. Resisting the urge to tell Gareth to shove his keys where the sun doesn't shine, I text back an acknowledgement, making sure I put an X at the end, and grab Thor's lead. I might as well drive over to the other side of the park, then I can drop the keys off and walk Thor at the same time, before my client arrives this afternoon. It seems that's all I'm good for these days, running errands.

I call Thor and manage get him into the car and head across the village, skirting the outside of the park. I don't see Gareth's van anywhere on the street outside the house, but that doesn't mean anything – parking on this side of the village is notoriously bad and the chances are he's had to park around the corner. I manage to squeeze the Mini into a tiny space close to the house, my back wheels just skimming the double yellow lines, and clip Thor's lead on, wincing as he stumbles when he jumps out of the car. Poor old boy.

'Hello! It's just me,' I call out, as I push open the freshly painted front door of the house Gareth is renovating. There is the smell of wet plaster on the air, and the bare floorboards of the hallway are covered in dust that rises up to cover my boots as I walk through. 'Gareth?'

'Through here,' a voice calls from the back of the house, where the recently renovated kitchen is. I frown slightly, it doesn't sound quite like Gareth's voice, but leaving Thor where he has slumped on the front door mat, I head through. As I enter the kitchen, my heart sinks. Aaron is leaning up against the newly installed work top, takeaway coffee cup in his hand.

'Oh, Rachel. How nice to see you,' he smirks into his cup before taking a sip, leaving a tiny curl of cappuccino foam on the tip of his hipster moustache.

'Is Gareth here?' I don't waste any time on niceties, eager to drop the keys off and leave now I know Aaron is here.

'Gareth? No. He stepped out for a bit.'

I look past Aaron to where a mobile phone sits on the counter. Gareth's mobile phone.

'Where is he? And isn't that his phone?' I reach for it, but Aaron moves it behind him, so that if I want it I have to lean round him. I pull back. I don't want to touch him. I don't want to get that close to him.

'Did you need him? He's just popped out.'

'So you said.' I grit my teeth in frustration. 'So, where is he? He asked me to bring over the keys to the Kingsnorth house.' I let the keys dangle from my finger.

'He had to go and get some bits from the builder's merchants. The plasterer is coming tomorrow and we said we'd provide the materials. I'm not sure Gareth needs those keys now.'

'Seriously?' Irritation scratches at my skin as I realize I've had a wasted journey. 'Listen, just tell Gareth ...' I trail off, watching Aaron's fingers as he spins Gareth's mobile on the work surface in front of me, almost taunting me. 'Did Gareth even send that message? Or did you send it to try and get me to come over, knowing that Gareth wouldn't be here?'

'What? Oh, Rachel, don't be so paranoid ... why would I do that?' Aaron shakes his head patronizingly, that annoying, smug smirk still playing about his lips.

'I don't know — to try and get me here on my own? Seeing as I won't go for a drink with you maybe you're just trying another tactic. Is Gareth even coming back here?' Panic rises as I realize I can't even call Gareth, to find out where he is and whether he's nearby. 'Look, I'm not in the mood for stupid games, Aaron. I'm leaving. Tell Gareth if he wants the keys he can come home and fetch them himself.' I flounce towards the front door, calling to Thor and hoping that my voice doesn't sound as uneasy as I feel.

Almost tripping over my own feet in my haste to get away from Aaron and that tense, uncomfortable vibe he carries with him, I make it all the way to the gates of the park before I am convinced that I can hear footsteps behind me. *Don't be so paranoid, Rachel.* Aaron's words ringing in my ears, I wrap Thor's lead tightly around my wrist and finger the keys in my pocket, slipping one between my knuckles to use as a weapon if I need to. The crunching of the dead leaves that have fallen from the huge oak trees that line the tarmac walkway gets louder, and I whirl around, key clutched tightly between my fingers.

'Hey, chill out.' Aaron is there, two steps behind me, his hands raised in surrender. It seems I'm not paranoid, after all. 'I just wanted to …'

'Why are you following me?' I demand. 'Was it you who sent that text? I'm going to speak to Gareth about this, you know that?' I lower my fist, suddenly feeling drained and exhausted.

'I just wanted to talk to you, that's all.' Aaron looks over his shoulder, towards an empty bench. 'Will you sit down with me, just for a second? I don't mean any harm, Rachel, come on. You know me.'

No, I don't rises to my lips but I keep the words tucked inside for fear of angering him. The park seems deserted, and we are alone on the bench. *I knew you, once, years ago, and even then, it was barely. I don't know you, or what you're capable of, at all now.*

'The thing is, Rachel,' Aaron says, leaning close to me, so close that I can smell his aftershave, and see the tiny hairs that peep out of his nostrils, 'I don't understand what you're doing with Gareth. I mean, why him?'

'What?' I am caught off guard, Gareth the last person I thought he would mention. 'What do you mean, what am I doing with him? I'm married to him, for God's sake. What does that tell you?' Indignation burns and my voice goes up an octave. 'And what's that supposed to mean – *why him?*'

'You deserve better than him, Rachel, and you're clearly not happy. You deserve so much more.'

'I'm perfectly happy as I am, thank you. Not that it's any of your business.'

Liar. I look away, suddenly worried that my affair with Ted is written all over my face.

'I could offer you so much more than he can.' Aaron gropes for my hand, his damp palm meeting mine and I pull back in horror, realization dawning. I was right, not Amy. He *is* a creep. 'I never got over you, Rachel. Why do you think I couldn't make a go of things with Harriet? Why do you think I came back here? It's only ever been you.'

Jesus. I try to swallow but my mouth is completely dry, my heart banging in my chest. I have to get away from him, just the very idea of him makes my skin crawl. This is worse than I first thought. He's not just a creep – he's obsessed.

'No, Aaron, it's never been me – we never had a relationship. You hung around with people that I knew at university – there was no friendship, no relationship, *nothing* between us – there's nothing to get over. I'm sorry if you ever felt that things should have been different between us.' *Why am I apologizing? I've never given him any reason to*

163

think we had something. 'You need to leave me alone, do you understand? I'll tell Gareth you're harassing me otherwise.' I stand; ready to run if I have to. Thor lumbers to his feet, wheezing. *Please, God; don't let me have to run.*

'Gareth will never find out, if that's what you're worried about.' His hand shoots out and grabs my wrist, gripping my skin tightly and making me cry out in shock. 'And let's face it, it's not the first time.'

'What did you say?' *He knows. Oh God, he knows about Ted.* Fear leaves a metallic taste in my mouth as I feel his fingers tighten, my heart hammering against my rib cage.

'I said, it's not the first time it's happened around here … look at him, for example. His wife legged it with her yoga teacher, apparently.' He drops my wrist, gesturing to someone walking towards us from the gates. I have to look twice, before relief overwhelms me as I recognize the familiar gait. It's Ted, wrapped up in a Barbour, wearing the scarf I bought him last week. The only time I've been brave enough to buy him anything. *Maybe Aaron doesn't know anything after all.*

'Everything OK, Rachel?' Ted has reached us and is looking at Aaron and me in turn, concern etched into his features. 'Is he bothering you?'

'No, it's fine.' I rub at my wrist where Aaron pinched the skin and tug the sleeve of my jacket down. 'Are you walking this way? Do you mind if I walk with you?' Latching on to Ted as a way to escape, I turn a blank gaze on to Aaron, determined not to show him how much he frightened me with that little display. 'Goodbye, Aaron. I'll tell Gareth what you said.' There is nothing Aaron can do, apart from smile and turn away, walking back towards the house Gareth is renovating.

'Shit.' I let out a shaky breath, once he disappears from view.

'What's going on, Rachel? Who is that guy?' Ted reaches for my hand, but I'm shook up, nervous, and I don't want anyone to see us together. 'Did he upset you?'

'Oh, God.' I scrub my hands tiredly over my face. 'I don't know if I can do this any more, Ted.'

'Don't say that,' he pulls me towards the wooded area behind the park bench, where we can talk away from prying eyes. 'I need you, Rachel.'

I sigh as he places his hand on the back of my neck, under my hair, sucking up the warmth from his skin as though I am starving. Which in a way, I am — starving for affection.

'That guy … he works with Gareth. I thought he knew about us, I swear, Ted, I thought my heart was going to burst in my chest. He's … creepy; he keeps following me, saying things to me. He scares me.'

'Do you want me to speak to him? Warn him off?' Ted's blue eyes gaze intently into mine, until I almost feel uncomfortable. I squirm out from under his hand, pulling Thor closer to me.

'No. Leave it. I don't think he knows, and I've told him that if he carries on I'm going to tell Gareth what he's been saying. But I just don't know if I can carry on with … all this. Us.' *The fear of discovery isn't exciting any more, and I hate the way I feel when I leave Ted's bed — disgusted with myself for my lack of willpower.*

'Don't say that, Rach.' Ted's mouth twists up slightly as though disappointed, before leaning in and kissing me until my breath comes in tiny gasps. 'I'll text you,' he says, before sliding out of the shadows of the trees into the park. I wait for five minutes, as Thor stares up at me balefully wanting

165

to be home in the warm, before I follow Ted, looking over my shoulder as I step out onto the path.

'Mum!' I'm so busy looking over my shoulder, I don't see Robbie on the path in front of me. 'What were you doing in the bushes?'

'Just taking Thor to do his business.' Panic makes my heart thunder in my chest and I have to concentrate on my breathing to make it seem as though I haven't just jumped out of my skin. 'I forgot the poo bags.'

'Ewww. Nice work if you can get it,' Robbie laughs. 'I'm heading over to Sean's for a bit – we've got college work to do. I'll eat there. See you later.' He leans in to kiss my cheek and I hold my breath for a moment, hoping that he doesn't smell Ted's scent on me. He waves over one shoulder as he strides away, and I finally feel as though I can breathe again. *What the hell are you doing, Rachel? This thing with Ted will be the end of you.*

I am stirring the curry, a cold glass of wine on the worktop beside me when Gareth gets home. For once, he comes through into the kitchen, instead of just heading straight for his office as he usually does. My thoughts whirl, and I slop curry over the side of the pan onto the hob in my frantic stirring as I wonder, panicky and nervy, if Aaron has told him about Ted and me. The more I thought about what he said to me earlier, the surer I am that he didn't say, *the first time it has happened around here.* I tut, and wipe at the hot glass on the hob, in an attempt to appear normal.

'Did you have a good day?' I ask, still wiping at the hob in a bid to avoid eye contact. 'There's wine open in the fridge.' I lay down the cloth and turn to the fridge, but

166

Gareth is already pulling the cork from the bottle and pouring himself a large glass.

'I had a shit day, thanks for asking,' he growls, and I turn back to the stove, resuming my stirring. 'Left my bloody phone at the Riverside house – you know, the one over the other side of the village? I had about thirty missed calls by the time I got back, I spent the rest of the afternoon trying to catch up.'

'You didn't need the keys to the Kingsnorth house in the end, then?' I keep my eyes on the curry as I ask, not sure I want to hear the answer.

'What? What keys?' Gareth frowns as he sips his wine. 'I never did need the keys to the Kingsnorth house. That house is finished – the estate agent has a set, and it's on the market.'

'Right.' My hands shake as I slide the plates out from the warming tray on to the work surface. 'My mistake.'

17

JANUARY – SEVENTEEN DAYS AFTER THE PARTY

'Come on, Mum,' Robbie slides a mug of tea in front of me, 'just eat a little bit. You don't have to eat it all.'

I pick up a slice of the toast he's made for me, forcing it to my mouth. I have no appetite, and everything I do eat turns to ashes in my mouth. Now, even Robbie has noticed, so I force the cold toast between my lips and chew, hoping I will actually be able to swallow it.

'See? My cooking isn't that bad, is it?' Robbie smiles as I give a tiny huff of laughter and bite into the food again. I have to make an effort, for him, if nothing else.

'What are you up to today? You're looking smart,' I ask, forcing the toast down with a big swig of tea. 'Oh, today is practice interview day, isn't it?'

'Yep. Can't wait.' He rolls his eyes, and tugs at the tie he's wearing theatrically.

'I got you something.' Getting up, I rummage in the drawer, searching for the tiny good luck token I bought him. 'Here.' I hand him the tiny silver keyring, a four-leaf clover. 'It's just a silly little thing from Dad and me, but we wanted to wish you luck, not that you'll need it – you'll be fine.'

'Thanks, Mum.' He turns it over in his hands, before attaching it to his door key. 'Fingers crossed it works.'

Glancing at the clock, I see it's almost eight thirty. 'You'd better go, you don't want to be late.' Robbie follows my gaze.

'Shit, sorry Mum. I have to go – you'll be all right, won't you?'

'I'll be fine, don't worry.' I have a plan of action for today – my next step in uncovering who did this to me. I might be scared, but I don't have to *stay* scared. That little bubble of rage that flared in my stomach when I talked to Amy about what happened is growing day by day. 'But listen, Rob … don't mention to anyone that Dad is away at the moment, OK? Don't say anything to Josh or any of your other friends.'

Robbie frowns, and I think he's about to say something before he changes his mind, instead just giving me a nod and a quick peck on the cheek before he flies out of the door. I know he probably thinks I'm paranoid, but I don't know who else Jason works for, and I feel slightly less exposed if people don't know that Gareth isn't home every night. I throw the remains of the toast into the bin, squashing the empty bread bag on top of it so Robbie doesn't see it later, and head upstairs to shower. As I place my foot on the bottom stair, the piercing shriek of the doorbell makes me jump, my heart stuttering in my chest. Cautiously, I pad silently over to the front door, peeping through the spy hole. I breathe a sigh of relief when I see who it is.

'Liz.' I smile weakly at the sight of my neighbour on the doorstep, looking slightly less perfect than usual. 'Is everything all right?' Her façade seems to have slipped this morning – her hair ruffles in the breeze as opposed to its usual rigid style, held in place with acres of Elnett, and she doesn't seem to be wearing any make-up – highly unheard of for Liz.

'I'm sorry to call round so early, Rachel.' Liz pushes past me in to the hallway, as though she can't bear to be outside for another minute. 'I've hardly slept, thinking about it all. I need to talk to you, it's about the party.'

'Oh.' I don't know what to say. 'Come through.' I lead her into the kitchen, and make more tea, even though Liz ignores it in her agitation.

'What did you want to talk to me about?' I hold my cup protectively in front of my face, my armpits prickling with nerves. I don't know what Liz wants to tell me, but I am frightened to hear it, I know that much.

'I'm so dreadfully sorry, about all of it,' she says, her hand shaking as she reaches for her mug. As she raises it to her lips, the tea slops over the edge, leaving light brown splash marks on her cream blouse. I move to grab her a cloth, but she waves it away, and I know then that she isn't herself, not at all. 'I feel as though it's partially my fault, I mean I had the party in the first place, and I'll be honest, when you first came to see me after that night, I wasn't entirely convinced that you … that it …'

'You didn't believe me,' I say flatly, 'so why are you here now? What's happened that's made you change your mind? I am assuming, of course, that you have changed your mind.' Unbeknownst to Liz she has just fanned that little flame of rage that burns low in my belly, the flame that makes it imperative that I find out who did this, and make sure they are punished. She looks suitably shamed, and takes another sip of tea to compose herself before she speaks.

171

'Obviously, I know now about Jason. I didn't realize at the time – I would never have employed him had I known that was his history ...' she sniffs, 'and then of course, Neil went crazy and fired everyone – so now, I have no gardener, no cleaner, I have to do it all myself.' *My heart bleeds.* I try to muster up some sympathy but fail miserably. 'I have to clean for myself ... that's how I found these.' She reaches down into her bag and pulls out a scrap of fabric. Her nose wrinkles with distaste as she pinches them between finger and thumb, throwing them down on to the table before wiping her fingers surreptitiously on her trousers.

'Is that ...?' I lean forward, my fingers catching the flimsy fabric and pulling it towards me. 'This is my underwear. The underwear I was wearing at the party. I couldn't find it the next morning ...' My cheeks burn with shame, and I can't meet Liz's eyes.

'I thought so,' she says quietly, reaching out to lay a hand on mine. 'I found a jacket in the pool house – a man's jacket. Lord only knows what people were doing in the pool house, I mean, it was freezing outside that night.'

'Yes,' I say, 'but what ...?'

She cuts me off. 'I found the jacket, thrown behind one of the chairs – it must have slipped off the back of it. I checked the pockets, thinking there might be something in there that might tell me who it belonged to, but ... well, there wasn't anything. Only these.'

'Only these,' I say absently, rubbing the fabric distractedly between my fingers. Somewhere, in the back of my mind I feel them being yanked down, the elastic digging in to my thighs before fingers tear it away, digging into my flesh, making me wince in pain. Wanting to kick, lash out, but

172

my legs refusing to co-operate. 'Excuse me,' I manage to mutter, before shoving my chair back and running for the downstairs bathroom where I throw up the tea, and the few bites of toast I managed to choke down earlier. Finally, my stomach empty, I splash cold water on my face and rinse my mouth out before returning to where Liz waits in the kitchen.

'I'm sorry, I just …' I breathe hard, the sight of the wispy, black knickers on the table making my belly clench in protest again.

'It's OK, I'm sorry for upsetting you, I just thought that maybe you'd want to know that I found them.' Liz's eyes fill with tears and I can almost forgive her for not fully believing me in the first place. 'I wasn't completely honest with you when we talked before, about the night of the party.'

'What do you mean?' I pull my hand back, flicking right back to feeling angry with her again.

'I know I told you who was at the party, Katie, Aaron and everyone, but the truth is … I have no idea who was there.'

'How can you have no idea who was at the party?' I feel my brows knit together in confusion, unable to understand where she's going with this. 'It was your bloody party!'

'I know who I invited, but I have no idea who actually came.' Liz averts her gaze, and her shoulders slump as she battles with what she says next, the words seeming to stick in her throat. 'I'm an alcoholic, Rachel. By the time you arrived at the party I was already well on my way to being drunk – I'd been drinking since about two o'clock that afternoon. Neil had to put me under a cold shower about an hour before our guests arrived, to make sure that I was at least sober enough to welcome everybody.'

Jesus. This is one revelation that seems to have passed the West Marsham rumour mill by. Liz has somehow managed to keep this well-hidden – I wouldn't ever have known, not on the surface, but now she has told me some things do come together to make sense a little. The way, when Josh was small, she would ask me sometimes to collect him from school, even though she didn't work, and I'd drop him off only to see her car on the drive. The faint, spicy aroma that seems to follow Liz around – a smell that now I think about it, reminds me of the Bloody Marys Gareth and I had for breakfast one Sunday morning on a romantic weekend away to Edinburgh.

'So, what are you saying?' I ask, my fingers tapping anxiously on the table top. 'That when you told me people were there, they might not have been?' My stomach does a slow flip as I try and process what she's telling me. I snatch my fingers away from the table as they drum harder and tuck them into my lap.

'I'm saying that … I didn't give the list of party attendees to the police – Neil did it. When you came over and I told you who I saw there, I was just reeling off whoever's name I could remember seeing on the list. I barely remember a thing about that night, Rachel.'

'So … you don't remember seeing anyone – even me?'

Liz shakes her head, a tear plopping on to her blouse and adding to the beige stains left by the spilt tea. I try to feel some sympathy for her, but I'm empty.

'And so … you said you saw Aaron there, when really you don't remember seeing him at all?'

'I don't remember seeing anyone. Neil is the one who said he saw these people; Neil is the one who gave the list to the police. Neil is the one you should speak to.'

I nod vaguely, my mind already racing. *Does this mean Aaron was telling the police the truth – he really wasn't at the party? Was he being deliberately vague with me, just to taunt me and upset me?*

'Thank you,' I say, nodding towards the fabric still left lying on the table. I don't know what else I can say; my thoughts are crashing and tumbling over each other in my mind. 'For bringing these over. And for being so honest. If you don't mind, I think I need to be on my own for a bit – get my head round things.'

'Of course.' Liz jumps to her feet – now she's done what she came here to do, she can't get away fast enough, it seems. 'Rachel, you won't say anything to anyone else, will you? About what I told you? I am getting help now, it's just … I don't want Josh to know.'

I think she's mildly deluded if she thinks that Josh doesn't know already, he's Robbie's age after all, but I just nod and promise to keep it to myself. Once Liz has left and I have the house to myself again I begin to think things over. I don't feel as though I am any closer to getting to the bottom of it all, and Liz's visit has muddied the waters somewhat. I did think, when I heard that Aaron had attended the party that he could be the one responsible – he hassled me for months before, after all – and I honestly believed that he lied to the police about not being at the party, but now I know that Liz didn't actually see him there, I'm not so sure. I only have Neil's word for it that Aaron was at the party at all.

Previously, it never even crossed my mind that Neil would have had anything to do with this – good old, dependable Neil, always there when you need a recommendation for a handyman or financial advice – but now a seed of doubt has been planted. Would he lie about

Aaron being there? Or did he just not remember things correctly? I'm not even sure that he and Liz know Aaron that well – Liz couldn't even remember his name when I asked her about the party originally – so why would Aaron be invited? Has Neil added his name to the list, knowing that I had problems with Aaron before Christmas?

Then there's Jason – another name that never occurred to me, not until Ted said he saw him at the party. Now, I find out that he's left Newcastle after being accused of a similar offence, not that that necessarily means anything, but it's something else for me to think about.

And then, of course, there's Ted. Ted, who said he'd call the police about seeing Jason, but didn't – why not?

A thumping starts up in my temples and I lay my head flat down on the cool oak of the kitchen table. I don't know what to think any more. Black dances at the corner of my vision and I sit up, pulling the underwear towards me, letting the flimsy fabric run through my fingers. Something catches my eye, and I stop, the hair prickling on the back of my neck. With clammy fingers, I lay the fabric out flat, so I can see clearly. There is a tiny stain, on the front panel, on the outside. Small, silvery and hopefully full of DNA. Raking my hands through my hair, I grab the phone and punch in the number I know by heart. It rings, and when the voicemail cuts in I hang up abruptly, not leaving a message. I forgot I'm not speaking to Amy, forgot that she can't be trusted, and my instinct was to call her straight away. My eyes flick to the kitchen clock, checking the time, and then I dial Gareth's number.

'Hello?'

'Gareth, it's me. Can you talk?'

'If you're quick, I'm about to go into a meeting,' his voice softens for a moment, 'is everything OK, Rach?'

'Yes, I'm fine. I'll be quick,' I say, racing to get the words out before he has to go. 'Liz came over. She found my underwear, the stuff I was wearing the night of the party. Someone left a jacket in the pool house and they were in the pocket. Gareth, there's a stain on it ... you know what that means?'

'Shit. Listen, Rach, don't do anything stupid.' The line muffles for a moment as though he's put his hand over the mouthpiece, and I hear him call out to someone.

'Gareth, are you even listening?' My voice is shrill, and I fight back the urge to scream at him, demand his full attention.

'What? Yes, I'm listening, I'm just saying don't do anything rash, OK? I thought we agreed ... Maybe just call ...' The line breaks up, crackling and stuttering filling my ears.

'What? I can't hear you ...' The line goes dead in my hand and I hang up. I don't need Gareth to approve what I'm doing. Dialling, I wait, my pulse sounding in my ears until I hear just the voice I need to.

'Hi, Carrie? It's Rachel Walker. You know you said if I brought you something solid, you might be able to do more, get the case moving again? I have something for you.'

18

NOVEMBER – SIX WEEKS BEFORE THE PARTY

'I'll be back in a little while.' I stand in the doorway to Gareth's office, the door ajar for once. He looks up for one moment, his eyes flicking over me but seemingly not taking anything in. He makes no comment about the fact that I am in my running clothes, no mention of the rain that pelts at the windows, and the fact that it's eight o'clock on a wet Tuesday evening in November, the darkness outside thick and velvety.

'OK.' With no interest in where I might be going he nods briefly, before he turns back to the papers in front of him, the screen of his laptop casting a white glow across his face. Bare branches from the tree outside whip at the window, and another gust of rain hits the glass. I wait a moment, just to see if he tells me to stay home, tells me that it's too cold and wet, that I shouldn't go running in the dark, it's too dangerous for a woman on her own. *If he tells me not to go, I'll stay home. If he tells me he doesn't want me out there on my own, I'll stop everything with Ted, and I'll stay home like a good wife.* But he says nothing, just reaches for the whisky glass next to the monitor, his other hand shoved roughly into his hair as his eyes run over the computer screen. Silently, I turn away, clicking the door closed behind me.

Twenty minutes later, I stand outside Ted's front door; the wind and rain driving towards me, pricking my skin like a thousand tiny needles and soaking through my clothes. My running fleece moulds to the shape of my body and my leggings stick to my calves, a thin stream of rain running down into my trainers. I shiver, rubbing my icy hands together, and wait for Ted to come to the door and let me in.

'Rach? Get inside, you'll freeze out there,' Ted glances over my shoulder to make sure we are unobserved before he ushers me indoors. The warmth of the central heating hits me as I step in, and I sigh with relief. 'When I said come over if you can, I thought you would drive over. Look at you, you're soaked. You shouldn't be out there, not in the dark, on your own.' *Oh, Ted.*

'It's OK – I made it here in one piece, it wasn't as bad as this out there when I set off. I thought if Gareth thought I was going for a run he wouldn't ask any questions.' Which, of course, he didn't. I don't tell Ted that if Gareth had asked me to stay home I would have done. Instead, I slide my wet trainers off, tucking them under the radiator in the hallway with the vague hope that they'll dry off a bit before it's time for me to leave, and let Ted lead me gently upstairs. He grabs a towel from the en suite, a huge, grey fluffy thing, and starts to towel dry my hair. Closing my eyes, I let myself drift for a moment, enjoying the feel of his hands in my hair, the lemony scent of his aftershave, and trying not to think of Gareth, at home, not the slightest bit concerned about me. Then, he's sliding my damp top over my head, a hand reaches round to unclip my bra, and I forget about Gareth, I forget how miserable I feel. I forget everything.

After, I hide under the sheets, pulling them up to my chin and feeling oddly self-conscious. Ted is downstairs making tea, and he's even draped my damp running clothes over the heated towel rail in the en suite so I don't have to put wet clothes back on. Guilt bubbles up, before crashing over me in a huge tidal wave, making me feel sick deep in the pit of my stomach, any feelings of pleasure already washed away by the self-loathing I feel now. I don't want tea. I don't want to lie here under Ted's sheets, with the smell of Angela's fabric softener still on them. I don't want to be here, in the bedroom that Ted used to share with Angela, her clothes still hanging in the wardrobe, the faint scent of her perfume still in the air as though ingrained into the furniture. Ted actually offered me something to wear, but the thought of wearing Angela's clothes, whilst carrying on an affair with her soon-to-be ex-husband, made me feel even cheaper than I did before. Ted doesn't seem to have made any effort to erase Angela from his life, even though she is the one who ran off and left him. The book she was reading before she hared off to start a new life with the yoga guy lies face down on the bedside table, the spine cracked, several of the page corners folded down to save her place as she read. I twist it round to see what book it is. *I Am Pilgrim*. I didn't have Angela down as a thriller reader – I thought she would be more of a Danielle Steel fan. Ted enters the bedroom, a cup of tea in each hand, kicking the door closed behind him.

'Sorry,' he smiles, holding a cup out to me, 'it's not very romantic, is it? I did think about opening a bottle of wine, but I didn't quite know how you would explain away the smell of alcohol to Gareth.'

'Oh, I doubt he would even notice,' I say lightly, and make up my mind to open a bottle as soon as I get home. A silence stretches out between us, and for the first time I feel a little awkward. Maybe it's because this is the first time we've been together in Ted's house, instead of some cheap hotel outside of town. Or maybe it's just that I've realized that having an affair with Ted isn't doing anything to fix my relationship with Gareth. All I know is that I shouldn't be here.

'Listen, Ted,' I say, thinking it's now or never, that familiar feeling of regret hovering over me. Perhaps it's time to tell Ted that we should think about stopping this thing, whatever it is between us.

'Rach, before you say anything, I just want you to know that …' Ted breaks off, linking his fingers through mine. 'I really enjoy spending time with you, you know. I know whatever we're doing here isn't ideal, but I'm in a better place, when I'm with you.'

'Ted, I …'

'I know things are hard for you at home, and I hope that when you're with me, it makes things a bit easier for you. I've found it hard adjusting to life without Angela, but being with you makes me feel less …' His fingers trace a pattern over the skin on my wrist, and I shiver despite myself.

'Less?' It's hard to form a coherent thought when he's making my nerve endings sing under my skin.

'Less of a failure. I just let her go after all, didn't I?' His mouth twists up in a sad attempt at a smile, but I can see the hurt in his eyes.

'I thought you and Angela breaking up was more of a … mutual decision? I know she left to be with Devon, but I always thought you thought being apart was the right thing?'

'I did. I do. We weren't right together; things between us had gone stale a long time before Angela ever met Devon. I don't blame her for leaving. But maybe I wouldn't have let her go so easily, maybe I would have fought a bit harder for Angela to stay if I hadn't met you.'

'God, Ted, you've known me for years. You can't say I had anything to do with it.' I give a tiny laugh, but it sounds hollow to my ears. The intensity of his voice unnerves me a little. I thought we both knew that this was just a bit of … something to make the days feel not so drab, not so long. Ted can't change the rules now.

'Well, you made things easier, let's just say that.' The thump of the front door slamming closed makes both of us jump, and I spill tea in the bed, my heart racing.

'Fuck, Ted!' I hiss. 'There's someone here!' Footsteps sound on the staircase and I look to Ted in panic. 'My phone is down there … and my trainers are in the hallway!' I feel sick at the thought of being caught, now, just when I've more or less made a decision to stop seeing Ted. He is already out of the bed, wrapping the huge, grey towel around his middle, and striding towards the door.

'Dad?' Sean's voice calls up the stairs and I close my eyes, feeling as though I might faint.

'Coming!' Ted opens the door a fraction and slips out into the hallway. I dive into the en suite, and start to pull on my still damp clothes, shivering slightly as the cold fabric meets my skin, and tying my hair back into a ponytail. Heart thumping, I crouch with my ear pressed to the bathroom door, trying to make out their conversation.

'Sean! What are you doing home so early?' *Tone it down, Ted, you sound like you've been up to something you shouldn't.* I would laugh, if I wasn't so terrified.

'Football was cancelled. The weather is too crappy, so they called it off. Are you OK?' I imagine Sean on the landing, frowning at Ted wrapped in a towel this early in the evening.

'Yeah, 'course. Just got a bit of a migraine coming, I think. I'm going to jump in the shower and get to bed early. Are you on your own?'

'Yeah, Robbie went straight home.' Leaning my forehead against the cool grain of the door, I close my eyes in relief. I just need to get out of here without Sean seeing me and I'll be home and dry. I hear the two of them chat briefly again, and then jump as the bathroom door handle rattles under my hand.

'Rach?' Ted hisses, and I step back to let him in.

'Jesus, Ted, I thought I was going to have a heart attack. Did he say anything?' I catch sight of myself in the mirror, cheeks pale with an odd ghostly glow from the weird trendy bathroom light Ted has installed. I let out a long shaky breath that I wasn't aware I was holding.

'No, it's fine. He's gone to his room – he didn't notice your trainers and your phone is still on the table in the hall. If you're quiet you can sneak out without him hearing.'

Ted leads the way, pushing the bedroom door open and checking the hallway, before waving me through. I feel like

I'm in a spy movie, only I doubt James Bond has shaky hands and a crampy belly at the thought of getting caught. Once at the front door, trainers safely back on my feet, I pull back slightly as Ted goes to kiss me.

'I'll call you,' I promise, ignoring his puzzled frown, before a quick glance up and down the street and I'm off, feet pounding along the pavement, the pulse that beats in my throat the familiar thud of my heart working to keep up with my feet, instead of the panicky thump of fear.

The rain has died down to a misty fizz as I run all the way home, stretching my stride and aiming for maximum push in order to work up a decent sweat. I've been gone for over an hour, so I want to make sure that I look the part when I arrive home.

'Hello!' I call out as I fall through the front door, suitably out of breath and hair plastered to my head in a combination of sweat and rain water.

'Hi Mum – good run?' Robbie appears in the hall, a bowl of noodles in one hand. 'You've been gone ages.'

'Not that long. And you were out when I left.' The beefy smell of the noodles makes my stomach roll, and I lean down to slide my wet feet out of my trainers for the second time this evening.

'Dad said. We got rained off, I've only been back for a bit.' He forks food into his mouth, splashing noodle sauce on his T-shirt.

'And already eating,' I laugh and ruffle his hair as he ducks away from me, the panic I felt at being caught earlier already slipping away into nothing, to be forgotten until the next time. Maybe Gareth did pay attention when I left the

185

house after all. I pause on my way to the stairs, goosebumps prickling along my cold arms as I reach the door to Gareth's office. I test the handle and it isn't locked – but when I inch the door open and stand there, damp and cold, Gareth isn't there.

Sighing, and shivering slightly in my damp clothes, I head upstairs eager to jump into a hot shower, but as I reach the landing Gareth calls my name.

'Rach? That you?' He appears in the bathroom doorway, warm light spilling out behind him, a cloud of fragrant steam wafting through the open door. 'Here, you must be freezing.' He stands to one side, and I squeeze past him into the bathroom, where hot water thunders into the tub. Huge clouds of bubble bath foam up under the tap, and a row of tea lights dance a flickering glow along the windowsill.

'What's this?' I turn to face him, a puzzled look on my face.

'I thought you might be cold after your run,' he shrugs, 'and I know I was a bit snappy earlier, so I wanted to do something nice for you. Shall I grab you a towel?'

I nod, feeling sick with guilt, and reach up to kiss him on the cheek. Stripping off my damp clothes, I slide into the hot water, goosebumps prickling all over my body as the warm water meets my cold skin, and I think, *this has to stop, before it goes too far, before someone gets really hurt.*

19

JANUARY – EIGHTEEN DAYS AFTER THE PARTY

I take a deep breath as I pull into the parking space, convenient in its proximity to the police station, almost as though someone is looking down on me, making sure everything goes smoothly and there is zero reason for me to *not* go ahead with this. The black underwear is encased in a plastic freezer bag on the passenger seat next to me, and my heart jumps in my chest every time I look down at it. I feel mildly unhinged, if I'm honest, as though this can't possibly be my life, can't possibly be happening to me. I tried to call Gareth back the previous evening, to convince myself that I did make an effort to be up front and honest with him, rather than for any other reason. I'll blank out the fact that I rang him when I knew he would have gone into his meeting and his phone would be switched off. Now, I clutch the plastic bag in one hand and my own handbag in the other, each containing things that will hopefully start to bring all of this to a close.

'Rachel. Come through.' Carrie doesn't keep me waiting, once I've asked for her by name, and she leads me through into an interview room. 'Sorry, it's a bit cold and drab in here. I didn't think you'd want to use the room we used … before. You said you've got something to show me?'

'Yes.' The air in here is chilly and I wish I'd worn something warmer, instead of just grabbing the first thing I touched in the wardrobe. 'Here. Liz Greene brought these to my house.' I pass her the freezer bag containing the underwear.

'She should have called me herself.' Carrie frowns, as she pokes into the bag with the end of her pen.

'She feels bad, for holding the party. Like she thinks she's to blame or something. She wanted to tell me herself.' I pause for a moment, wanting to tell Carrie what Liz told me about the list but not sure what reception it will get.

'And she found them where?'

'They were in the pool house, at the far end of the garden. She found a jacket in there, and when she checked the pockets to see if there was anything in them that could tell her who it belonged to, she found these. Carrie, there's a stain on them.' My eyes fill with tears and that familiar nauseous feeling washes over me. I haven't eaten since the toast I threw up yesterday morning and I feel light-headed, as though my head isn't quite attached to my body. Carrie tips the underwear on to the table and smooths it out with her pen, careful not to touch it herself. When she sees the stain, her mouth makes a little 'oh' shape and she raises her eyes to mine.

'You're one hundred per cent certain that these belong to you?'

'Yes,' I nod frantically, 'they're definitely mine. That's what I was wearing that night.'

'OK. This is good,' she says, and my heart does a little skip of excitement, 'I can get this sent away to be tested.

We can take a sample of DNA from the stain, and request samples from the guests at the party, then compare them – this will help get things moving again, Rachel. I'll also go and visit Liz again, I'd like to see that jacket.' She uses the pen again to stuff the underwear into a proper evidence bag, as I sit and watch.

'There's something else,' I say, blurting the words out. They ring around the room, breaking the thick silence between us. I lean down into my handbag, noticing that I have two completely different shoes on – both black, but different styles. I must be in more of a state than I realized. Tucking my feet under the chair and out of sight, I pull out my notes and lay them on the table.

'What's this?' Carrie frowns, as I flip the notebook open to the first page, the lines covered with my hurried scrawl.

'Notes,' I say. 'I've been making notes, about everything. Look, I understand, Carrie, I really do. I understand that without sufficient evidence there aren't any leads to follow, and I know that you're all busy on newer cases, but I thought that maybe I could just keep digging, try and find out what really happened, you know?' I flip the pages over to how her how much I've written, the things that I've uncovered.

'Oh, Rachel …' She holds out a hand to stop me, but I carry on flipping through, the pages slicing briskly through the air as I turn them.

'Look, see? Here's a list of names – I thought at first it was Aaron, because of how he bothered me so much before Christmas, but then …' I break off, remembering that she doesn't know what Liz told me yesterday. 'When Liz came to see me yesterday, she told me something. She said … she said she's an alcoholic. She doesn't remember anything about the party. The list she gave you was from Neil, not from her. He could have said anyone came … and I was thinking, why would they invite Aaron? They barely know him. What if Neil said he was there, to throw the scent off him?'

'Rachel, please.' Carrie's voice is firm, and she lays her hand flat on the page, obscuring the words. 'This isn't for you to investigate – let me do my job, OK?'

'But …'

'I know. I know exactly how you're feeling. You're feeling helpless and vulnerable, and you think that we don't care, but we do. We have to tread so carefully, Rachel, you have to let us do the work – if you don't there's a chance that if we do find him, any evidence we have could be compromised.' Her eyes meet mine and hold my gaze intently, not letting me look away. 'You have to trust me now. I'm going to take these,' she holds up the evidence bag, 'and I'm going to get them tested, and then I'll hopefully have some answers for you. You've done brilliantly to get them to me, and I swear to you as soon as I have *anything* for you, I'll call you. But please, Rachel, you have to let it go. You have to let me do the work, not you.'

'OK.' I nod, adrenaline fading and leaving me exhausted and drained. I get to my feet, anxious now to be away from here, away from the chilly air, the faint antiseptic smell that seems to cling to my clothes. There is a feeling of relief that sneaks up on me as I step outside, into the grey, chilly January air. I have given Carrie evidence, something tangible she can use to finish this once and for all, and I feel the burden on my shoulders become a tiny bit lighter. I slide into the driver's seat and rest my head on the steering wheel. Maybe, when this is all finally over, I'll be able to sleep for more than a few minutes at a time before I jolt awake, my heart thumping. Maybe I'll feel hungry again, craving the taste of rare steak and good red wine. A tap on the window startles me, and I utter a small shriek. Sean peers in the window at me, a look of concern on his face, and I lower the window.

'Rachel? Are you all right?' He looks up at the building behind us, the station casting a shadow over the pavement. 'Did something happen?'

'No … everything's fine. I just needed a moment.' I feel ridiculous, being caught like this, napping on the steering wheel, by my son's best friend. I give him a watery smile and flick away the hair that has stuck to my lip.

'Are you sure? I can help you home if you're not feeling well, you look dead pale.' He places his hand on my arm and I stare down at it, a rushing noise sounding in my ears. It morphs into Ted's hand, only it's not laid on the maroon wool of the jumper I'm wearing now, it's on my bare forearm. It's hot and I can hear music, Christmas music, even though it's New Year's Eve and surely, *surely*, Liz can't think that that is appropriate party music. We're all done with Christmas music now, time to move on! There is cigarette smoke on the air, and I feel sick, the tinsel and glitter of the baubles seeming to spin as I try and stay upright.

'… looking pale. Let me help you.' It's Ted's voice, and I want to shake him off, tell him Gareth is here somewhere and he'll kill us if he sees us together, but I can't seem to make my arms move in the direction I want them to. When I turn my head to try and tell Ted to leave me,

I'm fine, everything moves in slow motion and I feel nauseous, bile scorching the back of my throat.

'Rachel? Rachel!' Hearing my name brings me back to myself and all I am left with is the certain feeling that I am about to be sick.

'I have to get out.' I shove the driver's door open, catching Sean in the stomach, and lean into the gutter where I heave and heave until nothing is left. 'Oh, God, I'm so sorry, Sean. You didn't need to see that.' Fumbling in my pocket for a tissue, I spit uncouthly into the gutter before wiping my mouth, my cheeks burning with shame at showing myself up in front of Sean like this. He hands me an opened packet of Polos. I take one and pop it into my mouth, the cool mint flavour taking away the acid sting at the back of my throat.

'What happened?' His voice carries a tinge of concern.

'I'm not sure … a flashback maybe, to the night of the party? I could smell the cigarette smoke, hear the music …' I trail off, shivering as though someone has just walked over my grave.

'Did you remember something?' Sean's eyes are wide. 'We should probably go back in there and tell someone if you did.'

I shake my head. 'I don't know. I can't be certain that it was a memory or whether … I don't know.'

'Are you sure you're OK? Do you want me to come back with you?' Sean looks more than a little uncomfortable and while I would love nothing more than to be at home with a cup of tea (and a toothbrush) I want to be home alone, so I can think about what I just experienced. Was it a flashback? A real memory, or something I dreamed up? It felt *real*.

'I'm fine.' I wipe at my mouth once more with the tissue. 'Honestly. Maybe don't mention it to Robbie, though, eh? I don't want him to worry about me.' I smile weakly; sweat making my fringe stick to my forehead. Sean nods uncertainly and I jump into the mini and drive away before he can offer any more help.

I am sliding my key into the lock, still feeling shaken from my vomiting bout, when a voice behind me startles me making me drop the key with a noise of surprise.

'Mrs Walker?' The voice is softly spoken, with a faint hint of an accent and I don't recognize it. I turn slowly, coming face to face with Jason, the Greenes' ex-gardener.

'You? What do you want?' I demand, fear making my voice shrill. 'You shouldn't be here.' I look down to where my door key glints on the path.

'Please, I didn't come here to be … I don't want to hurt you,' he raises his hands in a surrender gesture, 'I just wanted to talk to you.'

'I don't think that's a very good idea. My husband will be home any minute.' I peer over his shoulder, as if looking for Gareth, and when he turns to look too, I quickly lean down and snatch up my key.

'Please. I need to explain to you about the night of the party, and what happened before. Why I had to leave Newcastle.' I pause in the action of sliding the key between my fingers.

'All right.' My curiosity is piqued. Why would he want to talk to me, unless he had something important to say? Surely if he didn't have any explanation for being there he'd be avoiding me like the plague. Especially now that

193

Liz has fired him. 'I'll listen to you. We talk out here, though, you're not coming in.' There's a good chance Mrs Gregory is watching us out of her window – she'll call the police if I scream loud enough.

'OK.' He rubs a hand raggedly over his stubble, and I notice the dark rings around his eyes. His face is thin and slightly baggy, as though he's lost a lot of weight quickly and I almost, *almost*, feel a pang of sympathy for him. 'I did come back that night,' he admits, watching me warily, 'but it really was only to get a saw that I'd left in the shed. I needed it for a customer after the Bank Holiday, one who would have sacked me if I couldn't do the job properly. It turns out he's sacked me now anyway.' He gives a sad little huff of laughter and shrugs. 'I didn't do anything to you, Mrs Walker. I'll admit that I was in the garden the night of the party, but for only a few minutes. It was just bad luck that I was seen. I didn't come anywhere near you though – I didn't see you or speak to you, I didn't even come into the house.'

'Right.' I think for a moment, trying to process what he's telling me, still unsure as to whether to believe him or not. 'You say you didn't see me – what about other people? Did you see anything out of the ordinary?' I ask. 'Anything that didn't seem quite right?'

'Nothing,' he shrugs again, 'but then I didn't look. You people aren't really my kind of people. Let's just leave it at that.' He wrinkles his nose with distaste, and I realize that we must seem over-privileged, money obsessed, and spoilt to him. 'I had nothing to do with any of this, and now people are spreading rumours about me, about why I left Newcastle and I'm struggling to get work.'

'Why did you leave Newcastle?' I ask, any fear I might have had of him forgotten for a moment.

'I was a teacher.' He blinks rapidly, as if his eyes are stinging. 'There was a girl ... a student. She thought she liked me, and when I told her it wasn't reciprocated, she told stories about me, said I did things that I didn't. Nothing was ever proved – I was found not guilty and she eventually admitted lying – but by then it was too late. I lost my wife, my job, my home, everything. That's when I moved down here; to get away from the gossip, to start over and now it's happening to me again. I told the police all of this, and they know it's true, but they don't care about telling everyone else the truth.'

'Why should I believe you? You could be telling me anything.'

'You should believe me because it's the *truth*!' His guard drops, and I catch a glimpse of desperation in his eyes, his mouth twisted in frustration, and in that moment, I *do* believe him. I recognize the look as the same one I carry, when I've tried to tell Gareth that I know something did really happen to me that night.

'I'm sorry, Jason. I didn't mean ... I didn't know.' There is a lump in my throat and I cough gently to clear it. 'I'm sorry this happened to you. I'll speak to Liz, on your behalf.' He gives me a nod and turns away without speaking again, his heavy, steel-toecapped boots leaving flakes of mud as he strides down the path, away from the house. I slide my note pad from my bag, reaching inside for a pen, and slowly and deliberately etch a thick, blue line through Jason's name, striking him from my list.

20

I let myself in, and immediately I know that someone has been in the house. I listen carefully, straining my ears to hear if Robbie is in his bedroom, but there is only silence. There is a feeling, a sense that the air has been disturbed, and I reach for an umbrella that is propped against the wall. It's not much, but it will have to do as a weapon, as I have nothing else if there is still someone in the house. Cautiously, I tiptoe along the hallway towards the kitchen, sweat beading on my brow and my breath coming in harsh pants, loud in my own ears. A metallic tang fills my mouth, the taste of fear, and I try to regulate my breathing.

'Hello? Robbie, are you home?' Nothing. The house is silent, and Robbie is definitely not here.

Pushing open the kitchen door, I hold up the umbrella, ready to strike if anybody is behind it. A faint hint of a citrusy scent reaches my nostrils, as I step into the room. The *empty* room. I cast my eyes about, but at first glance nothing looks out of place. Breathing in, the lemony smell hits my nose again, and a wave of nausea makes my stomach clench. Closing my eyes, I let the umbrella drop to the floor, one of the spokes catching my leg as I do so. I barely notice, so intent am I on trying to battle the flashback that rages behind my eyes.

That smell. So familiar, and yet at first I can't quite put my finger on it. All I know is that the smell is making my stomach turn, and when I close my eyes all I can see is the blue-and-white bedspread of Liz's spare bedroom. I gasp, my throat working as I try to swallow. Behind my eyelids, the vision plays out. The light is dim, it's dark outside and the orange glow from the street light is the only thing that lights the room. I feel hands pushing at my top, ruching the fabric up into my armpits, exposing my black bra and pale skin to the chilly air. A figure looms over me, but try as I might, I can't make out the features. My stomach flips, half with fear, half with the alcohol I've drunk, and I want to be sick. I try to push them off, try to buck my hips so I can roll out from beneath whoever is straddling me, their knees pressing hard into my rib cage, but my limbs feel leaden and won't move. Somewhere below me, I hear the thud-thud of the music and I turn my head to try and scream before a hand clamps over my mouth, the citrus scent filling my nose.

Now, back in my empty kitchen, that faint smell is still tainting the air and I lose the battle against the bile that rises in the back of my throat. I manage to reach the sink before leaning over and throwing up for the second time today.

'Jesus,' I breathe, grabbing an empty glass from the draining board and filling it to the brim with cold water. I rinse my mouth out with half of it and take a few sips from the water that remains. Running a shaking hand through my hair, wincing at the faint sheen of grease it leaves on my fingertips, I take a better look around the kitchen.

At first, I don't think anything is different; everything appears to be as it usually is. Then I notice the back door key. It lies on the work surface, next to the fruit bowl. Frowning, I move towards the back door itself. Usually, I leave the key in, a legacy of too many going missing, and Gareth's irritation at having to replace the lock. I place one hand on the handle and gently press it down. It doesn't move under my hand – the door is locked, just as I'm sure I left it. Robbie must have used the back door, then locked it and taken the key out without thinking.

I pick up the key, the metal cold against my hot, sweaty palm, and push it back into the lock. That may explain the key, but it doesn't explain the lingering smell of that lemon-scented aftershave. I take another sip of water, my mouth dry and my throat scratchy, and cast my eyes about once more. That's when I see it. The magnetic letters that have clung to the fridge door since Robbie was at preschool have been rearranged. Usually, they sprawl across the fridge in no particular order, holding up various reminders, appointments, and in the old days, school trips. Now, they spell out the words:

STILL WATCHING.

On shaking legs, tripping over the umbrella that still lies in the middle of the kitchen floor, I run upstairs, slamming my bedroom door behind me. I lean against it, the handle digging into my back as I press hard against the wood, convinced that any second now I'll feel fists hammering on the other side, as someone tries to batter their way in. Shit. Shit, *shit*. My hands cover my mouth as if holding in a scream. Does that mean he (whoever he is) has been in the house? Is he still there, hiding somewhere, waiting to jump out on me?

Calm down, Rachel. I suck in a deep breath through my fingers, letting it out slowly and repeating the action until I feel my blood stop thumping in my ears and my pulse returns to normal. I press my ear to the door, but there is only silence. Am I being paranoid? Maybe Robbie just got a new aftershave? But why would Robbie rearrange the magnetic letters? Is Jason really so innocent or was it him in the house? All of these thoughts run through my head, but none of them make me feel better, or any safer.

I have to get out of here. I flick my wrist to look at my watch. It's after lunchtime; Robbie should be home in a couple of hours. If I can just stay out until Robbie gets home, maybe things will be OK. I shake my head; once again tears are not far away. I need to speak to someone; I need some reassurance that I'm not going crazy, that everything is going to be OK.

I pull the cordless phone towards me from where it sits on the bedside table and dial Gareth's number. He's probably in a meeting, but I just need to hear his voice, even if he does tell me I'm being paranoid. I wait, nausea subsiding as the call connects and it starts to ring. I frown as I listen to the ring tone – it's the double ring of the UK. The call goes to voicemail and I hang up, feeling puzzled. Is Gareth back already? Did he get an early flight? Maybe he's going to surprise me.

I wait a moment, letting my pulse return to normal. *Gareth will be home soon.* We may not be getting along, and he may not be as supportive as I would have hoped, but at least I don't feel so … vulnerable, so exposed when he's here.

Feeling better for knowing that Gareth is on his way home, I dig in the wardrobe for my running skins and pull them on. Tying my hair back into a ponytail, I tug on my trainers and slide my door key into the tiny pocket in the back of my shorts. I can run, blow away all these paranoid thoughts, try and figure out if I even *am* paranoid, and with any luck by the time I get home Gareth will be back. Gatwick is only an hour away and if his phone has a double ring tone then he must be back, his flight *must* have landed. I fasten the rape alarm to my wrist and turn towards the edge of the woods. Carrie has the underwear now, and it's only a matter of time before a DNA match is found, and all this will be over. I won't be beaten by fear.

It doesn't take long to lose myself in the rhythm of my feet pounding the pavement, then the mulch of the dead, wintry leaves squelching underfoot as I turn into the woods. I stick to the trail closest to the edge of the woodland, the one that runs parallel to the pavement on the other side of the thin row of trees that marks the edge of the woods. My headphones dangle loosely on either side of my neck, irritating in the way they swing across my chest, but habit is to bring them and I don't want to wear them, too anxious to allow myself to shut myself off completely. Weak sunlight dribbles its way through the bare branches of the trees overhead, and as it touches my skin I could almost be convinced that spring is on the way.

My thoughts collide in time with my pulse, as I follow the winding trail thinking over everything I have discovered since the night of the New Year's Eve party. Everyone seems to have a different take on it, and everyone

201

seems to have their own reasons for not wanting to speak about that night. I remember Melody telling me that she was with someone she shouldn't have been. Liz, telling me about her problem with alcohol. Jonno's veiled comments about Gareth and how I should ask him about things directly. And then there's Aaron. I've only got Neil's word for it that he was at the party – and despite Aaron telling the police he wasn't there, he was deliberately vague with me when I asked him. Is he being vague for a reason, or is he just toying with me?

I stop, unscrewing my water bottle and taking a sip. My palms rest on my thighs as I lean over, gulping in great lungfuls of clean crisp air, before I start to run again. As I find my pace, I think I hear someone coming up behind me, and without looking over my shoulder I move over to the side of the path to let them through. The path is popular with joggers, cyclists and mums pushing their toddlers in all-terrain buggies and it's rare to run without crossing paths with a few people. I wait for whoever it is to overtake me, even slowing my pace a little, but the rustle of footsteps stays a small distance behind me, as though whoever it is is tracking me.

A prickle of fear runs down my spine and my breath catches in my throat. *Why won't they overtake me?* I speed up, hoping to out run whoever it is. One glance over my shoulder is all it will take for me to see who is behind me, but some irrational part of me, the part that is broken, the part that was smashed to pieces at a New Year's Eve party nearly three weeks ago, tells me not to look, tells me to run harder than I ever have before back to the safety of the main village road. I'm running at full speed now, my chest hurting, every breath painful as lactic acid builds up and makes my muscles burn. At the crossroads I sprint straight over, headed towards the bustling main road of the village. As I see the archway of branches that will lead me back to concrete, I risk a glance over my shoulder before tripping and crashing to my knees, my ankle twisting brutally as I fall.

I bite back the shriek that rises to my lips as pain shoots from my ankle to my knee. I look up to see my pursuer, but there is no one there, the pathway empty apart from a tiny grey squirrel that blinks beadily at me from the foot of a huge oak tree.

'Fuck.' I hiss the word out through clenched teeth, and rest my head on my knees as hot tears spring to my eyes. My ankle is already throbbing and swollen.

'Rach? Are you OK?' I raise my head slightly to see a battered pair of Dr Martens in front of me. 'Give me your hand, I'll help you up.' Amy stands in front of me, one hand held out.

'Thanks.' I take her hand and let her pull me to my feet, taking care not to put too much weight on the ankle I have twisted.

'Let me help you home.' Amy tucks my arm through hers, the warmth of her seeping through her jacket into my skin.

'I'll be fine honestly, it's just twisted.' My teeth are starting to chatter, and as it's not especially cold out I think it must be the shock of the fall. I try to put my foot down fully and let out a little hiss of pain, immediately taking the weight off it again. Amy gives me a sideways glance, her brows knitted together briefly before she shakes her head.

'I don't think so, Rachel. Look, I know you're not talking to me, but let me take you back to mine. It's closer than your house, and I've got some ice and some bandages we can use on that ankle.'

Without much choice in the matter I let Amy help me and we half walk, half hop in silence back to her house. Having Amy beside me is a comfort I've missed, but I still don't know how I feel about what she did – who does that to a friend? I trusted her and she sold me out for a few quid. She doesn't seem to know what to say either, and I am relieved when we reach her front door. She manoeuvres me into the cramped sitting room and gets me sat down with my foot raised. The pain pulses up my calf, making me wince every time I try to get comfortable, and I gulp down the painkillers Amy brings me. She returns to the room moments later with a tea towel wrapped around ice, and a box of bandages.

'I didn't do it, you know,' she says, avoiding my eyes as she holds the freezing tea towel to my purple, swollen ankle. 'Talk to that journalist, I mean. I would never do that.'

I hiss through my teeth as she holds my foot a little too tightly.

'But you had her card in your bag.'

'That doesn't mean I spoke to her.' She finally raises her eyes to mine, and I look away, not sure what to think. 'You jumped to conclusions, Rach. You saw one thing and put two and two together. Only, you didn't make four.'

'You really didn't speak to her?' I ask. 'She knew things that I had only told you.'

'Only me? Or Gareth as well? And Liz?' Amy drops the tea towel and moves back, to the armchair behind her. 'Not that I'm blaming them, but you can't just assume it was me that spoke to her.'

'Maybe,' I say, as I realize that Amy isn't the only one who I told everything to. I was so caught up in my own reasoning, once I saw the card in her bag that I never even stopped to consider that maybe it was someone else who talked. 'I'm sorry.'

'She wanted to talk to me,' Amy goes on. She picks up the box of bandages and I think that maybe I have been forgiven. 'But I told her to sling her hook. She must have slid her card into my bag on the way out. I wouldn't ever have told her anything, Rach. You're my friend.'

'I'm sorry I jumped to conclusions.' My eyes water, and it's nothing to do with the fat, swollen mess that my ankle has become. 'I've missed you.' And I have – so much. With Gareth away, and everyone around me seeming to keep secrets from me I've never felt so alone before.

'Missed you, too.' Amy grins, pinning the bandage with a flourish, before her smile dies on her lips. 'What's happening, Rach? You look exhausted.'

I tell her about Liz bringing the underwear to my house, and that Carrie has taken them for testing. Then I tell her about today, in the house. The overwhelming feeling that someone had been there, going through my things, leaving clues to mess with my mind.

'Shit, Rach,' she breathes, her eyes wide. 'You don't think …?'

'I don't know – I don't honestly know if he's there, watching me, waiting for the next time that he can …' I break off, the thought too frightening to complete. 'Or if I'm going mad. Seeing things that aren't really there.'

'And you spoke to everyone at the party? Asked them what they saw?'

'Nearly everyone. There's just one person – Katie Fielding. I haven't been able to get hold of her, so I'm going to go and see her later, if I can walk on this,' I gesture to my ankle, 'she's the only person I have left – let's just hope that she did see something, and she didn't realize it. I have to find out who did this, Ames – I have to finish it.'

An hour later, I hobble up the path having taken a cab from Amy's to home. I feel so much better, now I know that we are speaking again. And she believes me, that's the main thing – even if it does feel as though she is the only one. The light is starting to fade as I make my way up the path, filling the front garden with dusky shadows, and I feel apprehensive at entering my own home, even though every light is blazing inside. As I step into the hallway, I breathe in deeply, but there is no hint of the lemon scent that welcomed me home earlier. There is a light shining from beneath Gareth's office door, and I let out a sigh of relief. He's home. Even if he is shut away in his office, inaccessible to me, at least he is in the house if … whoever came in earlier, decides to come back. I shuffle along the hall to the office door, and gently push it open, but when I peer in, I realize it's not Gareth sitting at his desk.

'Rob? What are you doing?' Robbie's head snaps up and a deep shade of crimson starts creeping up from his neckline to his cheeks.

'Mum! I didn't know you were home.' He closes a drawer and gets to his feet.

'I was at Amy's.' I hobble further into the room and he frowns at me.

'What have you done?' He comes around to my side of the desk, spying the bandage wrapped tightly around my foot. 'Shit, Mum, what happened?'

'I fell over, running. Amy rescued me.' I give a tired smile. 'Where's Dad?'

'Dad? He's not back yet. Still in Croatia, isn't he?'

'I thought … what are you doing in Dad's office?' My mind feels fuzzy, and I wonder what painkillers Amy gave me – hopefully not her left over Tramadol.

'Just looking for … a ruler. I've got college stuff to do and I've lost mine. Come on.' He wraps his arm around my shoulder and I lean against him gratefully. 'Let's get you a cup of tea, and I'll order a pizza if you want.'

'Yeah,' I say, my gaze drifting to the pile of papers on the side of Gareth's desk, but I'm too tired and my ankle hurts too much to make sense of any of it all, least of all why Rob would be in Gareth's office, so I accept his excuse and offer of pizza and let him lead me into the kitchen.

21

NOVEMBER – FOUR WEEKS BEFORE THE PARTY

I am heading out of the vet surgery at the other end of West Marsham village, a very grumpy Thor walking along beside me. If he could talk, he'd probably be swearing – there is no dog that hates the vet more than Thor, even when it's something as simple as a worming tablet. I pull gently at his lead as he stops to sniff yet another lamp post on the way back to the car, relieved when he finally starts walking, albeit slowly.

The temperature has dropped right down now we are at the tail end of November, and although it's only six o'clock, ice crystals glitter on the pavement as I walk as briskly as Thor will let me to the ticket machine to pay for my parking. I hate the village car park at this time of night – tucked around the corner from the High Street, it is deserted by not long after five o'clock on a week night, and is poorly lit with plenty of shadowy corners, but this was the only time I could get an appointment for Thor. I chatter to him under my breath, as I tuck his lead into the crook of my arm, juggling my purse and the ticket in one hand, the cold making my fingers thick and clumsy. I am thinking about getting home, hoping Gareth has lit the fire in the front room, and whether I have time to cook something decent from scratch when I get in before the first of my evening clients arrive, so I don't hear the footsteps approaching, don't realize that anyone is standing behind me until I hear his voice.

'Hello, Rachel.'

I jump, my heart skipping in my chest as coins shoot out of my purse and roll across the tarmac of the car park.

'Shit. You made me jump.' I glare at Aaron, before stooping down to start picking up the coins I've lost.

'Let me.' He scoops up the last of the coins and hands them to me, his fingers lingering on mine for far too long. I suppress a shudder and start feeding the coins into the machine without thanking him. 'So, how have you been, Rachel?'

'Fine.' I yank my exit coin from the slot and start walking back to my car, Thor panting next to me.

'I haven't seen much of you, not since you visited me at the Riverside house.' He smirks, amusement in his voice.

'I didn't bloody visit you, and you know it.' I whirl around to face him, anger making my cheeks blaze red. 'I spoke to Gareth, you know. I told him that you lured me there, telling me Gareth wanted me to drop those keys off. I told him you've been harassing me.' But I've always been useless at lying, face to face anyway (I push away the thought of how I lie to Gareth every time I see Ted), and I can't quite maintain eye contact.

'Of course, you did. I'm just being friendly, Rachel, it's hardly harassment.' He raises one eyebrow, a smile playing about his thin lips as I scoot round to the other side of the car, hefting Thor on to the back seat and opening the driver's door. I wrench the door open, letting it slam shut behind me with a metallic thud, fumbling to get the key into the ignition with shaking fingers. I just want to get away from him, even sharing the same air space as him makes me feel uncomfortable. I drop the key somewhere in the foot well and grope around in the dark for it, finally snaring it in my fingers, but before I can shove it into the ignition the overhead light goes on and the passenger door slams. Aaron's aftershave fills my car, and I have to swallow to beat the nausea that washes over me.

'Get out of my car,' I say, trying to hide the tremor in my voice. I want to shrink back, press myself as hard against the driver's door as I can to keep as much distance between us as possible, but then he'd know I am afraid of him, so I force myself to sit in the same position, one hand on the ignition, fingers curled under so he can't see them shaking.

'Rachel. I'm just trying to be friendly, I told you that. Don't you think you're overreacting?' He puts his hand on mine and pulls it away from the ignition key. My mouth goes dry and I blink, scared to move. He rubs his thumb over the skin on my palm and I stop breathing, waiting to see what he does next. 'I told you I never got over you, didn't I?' I nod, and he tightens his grip on my fingers.

'There was nothing to get over, Aaron,' I say, every muscle in my body tense, ready to yank my hand away and get out, get away, as soon as he loosens his grip even a fraction.

'Maybe not for you, but there was for me.' He drops the smile, before turning to face me, my hand still wrapped in his fist. 'You forget, I know you, Rachel. I know everything there is to know about you.'

'What do you mean? You don't know me, Aaron. You've never known me.' I shake my head, wishing that Thor was a little younger, a little braver. Brave enough at least to bark and growl and maybe frighten Aaron off. 'I barely knew you then, and I barely know you now.'

'I *know*, Rachel.' He leans in close to me, and I can smell him, the aftershave, and something else, something more animal underneath. There is a tiny piece of something green stuck in his front tooth, and hysterical laughter threatens to bubble up, the way it always does when I'm trapped in a corner and don't know how best to react. 'I know about Ted.'

The laughter immediately retreats and my blood freezes. A chill runs down my spine and I cough, trying to buy myself a few seconds before I have to respond.

'What about Ted? There's nothing to know,' I manage to whisper, my head itching under my hat, and my scarf feeling as though it is strangling me. I've gone from freezing cold, to overheating in a matter of seconds. I need to get out of this car. Aaron adjusts his grip and I wince as he crushes my fingers. 'You're hurting me.'

'I know all about you and good old Ted,' he says in a hushed sing-song, 'aren't you a pair of love birds?' I shake my head, and try to pull my hand free of his, but he just holds tighter, and I have to give up for fear he'll break the tiny bones in my hand. 'Yes, you are, Rach!' He lets out a gurgle of laughter. 'Don't be shy about it – I saw you two at the pub, that day back in the summer. You might not have been obvious to other people but I knew, Rachel, I knew then that you and he were at it – or if you weren't then, you soon would be. And then you just confirmed it for me, after you came to the house. I saw you both, in the bushes. I saw him kiss you. That wasn't just a friendly peck, was it? Eh?'

I don't say anything. I keep my eyes down and hope that this is all he wanted – to scare me, and to let me know that he knows about Ted and me.

'So, I have an idea,' he says, in a conversational tone, 'I'm happy to do you a favour, Rachel. I'm willing to keep this to myself. I won't tell Gareth, OK?'

'Thank you.' Tears of relief spring to my eyes, and I give Aaron's hand a tiny squeeze, in the hope that now he'll let go.

'If you sleep with me.'

'What?' I pull back in horror, thinking that surely, *surely*, I didn't hear that right. 'What did you say?'

'I said, I'll keep it to myself about you and Ted, I won't tell Gareth that you two are friendlier than he would like, if you sleep with me. I think that's fair, don't you?' I can't believe him. He is serious. I see the vet leaving his surgery, turning the corner into the car park and headed towards the only other vehicle here.

'No. No way. Never.' I let out a gasp of disbelief, 'I can't believe you think … I would actually do that.'

'It wouldn't be the first time.' He leans in close to hiss the words in my face, spittle landing on my cheek, the pungent smell of garlic on his breath, and I know then, I know that I didn't mishear him the last time, he did say that.

'No!' I shout, and yank my hand out of his, banging it down hard on the car horn. 'Get out! Get away from me!' I fumble for the door handle, wrenching the door open, and the vet looks up from where he's unlocking his car.

'Are you OK? Mrs Walker — is that you?' The vet has thrown his bag into the car and starts to walk towards me. Aaron gets out of the Mini, holding his hands up in a gesture of surrender, an amiable grin on his face.

'It's OK, thanks. Lovers tiff. Women, eh?' He winks at the vet, who takes one more look at me before nodding and turning back to his own vehicle, no doubt his mind already on getting home. I stand, car key in my fist, ready to jab if Aaron comes anywhere near me, but he stays where he is.

'This isn't over, Rachel.' He gives me a wink this time, and turns and saunters away like nothing happened, leaving me wild eyed and panting, fear sending shots of adrenaline through my body, my hands and knees shaking. I get back in the car, lock all the doors, and sob.

Gareth barely raises his eyes from the laptop when I walk in half an hour later, not until I ask him to pour me a whisky.

'Tough day?' He raises his eyebrows at me, as though it's inconceivable that I, who no longer has to go into a *proper* office, who just gets to light candles and mix up oils for a job, should have anything other than the easiest of days.

'A bit.' I take the glass from him, and sip gratefully. The whisky burns on the way down, finally warming me up. 'Gareth, are we OK?'

'What do you mean?' A sharp tone to his voice, his hand pauses as he lifts his own glass to his mouth and he frowns, managing to tear his eyes away from the screen for one moment.

'Us. Do you think we're good together?'

'I don't really think about it.' Taking a sip of whisky, he goes back to the screen, shuffles some papers next to him.

The words smart a little, and I blink, blaming the water that comes to my eyes on the burn of the whisky.

'What I'm trying to say, Gareth, is are you happy?' *Am I risking everything for nothing? Should I just let Aaron tell you, and deal with the fall out, or do I try and salvage what we've got.* I do love Gareth, I do. I want to be with him, not Ted. I need to end things with Ted before it all gets out of hand. I have to make sure Aaron doesn't tell.

'For Christ's sake, Rach.' Gareth sighs and pushes his hand through his hair, leaving it standing up on top of his head in a little Mohican, before slapping his hands down on the desk. 'I'm really fucking busy right now, trying to keep the business going so you can live the life you do. Do we really have to talk about this now? Is this really important?' His phone beeps on the desk next to him, and he holds up a hand to silence me before I can speak. 'I have to take this.'

Knowing when I've been dismissed, I leave the office, closing the door quietly behind me and heading out in the freezing November air to the cabin at the bottom of the garden, to wait for my evening clients. The urge to call Ted, or to jump in the car and race over there, to feel his hands in my hair and him telling me it's OK to talk about my day, is overwhelming. But I don't. Instead, I light the aromatherapy candles and drain the whisky glass, making sure I am over the limit to drive, and text him. Tomorrow, I tell him, The Rising Sun Hotel at six o'clock. One more meeting. Then I'll break it off.

22

JANUARY – NINETEEN DAYS AFTER THE PARTY

Katie Fielding looks as though she's only just woken up when I knock on her door at ten o'clock the next morning, and she still looks better than I do. Shaken up by the idea that someone (*he*) might have been in my house, in pain from the throbbing that shot through my ankle every time I turned over in bed, I didn't manage more than a couple of hours sleep, until two o'clock in the morning when I finally caved in and swallowed two sleeping pills of Gareth's, left over from a particularly harsh bout of insomnia. There is still no word from Gareth, despite the UK ringtone on his phone yesterday, and that was another thing that kept me tossing and turning through the night. If he's back in the UK why isn't he home yet? I tried his phone several times during the night, but it went to voicemail every time. Now, I feel groggy, my head muffled by cotton wool, and I almost wish I hadn't taken them at all.

'Rachel, what are you doing here?' Katie's eyebrows, perfectly plucked, knit together in a frown and she angles her body across the door frame, making it perfectly clear that I'm not exactly welcome.

'Sorry to disturb you,' I say. Katie peers past me and I look over my shoulder, where behind me Jonno is leaving the house he shares with Melody across the street, unlocking his fancy Range Rover with a beep and a flash of headlights. 'Do you mind if I come in for a moment?'

'Um. OK. If it's quick.' Katie draws back and I step into the cool, white hallway. I've never been inside Katie's house before, despite the fact that she and Brett have lived four doors down from us for five years. Brash and loud, and quite a bit younger than the rest of us who live in the tiny, exclusive close of The Vines, they're not the kind of people that Gareth would encourage into our circle of friends. I did try, back when they first moved in, but Gareth vetoed me.

'I don't think so, Rachel,' he had said, quite pompously, when I suggested inviting them for dinner not long after they moved in. 'Not really our sort, are they? He's a bit flash and she's … well, she's got a tattoo.'

'So?' I had laughed at the look on his face. 'I've got a tattoo!'

'It's on the side of her head, Rachel. A tattoo, on the side of her head. She shaved half her hair off.' He'd shaken his head as if unable to comprehend why anyone would do that, and that was it, his mind was made up and I wasn't to go getting too friendly with them.

Now, her hair has grown out and the tattoo is hidden by a swathe of honey-gold, which ripples over her shoulders. She wears a spotless white tracksuit, to match the pure white décor in the house, and gold flip-flops on her feet despite the cold temperatures outside. A tiny diamond stud glints on the side of her nose.

'Not to be rude, Rachel, but why are you here?'

'I wanted to ask you about the party, on New Year's Eve. Can you chat for a minute? I won't keep you long.' I try and smile, but it's a bit wobbly and won't stay on my face.

'I don't really ... it's not ...' She swallows, and I feel my face crumple slightly. She's not going to speak to me. She presses her lips together and waits a moment, as if internally arguing with herself.

'OK. I heard that ... well, I heard that things hadn't been too great for you.' Katie's features soften, and that slight air of tension around her lessens.

'Yeah. Pretty shit, if I'm honest. Things have been ... difficult to say the least.' I bite down on my lower lip, almost frightened to ask her now she's agreed to talk to me. 'There are a few gaps in my memory of that night.' *That's probably the understatement of the year.* 'So, I wanted to ask you — not just you, I've asked Liz and Amy as well — but can you remember much about the party?'

She looks at me, warily, and takes a couple of breaths in before she speaks.

'Like what? I remember arriving, although I was a bit pissed before I got there. Brett and I were quite late, we'd been to that bar in town, you know the one that only opened recently? They had a big New Year's Eve party, it was something like twenty quid to get in but you got a free cocktail so we went there first.' She still has a slightly cagey air about her, as though there is something she isn't telling me. I tread carefully, cautious about what I say to her next. I don't want *her* to be cautious; I want her to talk without thinking, without censoring anything.

'Sounds great. Maybe I should have gone there instead.' I give a small laugh, but it has a ragged, grating edge to it.

'Sorry, I didn't mean … I'm still finding things a bit hard, you know?' Katie nods in understanding, and I press on. 'So, the thing I wanted to ask really, was did you see anything? Do you remember seeing me? And was I with anyone? I'm just trying to narrow things down a little bit.'

'You really don't remember anything?' Katie peers at me, curiously, as if by watching me intently she'll actually see that I don't remember. 'Mel said you couldn't remember the party, but I thought she was exaggerating.'

'No, I really don't remember much at all,' I say. 'A few things are coming back to me, but it's all a bit of a mess, nothing seems to really make sense.'

'Like what?' Katie's eyes darken with something like fear. 'What do you remember? Do you remember seeing me?'

'You? No. Not at all. I just remember little things – the thud of the music. The smell of someone's cologne.' *The fabric of my underwear being wrenched down over my thighs. A hand clamped tight over my mouth, so tight I can barely breathe.*

'Oh.' Katie lets out a breath, almost visibly relaxing. 'Well, I remember seeing you in the kitchen. You were talking to Liz, I think. I don't remember who else was there. Neil, maybe? I went out into the garden; you followed a few minutes later. Do you really not remember?' She has that panicky air about her again, and I rest my hand on her arm to calm her.

'I really don't. Katie, what happened? Was there someone in the pool house?' I try to keep my voice low and soothing, but part of me wants to shriek in her face, grab her and shake her and demand to know what she remembers.

'The pool house?' She looks confused. 'No, that was all dark. I was in the garden, and you came out, looking for a light for your cigarette. That's all. You didn't seem drunk, not

220

really. A bit merry, maybe.' So, Katie must have seen me before Gareth and I argued, before Ted found me. 'I was out there with … someone I shouldn't have been. Brett was inside somewhere with Neil, talking business. You saw us, even though we were tucked away behind the rose bushes. Oh God, Rachel, please don't tell anyone! Brett will kill me.' Her big blue eyes fill with tears and she grips my hand in between her freezing cold palms. She is strong for someone so thin.

'I can't remember,' I say blankly, trying to process what she's telling me. I remember someone else saying those exact same words … *with someone I shouldn't have been.* There is an almost audible click as everything falls into place. 'Melody. It was you and Melody together in the garden, wasn't it?'

Katie nods and covers her face with her hands.

'I need her, Rachel; she's the only thing that keeps me sane. Please, you can't tell anyone. This is why neither of us could come and see you, or speak to you; we just had to pretend that we didn't remember seeing anything that night. We could hardly say we were together, not with Brett and Jonno there. And we didn't see anything – we didn't see anything happen to you, Rachel. The last we saw of you was in the garden. You were OK then – a little bit tipsy but definitely not drunk.'

'I don't suppose you remember what sort of time that was, do you?' I ask, trying to piece together when they must have seen me. I have no recollection of it at all. Katie shakes her head, the back of her hand pressed to her nose as she sniffs.

'No, I'm sorry. Like I said, I'd had a few drinks before we even got there.' She lets out a juddery breath. 'You promise you won't speak to Brett about this?'

'I said I wouldn't say anything.' Irritated at her self-centered outlook, I pull a crumpled tissue out of my back pocket and hand it to her, so she can dry her eyes. Mascara runs in thick black streaks down her cheeks, and as she wipes it away a layer of foundation comes with it, leaving her face pale. 'Did you see Aaron there? At the party? You know, the guy who works for Gareth?'

'Him? No. He definitely wasn't at the party. Not for the whole night, unless he came early and left early.'

'How are you so sure?'

Katie looks at me closely, her eyes fixed on mine.

'Because he was at the bar, the one Brett and I started at. We saw him come in at about eight o'clock and he was still there when we left. Dancing with some blonde girl, he didn't look like he was leaving any time soon. He definitely didn't show his face at Liz's party. Not that night.'

Shocked, I make my way home in a bit of a daze. I was so sure that Aaron had something to do with all of this – even throwing his name out to Carrie as someone who might potentially want to hurt me. Although, after his behaviour in the run up to Christmas, who could blame me for thinking he might have had something to do with it? Now, I learn that he was messing with my head before, by not telling me outright that he wasn't at the party – presumably just to prolong my agony at not knowing.

I spend the afternoon slumped over the kitchen table, a glass of wine in one hand, my notes in the other. I don't know what to think. There is a thick blue line scored through Jason's name, and now a thick black line runs through Aaron's. The only names remaining are Ted and

Gareth. The thought of either of them doing this to me making me want to curl up into a ball and die.

I pull myself together enough to stash my notes away before Robbie comes home from college, and I am standing in front of the open fridge door, the chilly air clouding out around my face, making my nose itch with the cold when I hear the front door slam. I am trying to decide whether I can pull together something for dinner, or whether the rest of the bottle of white wine in the fridge door and yet another takeaway pizza will suffice.

'Rob?' I call, swinging the fridge door closed. I cup my hand over my mouth and breathe into it, hoping the smell of wine isn't too strong on my breath. 'Do you mind pizza again? Only …' I break off, as Gareth appears in the kitchen door way. 'You're back.'

'I'm back. Bloody hell, Rach, what's been going on?'

'What do you mean?' I frown, puzzled, before Gareth gestures to my foot, still bound up in a fraying bandage. 'Oh, I fell over, running. Where have you been?' If anything, Gareth looks worse than I do. He hasn't shaved, so a salt and pepper bristle covers his cheeks and chin. The skin on his face that is hair-free looks pale and slightly clammy, as though he needs a good night's sleep and a shower. The skin around his eyes is faintly purple, and could either by caused by tiredness, or bruising, it's hard to tell.

'Croatia. You know that.' He nods towards the fridge and, like the good wife I am, I reach in and pull out a beer, biting my tongue against the questions that rise to my lips. 'You look exhausted.' Something like concern passes over his face, and I give a weak smile.

'Yeah, bit tired.'

'You haven't still been chasing all this ... stuff, have you?' Gareth takes a mouthful of beer, his eyes never leaving mine. I pause for a moment, not sure what to say.

'I took the underwear to Carrie, if that's what you mean.'

'Oh, Rach.' I can't read the look in his eyes as he comes towards me and I freeze for a moment, not sure of his reaction, but he puts one arm over my shoulder and pulls me in to a one-handed hug. 'Has she said anything?'

'Not yet.' I lean in to him for a moment, enjoying the feel of his weight against me. It's been a long time since Gareth actively showed me any affection and I want to drink it all in before he removes it again. Like a pathetic little puppy, I shake my head, forcing the thought away. 'But listen,' keen to jump on the tiny bit of interest he has shown, I plough on, 'I know you didn't want me to keep my notes, and I know I promised I would leave it, but I'm so glad I didn't — Jason came to see me and told me exactly why he left Newcastle, and I found out that Aaron wasn't at the party after all ...'

'You mean exactly like he told the police?' Gareth drops his arm from my shoulders and moves away from me, his affection fading as quickly as it arrived. 'Only, when he says it, it's not the truth, you have to hear it from someone else? And what have you been doing? Knocking on the neighbours' doors, demanding to know what they know?' I say nothing, my eyes fixed on my feet, a slow, guilty blush creeping up from my neckline. 'For fuck's sake, Rach! I told you, God knows how many times, *let the police deal with things!*'

'But they're not!' I shout back. 'They ask a few questions and don't hear what they want to hear so they tell me there's no evidence ... and then that's it, whoever did it gets away with it.'

'Rach,' Gareth shoves his hand through his hair, 'you can't even tell them what did happen, because you can't remember. You can't even remember if anything did actually happen ... and now you're hassling the people around us. It's not right. The police have got the underwear, they can test for DNA – just let them do their job.'

'But I'm getting somewhere, if I hadn't spoken to Liz she might never have brought round my underwear in the first place and ...'

'I don't need this!' Gareth roars, throwing his beer bottle into the sink where it smashes into shards. I stop, my mouth hanging open in shock. 'Jesus, Rachel, you have no idea ... you have no clue what's going on under your nose, do you?' He scrubs his hands over his face, and when he pulls them away there are tears in his eyes.

'What are you talking about?' I whisper, my mind racing as to what he could mean. 'What's going on? Where were you yesterday? I rang you and it was a UK dial tone but you didn't come home last night.'

'Forget it.' Gareth turns to the sink and starts picking the shards of glass gingerly from the stainless steel. 'It's nothing, OK? I'm tired, I've been in non-stop meetings for days, and I just want to relax when I get home. I don't want people complaining to me that you've hassling them – I have to go into the office tomorrow and face Aaron, knowing that you've been questioning him about that night, even though he wasn't there. I know you've had a shit time, and I want to be supportive, but honestly, Rach?' He turns to face me and my heart flips at the desolate look on his face, 'we've had a really rough time lately, and I just want us to move on. I want things to be normal, you understand?'

Shell shocked, I nod but inside I am screaming, unable to comprehend why he doesn't understand how important it is to me to get this resolved. Only then will I be able to move on. I can't live my life in fear, constantly looking over my shoulder, paranoid in case he comes back.

'Fine,' I say, and leave him to his glass picking, not sure that if I stay in the same room with him, I can be certain not to tell him that things will never be normal, not until my rapist – because that's what he is, whoever he is, that's what happened to me, I know, even if I can't remember – is caught.

23

JANUARY – TWENTY DAYS AFTER THE PARTY

'I need to see you. Meet me at the coffee shop on the High Street?' The phone call comes early, the buzz of my mobile dragging me from a dream-ridden sleep, one that I'm not entirely unhappy to be woken from.

'OK. Give me half an hour.' I hang up, rolling out of bed and heading towards the shower, feeling groggy with lack of sleep. Yet another headache starts to thump behind my eyes and I grab two painkillers from the bottle next to the bed as I go, swallowing them dry. Gareth's side of the bed is untouched, and when I peer out of the window his car is gone from the drive. I assume he must have spent the night on the sofa bed in his office, and part of me is relieved that he didn't try to share a bed with me, not after the things he said last night.

I shower at speed, giving my hair a quick wash, wishing I could stay in for longer, leaving the conditioner on for minutes instead of seconds, attempting to make myself feel more like the old me. Instead, I hurry, pulling my clothes on even though my skin is still slightly damp, my leggings clinging and twisting as I tut in frustration, before rushing out of the front door, calling an apology to Thor for leaving him behind as

I go, his head raising briefly from his basket before he closes his eyes and goes back to sleep. I'm still late though, shoving through the door of the coffee shop ten minutes later than expected, my cheeks flushed with the cold and the rush to get here.

'Hey, I got you a latte. And a muffin.' Amy stands up to kiss my cheek, and I whip my hat from my head, static making my still damp hair stand out around my head like a halo.

'Thanks.' I take a sip, letting the coffee soothe me as I swallow, getting my breath back. 'What's the urgency? Why did you need to see me? Not that I don't appreciate an early morning phone call from you.' I smile to show her I'm kidding, but my stomach does an anxious roll as I wonder what she has to say.

'Something's happened.' Amy's green eyes are serious as she watches me over the rim of her coffee cup, and the smile dies on my lips. 'I wanted to speak to you before the gossip patrol are out, it's about Ted.'

'What about him?' The sound of his name gives me a little shiver, raising goosebumps on my arms, as I remember the flashback of Ted's hand on my arm at the party.

'He's been arrested.'

'What? Why?' *Oh, God.* I feel sick, saliva spurting into my mouth, and I swallow hard. I picture Ted's name, alongside Gareth's in my notebook, only in my head now there is a big neon light around it. Is this it? Is it all over? Thoughts tumble over one another in my mind before sense reels me in. *Wouldn't the police have called me? If they thought it was Ted who did it?*

'Oh shit, no … it's nothing to do with … God, sorry.' Amy reaches across the table, knocking her coffee over in her haste to reassure me that this is nothing to do with the party. 'He's been arrested for drink-driving.' She dabs ineffectually at the coffee spill with a tiny napkin.

'God.' I feel like I can breathe again, although my hands tremble slightly with the shock. 'That's awful, not like Ted at all.' I'm struggling to get my head around what Amy is telling me – Ted is usually just so *good*. This is completely out of character. 'What happened? How do you know this?' I have a million questions.

'I shouldn't really be repeating this, it came from Vanessa.' Vanessa is Amy's sister-in-law, who works at Kingsnorth police station – I'm not too entirely sure what she does there, something to do with administration, but I do know she walks around with her eyes and ears open, and often repeats things she shouldn't to Amy. This is the first time Amy has ever repeated anything to me. 'There was an accident – Ted went up on the kerb and clipped a cyclist. Well, I say clipped, he knocked the poor bugger right off. The bloke is in hospital – they think he's probably broken his leg. The problem with it all is that Ted didn't stop.'

'Oh no.' My hearts sinks – this is far worse than I first thought. 'He just drove off and left the guy there? What was he thinking?'

'I don't think he was … anyway; someone saw it happen and took Ted's number plate. They reported it, and obviously the plate came back in Ted's name. The police went straight over to the house and the car was on the drive. Parked terribly, but still on the drive. Apparently when he opened the door the stink of whisky on him was overwhelming.'

'So, what will happen to him?' I can't help but feel some sympathy for Ted, despite my suspicions about his involvement the night of the party – although what possessed him to get in the car after all that booze I have no idea. *Guilt?* A snippy little voice at the back of my mind asks, *has he got something to feel guilty for?* I take a hurried sip of my coffee, the dregs now lukewarm and horrid.

'I don't know. Dangerous driving charge maybe? There was blood on the steering wheel, and apparently Ted has a cut on his nose, so that kind of puts him there. They'll test the blood anyway to confirm it's his, and then that with the alcohol reading will probably be enough to get him a driving ban at the very least. That's what Vanessa thinks anyway.'

'This is awful. Poor Ted. Poor bloody cyclist. I should probably go and see him.'

'Who? The cyclist?'

'Funny. Ted, of course. Now that Angela isn't there he hasn't got anyone.'

Amy arches an eyebrow in my direction. 'Not your job any more, Rach.'

'No, I know. But he doesn't have anyone to talk to – and when something like this happens you need support. It's awfully lonely otherwise.' *I should know.* I lean down and pick up my bag from under the table. 'Thanks for the coffee – and thanks for letting me know. I shouldn't imagine Ted has too many people feeling sorry for him at the moment.'

'Rachel Walker. I have an appointment at ten thirty with Mr Durand.' I give the receptionist a confident stare and dare her to argue with me. I am at Ted's office on the other side of town, fudging my way into an appointment so I can talk to him.

'I can't find it on the system, Mrs Walker. Are you sure you have the right day?' The receptionist eyes me coolly, and I shake away the idea that she knows who I am, knows that Ted and I were having an affair a matter of months ago.

'It might not be in the diary. I made the appointment with Mr Durand himself.' She holds up one finger as she makes a call, presumably to Ted. She speaks quietly into the receiver, her eyes never leaving my face, before pointing me in the direction of Ted's office. I smile sweetly, and make sure I slam Ted's door a little behind me.

'Rachel ... what are you doing here? You don't really have an appointment, do you?' Behind his desk, Ted looks confused and more than a little battered, a tiny sticking plaster on the bridge of his nose, the green and purple of a bruise radiating out from beneath it, spilling down towards his cheeks.

'I heard what happened, Ted. At least, some of it anyway.' I cross the room to him, wanting to touch the tender skin on his nose, but something stops me. Perhaps the tiny ripple of fear that snakes along my arms, raising goosebumps on my skin, as I once again remember his name etched into my notes. 'Are you all right?'

Ted sighs, wincing as he gingerly presses his fingers to his bruised nose.

'I'm an idiot, Rachel. I drank too much, hit that poor guy and then panicked. I drove home, for goodness' sake – I didn't even stop to make sure he was OK.'

'Everyone makes mistakes, you just have to take the punishment.' I sound unfeeling, a harsh edge to my words. 'What on earth made you drink so much?' I have to know – if it does have anything to do with the party, something he's keeping secret, maybe now he'll have to talk, burdened by guilt and unable to keep it in any longer.

'Angela.'

'Oh.' I wasn't expecting that.

'She called and said that she's booked Sean's flight for the summer. Then she told me that she and Devon would

231

be taking him to view colleges, and helping him with his applications. He can't wait to leave! It's all he's talked about since she rang. She's keeping him there, Rach. She's going to take my boy away from me.' Ted looks at me, despair in his dark eyes and I reach out a hand to him.

'There'll be visits,' I say, 'it'll be difficult, but it's not as though you won't ever see him again.'

'You don't get it, do you?' Ted yanks his hand from mine, pushing me away, anger radiating from every pore, and I glance nervously towards the door, making sure I have a clear escape route. There is something disconcerting about the way he expresses his anger, and I lick my dry lips nervously, wanting desperately to leave. I wish I'd never come at all. 'I've lost everything, Rachel! Angela left – it hurt, but I could deal with it, it wasn't working between us. Our marriage had been over for a long time before she moved in with Devon. Then you ... I thought we had something.' His eyes lock on mine and I feel a flutter of fear in my chest. 'I thought you were different, Rachel. I thought we would be together eventually, but you called it off. Yeah, you said it was a bit of fun and you loved Gareth, but I knew you were coming round to the idea of us being together permanently. Only then, you left me too. And now ... Angela wants to take my son from me, leaving me with nothing.'

'Ted, please calm down,' I hold my hands up, trying to quieten him down and keep my voice from shaking. 'Sean is eighteen. He's an adult. He doesn't have to go if he doesn't want to, and even if he does, if he wants to come home then he can. He might not even want to go, have you asked him?'

'She's put all sorts of ideas in his head – he's already talking about packing, booking flights. And no wonder, it's not like life at home with me is as appealing, is it?' His voice breaks, and he shoves his hands through his hair. 'This is it, Rachel, I'm going to be left with nothing. No wife, no lover, no son. And what's coming next? No driving licence? Then what? No job? How can I do my job without a car? Maybe this is it. Maybe I'll get what I deserve.' Regret etched onto his face, Ted puts his head in his hands. 'God, I never should have got involved with you.'

'I think maybe you need some time alone.' My back presses against the closed door, my hands shaking. 'I'll let the receptionist know you'll be a few more minutes, OK?'

Without waiting for him to answer, I turn and open the door, rushing down the corridor towards the exit. My heart hammers in my chest and my legs feel like jelly as I make it back to the car, sliding into the driver's seat and pressing the locks down. I would have said before that Ted always keeps his cool, very rarely – if ever – losing his temper. If anyone had asked me before if I had seen Ted flip out the answer would always have been no. Something in the way his face changed so quickly, the way he went from composed to pure rage in the blink of an eye has caught me off balance and made me think that maybe I don't know Ted as well as I thought.

Maybe I'll get what I deserve. The words spin through my mind, and all at once I am back there, at the party. Faces whirl past me in a blur, Katie Fielding, her hair tied up in a fancy, glittery up-do, Melody, a drink in her hands, something with a sparkler and a straw. Then, hands gripping my upper arms, and I am wincing with the pain, struggling to get free. Cigarette smoke fills my nose and throat and I want to gag, the ashy taste on my tongue suffocating me. Kicking out, a flash of my silver sandal as I try to lash out, only my foot doesn't move the way I want it to. A head leans in close, hissing in my ear, '... *this is all your fault, I'll make sure you get what you deserve.'* My arms and legs don't want to move properly, as though they are filled with lead or cast in concrete, heavy and unwilling. I want to scream, it catches in my throat and I think, *yes, someone will hear me, someone will come,* but it doesn't break free of my throat and then I am on the bed, his hand clamped over my mouth, holding the scream tight inside me, that citrusy lemon scent filling the air.

Back in my car, I cry out, fumbling with the door handle, desperate for fresh air. I half fall, half stagger out of the car, landing on the edge of the kerb on my knees, the shock of the pain making me gasp. There is a rip in my leggings, right on the knee cap, and a thick, maroon ooze of blood starts to run down my leg, tiny pieces of gravel sticking to the graze.

Slowly, I get to my feet, feeling shaken and drained, dusting away the tiny pieces of dirt that cling to my palms. I can almost smell the cigarette smoke on the air, taste the Christmas canapés on my tongue, it feels so real when I'm back there at the party. A little more of that night comes back to me with every flashback, and I just wish I could see his face, or get some hint as to who he really is. I draw in deep lungfuls of cold, crisp January air, dabbing at the cut on my knee and avoiding the gaze of curious passers-by, until I am calm again, my heart rate back to its normal pace. You might think that every flashback, every memory that I manage to piece together would batter me down, until there is nothing left of me, but I'm determined not to let it. I think of my notebook, tucked away and hidden from sight *(from Gareth)* behind the cookery books on the bookshelf in the kitchen. I need to take every piece of information that comes to me when I'm caught up in the horror of these memories, and make it work for me – use it to make sure I take this bastard down.

24

DECEMBER – THREE WEEKS BEFORE THE PARTY

The handles of the carrier bags cut into my palms, turning my fingers white from lack of circulation as I stagger up the road from the bus stop. It's only two weeks until Christmas, the only Saturday I have free between now and then to get my Christmas shopping done, and it's typical that my car wouldn't start when I got back to the car park. Even more typical that I forgot my mobile, left on the kitchen side unit when I left the house in a hurry this morning, so keen was I to get the shopping over and done with, so I couldn't even call Gareth and ask him to come and fetch me. Not that he would have come – he and Robbie were supposed to be going to watch West Ham v Chelsea, although as I approach the house, shifting the bags from one hand to the other for some slight relief, I see his car is still in the driveway. I don't think anything of it – he probably decided to get the train in, thinking the crush of the Christmas shopping crowds on public transport would be less hassle than the traffic jams on the roads.

It's a shock then, when I finally manage to juggle my door keys and the hundreds of bags I've carried home and let myself in, to see Gareth standing in the hallway.

'Oh.' I drop the bags to the floor and massage some life back into my aching fingers. 'I didn't realize you were home – I've had to leave the car in the car park, it wouldn't start …'

'Shut up, Rachel.' Gareth's voice is brittle and hard, as though he's holding something back.

'What?' I stare at him, open-mouthed. 'You can't speak to me like that.'

'I can speak to you any damn way I please.' His mouth slashes a grim line into his face, and I can't place his expression. If I had to choose, I would say something close to hate. My eyes drift downwards, to where I spy my mobile phone clamped in his right hand. All of a sudden, the atmosphere changes, becomes so thick that you could cut it with a knife. Shivers race down my spine and my heart rate speeds up, fear racing through my veins.

'Where's Robbie?' I whisper, anxious that he will be a party to whatever happens next.

'Now you wonder about Robbie!' Gareth lets out a harsh bark of laughter. 'You probably should have thought about him before, you know. He's out – thankfully – I wouldn't want my boy to hear this.' He looks at me closely. 'Out with the girls last night, wasn't it? That was the excuse.' He juggles the phone from one hand to the other as I look on, nervously.

'I was out with the girls. You can call any of them.' I really was out for a few drinks last night with the mums from my NCT group. Eighteen years on and we still meet for drinks every six months, to gloat about our children's

236

achievements under the guise of friendship. Gareth slides the unlock button on my phone and taps at the screen.

'*Tomorrow night. Seven p.m. I'll tell him I'm going for a run. Can't wait to see ALL of you x*,' he reads out from my text screen, 'sent to someone named "T".'

My breath sticks in my throat and for a moment I feel as though I'll never be able to breathe again.

'When did you send that, Rachel? When you were knocking up a bowl of pasta for Robbie and Sean last night, pretending you give a shit about their day? While you were putting your make-up on? While you were sitting across the table from me, telling me you wouldn't be late home because you think it's time to call it a day on the NCT drinks? When all the time you were lying. To me *and* to our son.' By the end of the sentence his voice breaks, devastation showing on his face as I struggle to hold back the tears that spill down my cheeks.

'I never sent that text,' I say, reaching out a hand that he ignores. I know I didn't send it, I never would have sent Ted something so explicit and *obvious*. 'I never sent it, I swear.'

'You can swear all you want, Rach, only I called the number.' A blaze of triumph sparks in Gareth's eyes. 'Do you want to guess who answered? He was mighty pleased to have your name come up on his call screen.' He steps closer to me, uncomfortably close, shoving the phone in my face.

'Oh no, Gareth, please I can explain …' Taking a step back to widen the gap between us, I cover my mouth with my hands, trying to hold in the scream that itches to escape the back of my throat.

'Explain? Explain what? That poor old Ted, Ted fucking Durand, that sad little man whose wife left him, who everyone has been feeling sorry for, has been fucking my wife?' Gareth's voice is quiet now, scarily calm and I am more unnerved by this than I've ever been when he's lost his temper before. 'Is that why she left him? Because of you? Because she found out you were just another old slut, eager to jump in his bed?'

'No!' I shout, swatting the phone away from my face. 'It wasn't like that! I'm not a slut.' I tilt my head back, blinking back the tears that sting my eyes. 'Angela was gone before ... before anything happened.'

'Oh, well that's OK then, isn't it?' Gareth snorts, his face an alarming shade of red as he allows anger to sweep over him. 'So Ted was a free agent ... it was just you who had commitments, only you who was actually still married.'

'Please, just let me explain. I can tell you everything if you just let me explain.'

'There's nothing to explain!' Anger radiating off him with a white-hot heat, he comes towards me and I flinch, but it's too late as his raised hand cracks me across the cheek and he storms away from me, leaving me shocked and frightened, a large red handprint raising itself on my white, chilled skin.

I cower on the stairs for a moment, my cheek smarting with pain and my eyes filled with hot, stinging tears. I should have known that this moment would come – I promised myself over a month ago that I would call it off with Ted, after we nearly got caught that time, but something made me go back to him time and time again.

I hear the sound of Gareth opening cupboards, and the noisy slosh of liquid into a glass. Much as I don't want to, I have to go in there and explain to him how things were. I have to try and salvage something from the ruins of our marriage, for Robbie's sake if not my own. Slowly, I push myself up to standing, catching a glimpse of my face in the hallway mirror as I do so. A purple mark already sprouts under my eye, and I foresee a couple of weeks of daily make-up routines to cover it.

'Gareth,' I say quietly, as I enter the kitchen to see him slumped, head in his hands, at the kitchen table. 'Please just let me explain.' He waves a hand in my direction, but doesn't speak, just raises the glass to his lips.

'It wasn't like you think with Ted. I didn't … I don't love him. It didn't mean anything to me.' Gareth raises his head to look at me, his eyes red-rimmed, his mouth twisted in a grimace of pain, and I hate myself. 'I was lonely – you aren't ever around, and when you are here, it's like you don't want anything to do with me. I talk to you, and you blank me, telling me you never heard what I said, but all I feel is that I'm not good enough, not interesting enough for you to pay attention. You shut yourself away in your office and don't tell me anything; you don't want me to help out with the business any more. On the rare occasion we do sit in the same room, you spend the entire evening on your phone, doing God only knows what. I was so desperately *lonely*, Gareth, I just wanted some affection, to be made to feel as though I am worth something, to someone.'

'So, this is all my fault?' His voice breaks, and I understand that it's me that has broken him. 'I made you feel shit, so you went somewhere else, is that it? Fucking hell, Rachel.'

'I'm not blaming you; I know this is all my fault. I'm just trying to tell you how I felt … I don't love Ted, I love you. I want to be with you, but I felt as though you didn't want to be with me.' There is a pain in my chest so sharp, that I am convinced it is my heart breaking. *How could I have been so stupid? How could I have done this to us?*

239

'You could have just talked to me. You could have just told me how you felt and we could have fixed it. How can your running off and jumping into bed with Ted Durand fix anything between us?' He slams the heavy crystal glass down on the table, making me jump. 'Jesus, Rachel, you have no idea about the shit I'm dealing with at the moment, do you? I'm trying to support our family, and you ... Aaron said ...'

'Aaron?' I cut him off, sharply. 'Is that where this has all come from? Did that bastard tell you to check my phone?' *Did he somehow get hold of my phone and send that text to Ted, purely so Gareth would see it? I know I didn't send that message.* My blood runs cold as I realize that Aaron did what he threatened – and he's clearly more dangerous than I ever thought he could be. 'There are a few things you should know about Aaron,' I say, determined not to let Gareth believe whatever shit Aaron has spouted at him. 'You should know that he's been threatening me.'

'Oh, come on, Rachel.'

'It's true!' My voice rises, and I struggle to get myself back under control, Gareth won't believe me if I can't even tell him without getting hysterical. 'He saw me with Ted at a pub. He called me over to the Riverside house, pretending to be you – remember that time, with the keys? – he tried it on then, telling me he never got over me.' Gareth frowns, but doesn't speak, so I carry on. 'Then, when I took Thor to the vet, he locked himself in my car with me and told me that if I didn't sleep with him he would tell you I was having an affair with Ted.' I stop, eyeing Gareth expectantly to see his reaction. I am stunned when, a few seconds later, he starts to laugh.

'Fucking hell, Rachel, I can't believe you would stoop this low.' He shoves his chair violently back from the table and scrubs his hands through his hair. 'That you would actually concoct some ridiculous story about Aaron to try and get yourself off the hook.'

'It's not some ridiculous story, it's the truth – and I told you about Ted, didn't I? I got caught, Gareth, and now I'm trying to be honest with you to try and save what little we have left.'

'Why the hell would Aaron proposition you like that? I've known him for years, he *works* for me, he's my second-in-command. I've talked about making him a director, for God's sake, why would he risk that? Tell me.'

'I don't know, Gareth,' I cry, frustration welling up, 'all I know is that's what he said – he would tell you if I didn't sleep with him.'

'Aaron didn't tell me anything,' he says, as he walks away from me, back into the hallway. He reaches into the cupboard under the stairs, pulling a jacket from a hook. 'You left your phone behind, and you got a text. Apparently, Amy found your scarf at hers after the last time you went over. I was going to text her back to say I'd collect it for you because you were out shopping, and instead I found your text to Ted.'

'But you said, *Aaron said* … I thought he'd …' I trail off.

'I was going to say that Aaron said maybe I should encourage you to take a bit of time off – maybe the two of us go away for a weekend – he was worried that you didn't seem yourself lately.' He gives that strange bark of laughter again, harsh and grating. 'Looks like he was right.' He tugs his jacket on roughly and snatches up his keys from the table by the door.

'Gareth, wait.' I snare his jacket between my fingers, tugging at it to make him stay. 'Where are you going? Can't we talk about things?'

'I'm going to see Ted,' he says, and sharply shakes himself free, slamming the door in my face.

As soon as his car leaves the drive, I call Ted.

'Rachel!' Ted's voice is warm, pleased to hear from me, the complete opposite to Gareth. I feel a tiny pang before the sick, queasy feeling brought on by guilt swarms over me. 'You're not cancelling tonight, are you? I think we got cut off earlier when you rang.'

'It wasn't me that rang you. He knows, Ted,' I say, urgently, 'Gareth knows and he's on his way. I told him everything.'

'What? Why? He's on his way?' Ted sounds hurt and more than a little confused. 'Why would you tell him about us? Does this mean …?'

'He found a text on my phone … it's … ugh, it's a long story, but he knows and he's on his way to see you.'

'What did you tell him?' For a moment, I think I hear hope in Ted's voice, but I am too frightened of what Gareth is about to do to him to dwell on it.

'Everything. It's over, Ted,' I say in a rush, 'that's it. It's over between us; I can't see you any more. I told you I wouldn't ever leave Gareth. Don't call me, don't try to see me. And it might be an idea to go out before Gareth gets to you.' I don't wait for him to speak; I just hang up, my nerves jangling.

I pace anxiously for what feels like hours, before I shut myself in the living room as darkness falls. I have tried to call Gareth, but his phone is going to voicemail and I am reluctant to leave a message. Robbie comes in, eats, and goes to his room; blissfully unaware that anything is out of sorts between his parents, as I hibernate in the living room, not wanting him to see the mark on my face. Finally, I hear the click of the front door closing and Gareth appears, dishevelled and tired, shadows marked on his face by the glow of the small lamp I have switched on.

'You're back.' I go to stand up but he raises his hand to me, so I sink back into the armchair. He comes across the room, kneeling at my feet, and places one hand on my face. I feel the slight throb of my cheekbone under his fingers, where he hit me, the bruise already a bright range of purples and greens.

'I'm sorry … for the way I behaved earlier,' he says, 'I was angry.'

'I know,' I say, not telling him it's OK, because regardless of what I did, it's not OK. 'Did you see Ted?' I don't want to ask but I am scared, frightened in case Gareth has done something we will both regret.

'Don't even think about Ted,' his voice hardens, 'I mean it, Rachel, if we're going to make this work, you can't even think about him. You can't see him, you can't speak to him. Not if we're going to get through this.'

'OK.' I nod frantically, the bruise on my face rubbing against his hand, the pain making tears spurt to my eyes. 'I promise, I won't have anything more to do with him. It's you I want to be with. It's you that I love.'

Gareth gives a sharp nod and strokes his fingers gently against my bruised cheekbone, before he gets to his feet and leaves the room. I hear the dull thud of his office door slamming shut behind him and I am left alone in the dark, wondering how on earth we will ever recover from this.

25

JANUARY – FOUR WEEKS AFTER THE PARTY

I'm not stupid. I know Gareth is hiding something – his outburst the night he came back from his trip just reinforced my suspicions – the only thing is what? I can't shake the creeping feeling that it has something to do with the party – he still hasn't confessed to grabbing me by the arms that night, and as far as I know he is still unaware that I know about it. He's been even cagier than usual since he came back from Croatia. Why did he want to leave the party so urgently? And what did he do after I refused to go with him? I know he grabbed me, but did he go further than that? Is that why he wants me to drop my own little investigation into that night – is he scared that I'll uncover something that will incriminate him? The very idea of it makes my stomach turn and I have to take a deep breath, breathing out slowly and counting to ten, just to stop myself from losing my mind. He has worked from home for the past ten days, ever since he got back from Croatia, and part of me thinks that perhaps he knows that I'm just biding my time, waiting until he leaves the house so I can get into his office and have a good snoop around.

Today though, seems to be the day. He's been holed up in there for most of the day, I've heard him muttering and occasionally, his raised voice, as if talking to someone on the phone. Now, I hover in the doorway, a cup of tea in my hand, which he clearly isn't going to drink.

'Are you going out?' I ask, innocently. 'I brought you a cup of tea, it's been a while since lunch.'

'No, thanks.' Distracted, he shoves some paperwork into his laptop bag, before surveying the chaos that is his desk, pushing his hands through his hair. 'Yes. I'm going out. I've got a meeting, I won't be long.'

'Will you be back for dinner?' I need to gauge exactly how long I think I'll have before he returns. The last thing I need is to be caught rummaging through his desk drawers – how on earth would I explain it? *'Sorry, Gareth, just going through your things to make sure it wasn't you that attacked me at Liz's party. Shall we get a takeaway?'*

'Probably. I don't know. Does it matter?' He frowns at me, grabbing one last file from his desk before coming to the doorway. Nudging me out of the way, he pulls the door closed and locks it, tucking the key into his jacket pocket. He pecks my cheek, and I almost spill the tea down my top.

'See you later,' I say quietly as he rushes along the hallway, slamming the front door behind him, my mind already racing. *Why has he locked the door? What is it that he wants to keep from me? And how on earth can I get inside?*

I wait fifteen minutes, sipping at the tea I made for him just in case he's forgotten anything and comes back for it, but he doesn't return and I start to relax, thinking the coast is clear. Headed to the junk drawer in the kitchen,

I rummage around looking, *hoping*, it'll be as simple as finding a spare key to the office, but no, of course it isn't. He's hardly going to lock me out, and then leave a key for me to find. I realize that this is going to be a lot harder than I thought.

At the back of the drawer I find a hair grip – I'm no lock picker, but how hard can it be? Several Google searches, a quick You Tube tutorial and one hell of scratched up lock later, I find out that it actually is really, really, hard – but can be done. Flushed, and more than a little sweaty, I check the time on my watch as I let myself into Gareth's haven. Ten to five. It's taken me over an hour to get into the office, and I am terrified that he's going to be home at any minute. *No time to waste, Rachel.* The sky is ablaze with reds, purples and pinks as the sun starts to make its way down, and I open the window blind where Gareth usually half closes it, so I have an unobstructed view of the street outside. I know this gives anyone outside an unobstructed view in, but I'm hoping that I see Gareth's headlights approaching before he sees me. Satisfied that I have everything in order, I turn to the desk.

Organized chaos. That's the only way I can describe it. There is a tiny square of clear space where his laptop usually sits, only he's taken it to his meeting. Not that it would be much use to me – he password protects everything and I have no idea of what they could be, nor do I have the time now to try and guess them.

I turn my attention to the paperwork on the desk but rifling through there is nothing out of the ordinary. Plans for new houses, planning permission correspondence and quotes from suppliers make up the bulk of the paperwork –

nothing sinister there at all — and why would there be? He's hardly likely to lock the door but leave everything out on his desk for the world to see. Sitting in his chair, I wheel it close to the desk, and try the drawers. It is absurdly warm in here, and I puff my sweaty fringe out of my eyes as I tug on each drawer. The top two open easily — filled with spare pens, staples and other little bits of stationery, there is nothing out of the ordinary. I push aside a small stack of window envelopes and uncover a photograph.

Raising a hand to my mouth, I gently ease it free, tears burning at the corners of my eyes. It's a copy of our wedding photo. Taken nineteen years ago, we both look young and happy, full of excitement at what the future holds for us. I'm not sure how we got to here — me, searching his office for evidence that he drugged me and attacked me, him barely having the time to look my way. He certainly doesn't look at me the way he did in the wedding photo any more. Swallowing down the lump in my throat, I tuck the photo back in its place and close the drawer.

The bottom drawer is the one that won't open. Frustrated I tug at it, but it won't budge. I go back to the unlocked drawers, searching for a key tiny enough to fit the lock but there's nothing, not even taped to the top of the desk, like I once saw in a movie. Dejected, I sit back, wiping at the beads of sweat that prickle on the back of my neck. The hairgrip I used to get into the office lies on the biggest stack of papers in front of me. I could do it again, couldn't I? I have to try, but please God, don't let it take me another hour to get into it, Gareth would be sure to be back by then. With slippery fingers I get to work, and either I'm getting better at this, or this lock isn't so complicated, as it doesn't take me long to get in. Hurriedly I yank the drawer open and reams of paper come spilling out, across the polished wooden flooring.

'Shit,' I mutter to myself, leaning down to scoop up the errant paperwork, freezing as I read the letter on the top of the pile. It's a bank statement for our joint account. We both have our own separate accounts, plus one in both our names that we both transfer money into to cover the bills. As I scan quickly down the statement, I see the balance is far less than I was expecting. Frowning, I go back to the top and reread. My payment has gone in as usual, but it doesn't look as though Gareth's has been transferred. In fact, my payment has barely covered the overdraft on the account. Feeling slightly sick, I rifle through the paperwork until I find the statement for the month before. I remember, mid December, saying to Gareth that I hadn't seen the statement, and that I was going to call the bank and ask for a copy. He'd said not to worry, that he was going to the bank the following day and he'd get one then, so I'd put it out of my mind. Now, I see why he didn't want me to see it – his payment hasn't been transferred for the previous month either. My heart starting to thump in my chest, I shuffle the papers into some sort of order, and start to comb through them methodically, feeling more and more ill with every page I turn.

'FINAL DEMAND' screams out in violent red font on white paper, as I pull a sheet of A4 from its envelope. I shake the letter open to read that it is a final demand from the electricity company, telling us that we have seven days to make payment in full before legal action will commence. It is dated the twenty-seventh of December.

My heart starts to pound in my chest as I start sifting through the mountain of bills that have overflowed from the desk drawer. Final demands from both the gas and electric companies, with a bailiffs' letter from the electricity company telling Gareth that they will be seizing goods.

As I rifle through the post, many of the letters unopened, I find two from the bank, one informing Gareth that they are calling in the overdraft on his current account. I read, and reread the letter in horror, before tearing through the mound of paper to find his personal bank statement. It's even worse than I could have imagined. There is nothing in his account at all, and he's so far into an overdraft that I wasn't even aware he had, that I have no idea how he'll ever pay it back. The second letter from the bank is informing us that as no mortgage payments have been made for three months, despite repeated requests for contact none has been forthcoming, and therefore they have no option but to repossess the house.

I am unaware that I am crying, until large, wet splashes hit the letter, making the ink run. *How has this happened?* I've been transferring my bill money every month without fail, trusting him to do the same – and he must have been deliberately hiding the mail from me to make sure I didn't find out exactly how much he's fucked up.

Anger bubbles up, and I yank the remaining paperwork from the drawer, barely reading each letter, tearing through them, the fear and anger chugging through my veins with every letter I read. There are casino slips, betting forms from various different betting shops, and most horrific of all, a ream of IOUs to Jonno Barker, for various sums ranging from five hundred pounds to two thousand pounds, dated August onwards – from the week before the barbecue. No wonder Gareth wanted to leave Liz's New Year's Eve party when Jonno arrived – and that must be what Jonno meant when he told me to speak to Gareth. Gareth owes him thousands of pounds.

Shaking, I start to collect all the evidence together, when a tap at the window scares the living daylights out of me. Darkness has fallen while I've been reading through Gareth's secret hoard of bills, and now a white face is outlined at the window through the open blinds. I utter a little shriek as I see it, before placing my hand to my chest. It's Sean, presumably here to meet Robbie. I haven't heard Robbie come in, but I've been so engrossed I wouldn't have heard anything. Sean gestures to the front door and I nod, and he appears before me a few seconds later.

'Are you OK, Rachel?' He leans against the doorframe, the tip of his nose pink with cold. I shiver as he brings a gust of fresh air in with him. 'You look like you've been crying.'

'No, it's … oh, God.' I scrub my hands over my face.

'Is everything OK? Did something happen? Like, I mean, with your … with what happened at the party?' He looks uncomfortable, not wanting to meet my eyes.

'No, nothing like that.' I fumble in my pocket for a tissue to blow my nose.

'Mum?' Robbie appears in the doorway, over Sean's shoulder. His gaze goes to the pile of papers in my hand, and he sucks in a breath. 'You found them.'

'You knew about this?' I have to fight to stop my voice from rising to a shriek. 'Did your father tell you about these bills? About the fact the we are about to lose

251

everything?' I am fighting to keep control, my emotions running so high that I don't know what will come out of my mouth next.

'No!' Robbie says, sliding in past Sean to stand next to me. 'I found them on my own ... I sneaked in here one day when he was busy, I wanted to borrow his laptop while he was out, and I knew he wouldn't let me if I asked him. I found all these bills, but I couldn't say anything to him, he'd go mad that I'd been in his office. I didn't know what to do.'

'And then when I found you in here that day? The day I fell over in the woods.'

'I was looking to see if there were any more bills – or if he'd started dealing with stuff. I wanted to help.' Robbie's cheeks flush pink.

'Oh, God, Rob. Why didn't you talk to me?' I scrub my hands over my face, not knowing what to do, what to say. There is no way that this can be easily fixed. I need to see Gareth. This was the last thing I was expecting to find – and while I am relieved that I didn't find anything relating to that night, relieved that I can cross Gareth off the list, leaving only Ted's name remaining – all I can hear is the sound of my life falling apart around me. And that's when the telephone rings.

26

I snatch up the receiver, fire burning in my belly, thinking, *god damn you, Gareth, this had better not be you, because I cannot be responsible for the words that come out of my mouth.* I practically bark into the receiver,

'Hello?'

'Rachel? Is that you? This is Carrie — from Kingsnorth station?' Her voice is hesitant, and I realize she only half-recognizes my voice.

'Carrie! Yes, it's me.' At her name both the boys' ears prick up, and they fall silent from where they have been murmuring between themselves.

'Can you talk?'

'Yes — has something happened?' My heart rate starts to speed up, and my sweaty fingers slip on the telephone receiver. I juggle it to the other hand, wiping my palm on my jeans.

'It's about the DNA sample that we took from your underwear,' she says, and the bottom falls out of my stomach, as though I've ridden a lift too fast, leaving me shaky and nauseous. 'There was an incident a little while ago that led to us obtaining some DNA evidence from another case. We ran the sample through the database and got a hit against the sample from the underwear.'

'Oh.' I sink into Gareth's desk chair, my legs no longer able to hold me up. The leather creaks reassuringly under my weight. 'You mean ...'

'Yes,' Carrie's voice is strong and clear in my ear, 'we got a match, Rachel. We've found a match to the DNA on your underwear from the night of the party ...'

'Who is it?' I demand, shock draining away to leave me alert and angry, angrier than I think I've ever been. 'Is it someone I know?'

'It is someone you know, but I need to explain ...'

'Who? Just tell me who.' I cut her off. I don't want to hear a long explanation; all I need to know right now is who did this. I wish Gareth were here.

'The sample we ran that came back as a match to your sample came from Ted Durand ...'

'What?' I whisper, and as I catch sight of myself in the darkened window, I can almost see the colour draining from my face. Ted. The final name on my list, the only one I couldn't draw a line through. Ted, who I trusted. Ted, who thought we had a future together. My thoughts scramble, and I am almost unable to process what I've heard.

'Rachel? Rachel, are you still there?' Carrie's voice sounds in my ear, rich with concern and I nod, before remembering she can't see me.

'Yes,' I murmur, my hand covering my mouth, 'I'm still here.'

'Listen to me, Rachel,' her voice is serious, an underlying edge of steel running through it, 'it's important that you listen to me now – Ted Durand didn't do this to you.'

'But you just said ...'

'The sample came back as a match – but it's a familial match. Do you understand what that means, Rachel?

It means that although it was Ted's sample, he didn't do this – the DNA wasn't a complete match. It means the person responsible for your rape is a close, male family member of Ted's. Now, I've got officers on their way to Ted's house now but it's very important that you …'

'He's here,' I say, taking great care to keep my eyes away from Sean, training them hard on Robbie's face. 'Yes. That's right, he's here now. I'm not on my own.'

'Shit,' I hear Carrie swear and then shout something to someone in the background, 'Rachel, don't hang up …'

I drop the phone, crashing it back on to the stand as I try and get to my feet, nausea washing over me. Black spots dance at the corner of my eyes, and then, it's as though a curtain falls away and I remember everything.

'I'm not leaving, Gareth! It's bloody …' I try and look at my watch, but it twists loosely on my wrist and I can't keep it still long enough to catch the time. 'It's only just midnight. Just stay for one more drink.'

He grabs me by my upper arms and I wince – he's hurting me, his fingers digging hard into my bicep and I try to pull away but he's just too strong.

'For God's sake, Rachel, just do what I bloody ask you.' He almost shakes me, before looking over his shoulder, to where Jonno Barker is advancing towards us, a grim smile on his face.

'No. I'm not leaving. Just go if you're going.' I manage to struggle free and Gareth looks at me with something like disgust.

'Fine. Suit yourself.' He pushes past me and disappears in the throng of people filling the downstairs of Liz's house.

I make my way to the back of the kitchen, a little tipsy and fighting the start of a headache. I would have left with Gareth, if only he hadn't been so bloody about it – all he had to do was be decent, instead of being so damn bossy all the time.

Someone, I don't see who, hands me a glass of red wine and I gratefully swig from it, the heat of the wine and fuggy air of the room making my cheeks glow red. It's not long after that I start to feel poorly – I vaguely remember Ted trying to help me as my legs fail to carry me properly, then his voice as he tells me he needs to take a call. The next thing I know, I am on the bed in Liz's spare room, hands yanking at my leggings and my knickers, trying to kick him off but my legs refusing to co-operate.

'Get off me,' I wheeze, sick scorching the back of my throat as I try to twist away, bucking my hips … only nothing is working properly.

'You bitch, you total, utter bitch.' The voice hisses hotly in my ear. 'You think you're so fucking great, don't you? Let's see how great you really are.' Hands pull my thighs apart and tears run down my cheeks as he forces himself between my legs. 'You'll get what you deserve, you whore … you fucking, god damn, home-wrecking whore.'

I try to scream, twisting my head away but his hand clamps down over my mouth and I smell that lemony aftershave. He's too strong, and my limbs are like lead … all I can do is lie there and wait for it to be over.

'Mum?' Robbie kneels in front of me, my hands held tightly in his. 'What is it? What's happened?' I pull my hands away and shakily get to my feet, my eyes never leaving Sean's face.

'It was you,' I whisper, as Robbie looks on in confusion, 'it was *you*. You did this to me.'

'Mum? Sean?' Robbie looks from me to Sean and back again, his voice shaky as realization starts to dawn. Sean steps forward, his chest puffed out, but I stand my ground.

'It was me.' A smirk plays about his lips, and I have to swallow hard in order to not be sick. 'You deserved it.'

'What? You did this, to my mum? After everything she's done for you?'

Robbie draws back his fist, but he's too late. Sean has Gareth's paperweight in his hand; he must have palmed it while I was on the phone, knowing as soon as I said Carrie's name that it was all over. In one swift move, he raises his arm and cracks Robbie across the face, sending him to the floor.

'Rob!' I rush to him, his poor cheek already bruised and bleeding. He lies dazed on the floor, one hand cradling his face.

'I'm all right, Mum,' he says, blinking as he struggles to a sitting position. 'Just get away from him, don't let him hurt you.' He looks up at Sean. 'Why? Why did you do it, Sean?'

Sean smirks, but two spots of colour blaze high on his cheeks. 'Do what?'

'You *raped* me,' I whisper, bile rising in my throat.

'Rape?' He raises his eyebrows. 'Prove it was rape, Rachel. You've got a reputation for sleeping with people you're not married to ... and you can't even remember a thing.'

'You drugged me!'

'Did I? There's no proof of that either, is there?' His voice is a little unsure, but that smirk still sits firmly on his face.

'Why though, Sean?' Robbie's voice is thick with tears, as he lies on the floor, blood dripping from his split cheek.

'Like I said, she deserved it.' As his words reverberate around the room, his bravado seems to waver for a second.

'What do you mean, I deserved it?' I get to my feet, throwing another look of concern towards Robbie. His cheek is bruised, but he's alert. Stepping towards Sean, even though my heart is in my mouth, I front up to him meeting his gaze full on. *I will not be afraid.*

'You *deserved* it, Rachel, that's what I mean!' Sean's eyes are shining with tears, as he raises his voice. 'You're a whore, a slut, a home-wrecker, someone who loves nothing more than ruining other people's lives. I saw you with my dad.'

'This is about Ted?' While every fibre of my being tells me to get out, to get away from Sean, I know this might be my only chance to find out his reasoning behind all of this.

'I saw you with him, in the summer. At the barbecue, you came out of the toilet and he came out just after. Your shirt wasn't buttoned properly, and he had a smudge of lipstick by his mouth. I knew what you'd been up to, I'm not stupid. My mum was never going to come home if she found out what my dad did with you, you dirty cow.' For a moment, he looks like the small boy I remember, before his face hardens again.

'Your mum was already gone by then, Sean. I had nothing to do with your mum leaving your dad. It was already over between them.'

'Yeah, you'd think, wouldn't you?' Sean smiles, but there is a manic edge to it, and his eyes glint dangerously in the lamp light. 'Only, I overheard that too. Remember, Rachel? The night you and my Dad nearly got caught?'

I glance down to where Robbie looks up at me, fear and confusion and hurt written all over his face.

'I heard my dad telling you that if it hadn't been for you, maybe he would have fought harder to get my mum back. For us to be a proper family again. Only you had to come along and fuck things up, didn't you?'

'But you were so concerned — that day when I threw up ... the day I bumped into you by the park and you walked me home. If you hate me so much, why do that?'

'I had to keep in there, didn't I? My dad wouldn't discuss it, so how else was I supposed to know if the police had any idea of what had happened? Of course, you couldn't stop yourself from spilling your guts, self-centered bitch that you are.'

Disgust crawls over his features, and I shiver at the hate I see in his eyes.

Standing next to the desk, I inch my fingers closer to where Gareth's letter opener lies behind a stack of papers. Visible to me, it is hidden from view from where Sean stands. I must have something to protect myself and Robbie, if the need arises. Sean is all over the place and he's already hurt Robbie once. A thought strikes me, and I glance down at Robbie, my faith in him shaken a little. He seems as shocked by this turn of events as I am, but there is something that niggles at me.

'You said you weren't at the party,' I blurt out, my fingers finally closing around the handle of the opener. 'Robbie said you were both at your house for the entire evening.'

'Ha. Good old Rob — gave me the perfect alibi!' Sean steps around the side of the desk, just as I whip the blade behind my back. 'Tell her, Rob. Tell her how you lied — tell her how her own son gave her rapist an alibi.' He leans down and pulls Robbie to his feet, despite the slight height advantage Robbie has over Sean, Sean seems to have superhuman strength as he pulls Robbie to standing with no effort at all.

'Mum …' Robbie stutters, tears streaking his cheeks, 'I'm sorry, I didn't know …'

'*Tell her*,' Sean roars, delivering a blow to the side of Robbie's head. Robbie cowers, trying to cover his hand with his hands, but Sean pulls him round to face me. 'Go on, tell her.'

'I … l … l … lied,' Robbie wheezes out, his face contorted by fear, one eye already closing with the force of Sean's punch as Sean holds him by the hair. 'I told them we were home at Sean's all night. I was, I was there all night, but Sean went out at about midnight, just after. He told me he was going to go and score some weed.' He swallows painfully. 'I told him I'd found the bills in Dad's drawer and I was worried. I wanted to make some money that I could give Dad, to help out a bit.'

'Oh, Rob,' I say quietly, my heart breaking.

'Sean said he could score some weed and then I could sell it on at college. I thought I was doing the right thing. But Sean couldn't get any. Now I know why.' He breaks off, his voice strained with the effort of holding back tears.

'It all just fell into place,' Sean shrugs, and the blood turns to ice in my veins. He planned everything down to a T. 'Rob told me about the money and I thought, *yes! She'll lose her house, all her stuff. People will look at her like the piece of shit she really is.* All I had to do was let Gareth know what you'd been up to, and then he would leave you as well – you really should keep a better eye on your mobile, Rachel.'

'That was you – you sent that text for Gareth to find?' I adjust my grip on the blade behind my back, ready to strike if I need to.

He rolls his eyes. 'Yeah, I sent that text from your phone to my dad – it was a bit awkward – you nearly caught me!' The light tone drops from his voice and his eyes go flat and blank, causing an icy finger to run down my spine. 'Only it didn't work, did it? Gareth still didn't leave you – he still stayed for more, meaning I had no option but to up my game. I had to find a way to destroy you – to make you repulsive to everyone around you. What is it about you, Rachel, that these men find so attractive? I mean, I didn't think you were that good in the sack – bit unresponsive, you know?' He gives me a wink, and twists Robbie's hair in his fist, so he can't move. 'And then ... well, I started enjoying myself. For someone who reckons she's such a strong, independent woman, you're remarkably easy to frighten, Rachel.'

'All of it was you, wasn't it?' I whisper, everything falling into place. 'The letters on the fridge – I saw you, that day, outside the police station. Had you just come from my house? You'd been inside my house, leaving a threatening message, and then straight after you were there, looking after me while I threw up in the gutter ...' My stomach twists at the realization that Sean is responsible for everything, not just what happened that night at the party.

He gives another little shrug, like it's no big deal. 'Just my luck that Jason turned up on your doorstep that day too, eh? That was a stroke of luck – made him look dead suspicious.'

But I am not listening, lost in my own thoughts, adding up all those moments that conspired to make me think I was losing my mind.

'And the car ... you must have scored that word into the door before you rang the bell to call for Robbie, acting like nothing happened?' I shake my head, trying to piece it all together, my eyes never leaving Robbie as Sean holds him tightly. 'And when I was running … that was you too, wasn't it? Following me, making sure I could hear your footsteps behind me. What would you have done if I had turned round and seen you?'

'You wouldn't have done,' he says arrogantly, 'you're not the strong, independent, good-hearted person that you like people to think you are, Rachel. You're dark inside – selfish, greedy and manipulative, only out for yourself. You deserved everything I gave you.'

'How fucking dare you?' I murmur, the rage that has slowly been building the entire time Sean has been talking boiling up and over the edge, taking me with it. A red mist descends, and I know that now it's him or me – one of us has to finish the other, for good.

'What did you say to me?' He glares at me, raising the paperweight once more, ready to bring it crashing down on Robbie's temple. 'Be careful, Rachel, you only have one thing left to lose now.' He smirks down at Robbie and I use his distraction to my advantage.

'I said, *how fucking dare you!*' I roar, as I fly towards him, letter opener raised in my fist. 'How fucking dare you threaten to take my son from me? How dare you try to ruin my life? You think this is it? You think I'll just curl up and die in a corner? You will *never* break me, you piece of shit, and things will *never* go back to how they were before.' In his surprise, he drops Robbie to the floor, and I thrust the tip of the letter opener against the cool white of his throat.

'You are nothing more than a *child*,' I sneer, grateful that from the angle of his head he can't see the way the blade shakes in my fist, adrenaline coursing through my veins, 'a child, who understands nothing of the adult world. Your mother didn't want to be part of your family for her own reasons, nothing to do with me. And you may have hurt me, you may have frightened me, you may have made me suspicious of everyone I've ever been close to, but you … DO … NOT … WIN, do you understand me?' The tip of the blade breaks the skin of his throat, a tiny bubble of red appearing at the tip. Mesmerized by the maroon burst, I have to stop myself from pressing harder, from thrusting it deep into his artery.

'Rachel! Stop!' The door flies open and hands grip me by the upper arms, pulling me away from him. I turn to see two police officers, striding towards Sean, handcuffs in hand. Gareth is behind me, his hands on my arms keeping me from flying back towards to Sean, while Carrie stands in the doorway. I drop the blade to the floor, leaning back against the reassuring warmth of Gareth. He spins me to face him, pulling me tightly into his arms, as I start to sob, the fear of the past three months rising into a tidal wave of emotion. A moment later, I feel another set of arms come around me as Robbie stands with us, and we watch, as a family, as Sean – childhood friend, once part of our family, now unrecognizable as the small boy I welcomed into our home – is led away. Finally, it's over.

27

EARLY FEBRUARY – FIVE WEEKS AFTER
THE PARTY

It's a damp, drizzly afternoon, the light already fading from the day even though it's not even three o'clock yet when my world shatters for a second time in as many months. Gareth is home, not quite ready to go back into the office after the events that took place just a few days ago, and it is he that opens the door when the doorbell rings, startling us both. I sit on the edge of the couch, unable to relax, hoping that he can get rid of whoever it is. There has been an endless stream of phone calls and visitors, mostly Helen Faulkner wanting to write a follow-up piece, now that Sean has been arrested, her white blonde hair bobbing past the front window every other day, it seems. I have refused to see or speak to her every time, and I'll refuse again today. But it's not Helen Faulkner that Gareth leads into the dimly lit sitting room.

'Carrie. Hello.' I get to my feet, my heart leaping in my chest. Surely, she must be here to give us news? Suddenly, irrationally, I feel as though I don't want to hear whatever she has to say. 'Shall I make some tea?'

'No, I'm fine. Thank you.' Carrie says, with a weak smile. 'I have an update for you, Rachel.'

I nod, without speaking, and then suddenly Gareth is beside me, his arm around my shoulders, awkwardly. I shrug him off and take a seat. There is no me and Gareth, not right now, probably not ever again – I don't have the headspace to think about what he's done, the lies he's told. Not yet. Until I can, I am struggling to tolerate his presence.

'Rachel.' Carrie sits down beside me, her knees almost touching mine. 'I'm here because there's been a development.' She takes a deep breath. 'Sean Durand has been granted bail.'

'Bail?' I feel my breath stick in my throat in horror, the ground lurching beneath my feet. 'How? How can they grant him bail?' I feel sick, icy fingers of dread at the back of my neck. *He's not locked up. He's out there, somewhere.* I fight to draw in a deep breath, hunching my shoulders, panic threatening.

I feel Gareth's hand come down between my shoulder blades, rubbing my back and despite how I feel about him, his touch calms me and I manage to breathe again.

'How, Carrie?' he asks, his words echoing mine, his hand moving down to mine, our fingers linking. 'How can they let him go after what he did? His mother lives in the US – did you know that? What's to stop him from leaving the country?'

'Let me explain,' Carrie says. 'I'm so sorry, I know this is very difficult for you both … but I'll tell you everything.' Gareth nods, his face ashen. I swallow hard, a thick lump of – something – rage, or maybe fear sticking in my throat and I wait to hear what Carrie has to say. 'Sean has been released on conditional bail terms. This means that he must return to his known address to live – Ted has agreed to this. Sean has to hand in his passport to the police, so there is no chance of him absconding to his mother. He has to agree to not contact either you, Rachel, or Gareth or Robbie, and he must report to Kingsnorth police station every Monday afternoon at four p.m. He has agreed to all of these conditions.'

'So, he just ... walks free? Is that what you're telling me?' My eyes widen with horror. The idea of Sean walking the streets, as though nothing ever happened chills me to the bone. He was supposed to be punished – he ruined my life, and he was supposed to pay the price for that.

'It's not that he walks free, Rachel,' Carrie says, 'but yes, he will be at home, not in prison. But he cannot contact you under any circumstances, OK? And if you're at all worried, or if he does attempt to contact any of you, you can call us immediately.'

'No, this isn't good enough, it isn't fair ...' Gareth starts speaking but I tune him out, lost in my own thoughts, lost in the idea that I could bump into Sean on the streets of West Marsham, that he is free to carry on living his own life. *But only until he's sentenced*, a little voice speaks at the back of my mind. I don't know a lot about the British justice system, but I do know that rape can carry a hefty sentence. *Once he's behind bars, that's it – he can never touch anyone again. He'll be properly punished.*

'Rachel?' Carrie is looking at me with concern, her brows knitted together in a frown. 'Did you hear what I said?'

I shake my head. 'Sorry. What did you say?'

'Sean's pleading not guilty, Rachel. There's going to be a trial.'

Not guilty. The words tumble over and over in my mind as I lay in bed, watching a shaft of moonlight move across the ceiling as sleep doesn't come. I asked Carrie how he could plead not guilty, when I heard him admit everything, when

267

the DNA sample came back linked to him, and her only explanation is that he is going against the advice of his legal team, presumably to cause maximum distress to me.

I'll now have to go through all of it again, in court, and hope that a jury believes me over him. There is a hard knot in my stomach, built of rage and fear, at the image of him in my mind shaking his head, smug grin on his face, mouthing the words *not guilty* over and over. I was so sure that this ordeal was finished – once I saw Sean being led from the house, flanked by two police officers, I thought it was all over, and I was safe. Sean was in custody and he would never be able to hurt me again. And now … now I realize *it isn't over*. It will never be fully over until I finish it myself, just as I said I would all those weeks ago in Amy's sitting room.

Every night I toss and turn, craving the oblivion of sleep, but it eludes me until I barely know who I am any more. Thoughts of Sean consume me, the memory of his hands pushing me down onto the bed, the smell of his aftershave, the fear I have felt every day since I woke up in Liz's spare bedroom. After too many sleepless nights to count, I know what I must do. The only person who can make sure I'm safe is me.

I creep out of the house early one morning and walk over to Ted's house. My hands shake as I watch as Ted leaves the house in a rush, tie flying, coffee mug in hand as he jumps into the car and screeches away, obviously late for work. I watch as, two hours later, the curtains open in the front room, and Sean appears, clad only in a T-shirt and boxer shorts, clearly having just woken up.

I watch as, later on that day, he walks down to the shops – not the ones closest to the house, he can't shop there now, as they'll all be gossiping about him – but the ones towards the outskirts of the village, raising a hand in a vulgar gesture to someone who beeps as they pass him.

I watch, day after day, night after sleepless night, sick with exhaustion and worry, as Sean carries on about his business, no burden evident on his shoulders, no remorse etched onto his face. I watch as he greets Amy as she leaves her flat, smirking as she gives him a look of disgust and turns her back. I watch as he greets a teenage girl in the park, leaning down to pet her dog and I want to scream at her to *run, don't you know what he's done? Don't you know who he is?*

Until, finally, I don't need to watch any more. The timing is right, at last. In the park – the one where I walked Thor, met Amy, kissed Ted – I sit on the bench at the end of the path, the light almost gone as another chilly winter's evening sets in. The secluded bench, closest to the trees. Huddled up in a black hoody, scarf, and woolly hat pulled down low over my hair, I watch for the last time, as Sean's shadowy figure enters the park, at four forty-five on Monday afternoon. He is walking home from his appointment at the police station, headphones in, intent on getting home before full dark. I watch as he approaches the bench, the trees behind casting ever darker shadows as the sun sinks completely below the horizon and I get ready.

Sean was right about one thing. There is a darkness inside me. I slide my hand into the pocket of my bag, my fingers wrapping around the cool blade of the knife I now keep there, its chill metal reassuring against the warmth of my fingers. This whole thing started with me. I'll make sure it ends with Sean.

ACKNOWLEDGEMENTS

Bringing this book to life has been a real labour of love, and there were times when I wasn't sure it was ever going to be finished (anyone who says second book syndrome is the worst has obviously never suffered from third book syndrome!), but here it is, and there is a whole army of people that I need to thank…

Kate Mills, my bloody awesome editor – thank you for letting me write what I wanted, for your guidance and your patience and for generally being Queen of F*cking Everything.

Lisa Moylett – if Carling made agents… This book would definitely never have made it without you and the fearsomely brilliant Zoë Apostolides – thank you for telling me I could do it when I didn't think I could. I'm so lucky to be part of the CMM family.

Lisa Milton and the whole HQ gang – I still have to pinch myself a bit that I am part of this fantastic publishing crowd, and I'm so grateful for all the hard work you put in to make our books the best they can be. You guys rock.

My lovely author friends, especially Christie Barlow, B A Paris, Roz Watkins, Darren O'Sullivan, Rachel Dove and Vicky Newham – thank you for letting me know

I'm not alone in my weird quirky rituals, (and for the wine – thank you for all the wine!).

My sisters, who show their support every time I write a book, by asking me what I'm having for dinner every day and sending me inappropriate cartoon drawings.

And finally, my crew – Nick, George, Izzy and Oscar. I couldn't do any of it without you.

Turn the page to read an extract from the quarter-of-a-million-copy bestseller *Between You And Me,* a psychological thriller with a twist you won't see coming…

'Compelling, chilling and an incredibly impressive debut'
Alexandra Brown, author of The Carrington Series

between
you
and me

LISA HALL

Prologue

It happened so quickly, and now there is so much blood. More than I ever thought possible. One minute, he was shoving me backwards, into the kitchen counter, the air thick with anger and words spoken in temper that could never be taken back. The next, he was on the floor, the handle of the knife protruding from his ribs. I don't even remember picking it up, only that I had to stop him. I back away, pushing myself up against the cold, granite surface, across the room from where he lies. I feel light-headed and sick, sweat prickling along my spine. He reaches up to me with a shaky hand, slick with his own blood, and I draw back even further. He is slumped on the floor, back resting against the kitchen counter, a lock of hair falling over his brow. He is pale, a sheen of sweat shining on his forehead. A coppery, iron tang fills the air and I want to retch. Turning, I lean over the kitchen sink, where I heave and heave but nothing comes up. I wipe my mouth on a tea towel and push my shaking hands through my hair. I need to try to think calmly, rationally. I need to phone for an ambulance, and I need to get my story straight. I'll tell them that he slipped and fell on the knife, a brutal, heavy knife usually used for carving the Christmas turkey, not carving into other people. That we weren't arguing, just talking. It was an accident; one minute he was fine, the next he was on the floor. I'll tell them that I didn't see what happened — I have to protect myself. I can't tell them that I snapped. That a red mist descended and for just a few seconds I felt like I couldn't take it any more, the shouting, the aggression and the lies. That in just a split second all rationality left me and I grabbed the knife and thrust it firmly into my husband's stomach.

Chapter One

SAL

The first time you hit me it was a shock, but not a surprise. Surely, this is the natural progression of things? Starting with the little things, like wanting to know where I've been, who I've spoken to, escalating to a little push here and a shove there, until now, when a slap almost feels like a reward – and I'm thankful that it wasn't something worse, that there are no bones broken this time.

I remember the first time I saw you. Nothing on earth had prepared me for it and the sight of you hit me like a punch in the guts. Is that ironic? You stood there, in the Student Union bar, talking to a guy on your course I had seen around campus previously, a pint of Fosters in one hand. The sun was streaming in through a window behind you and you looked majestic, standing tall in a faded pair of Levi's and battered Converse, your fair hair standing out around you like an aura. I was with a group of people from my own course, planning on spending the evening with them, hashing over that day's lectures over a few drinks and then maybe heading out for a bite to eat. Once I saw you,

I knew my plans had changed and that I had to pluck up the courage to approach you. How would things have turned out if I hadn't asked you if you wanted another pint? If you hadn't accepted, and we hadn't spent the entire evening holed up in one corner of the SU bar? If I hadn't answered your call the next day and accepted your invitation to lunch? If we hadn't spent the whole of that following weekend together, in your flat, ignoring your roommate, the phone, the world outside?

Maybe I would be married to someone who doesn't think it's OK to hit me. To throw things at me if I have a different opinion to the one I 'should' have. Someone who doesn't think that being happily married means the other half of the partnership toeing the line at all times, no questions asked. Maybe you would be settled with someone else, someone who knows the right thing to say and the best way to handle you. Maybe you would be with someone you don't think defies you at every opportunity, although I don't, I really don't. You just think I do, regardless of what I do or what I say. Maybe both of us would be happier.

Chapter Two

CHARLIE

A file the size of a house brick lands on my desk and Geoff appears, throwing himself down in the chair opposite mine.

'Another bunch of stuff for you to work through – looks like you're not going home early tonight!' he wheezes, his face bright red as he struggles to catch his breath. Geoff is the size of a house himself, his enormous belly straining at the buttons of his grubby white shirt. Geoff is a colleague, my equal, but as he's fifteen years older than me, he treats me like a five-year-old. The man has a serious lack of ambition, and a serious case of body odour.

'Honestly, Geoff? It's 8pm – surely you don't think I'm even considering going home yet?' I give a little laugh as I pull the file towards me and start leafing through it; despite the fact I still have a ton of paperwork next to me that needs going through before I can even consider leaving the office. I feel the beginnings of a migraine tapping at my temples, no doubt brought on by tiredness from a 5am start and the stress of the never-ending paperwork that comes with the case I'm working on. The pressures of being a corporate lawyer are well known – the long hours, the stressful cases that take over our lives and eat into our personal time with our families – but it is all worth it in the end. The salary and benefits make sure of that.

'Well, don't stay up too late. You don't want to leave that pretty little family of yours too much; someone else might snap them up!' Geoff heaves his massive bulk from the leather chair across the desk from me, leaning over to ruffle my hair as he leaves.

'No chance of that, Geoff.' I grin at him through gritted teeth, the thud of my headache growing louder and making me wish I could slap his meaty fingers from the top of my head. He breezes out of the room, as much as a twenty-stone, fifty-year-old corporate lawyer can, and I reach for the phone. I dial our home number, leafing through the new documents while I wait for Sal to pick up. Engaged. I hang up and redial, using the mobile number. It rings and rings, and I picture it sitting on the kitchen side where Sal always leaves it, the hideous Johnny Cash ringtone that Sal insists on blaring out. It rings out and goes to voicemail.

'Sal, it's me. Who the fuck are you talking to? Call me back.' I slam the receiver down, and lean back in my chair, grinding the heels of my hands into my eyes to relieve the pressure that beats away there. I don't need this shit – I have enough on my plate to deal with in the office, without wondering who the hell Sal is talking to at eight o'clock at night.

An hour later, when my call still hasn't been returned, and I've tried the house phone numerous times, but to no avail, I bundle up the files and stuff them into my briefcase.

I can't concentrate on work all the time I am wondering why Sal isn't answering the telephone. All sorts of scenarios cross my mind, ranging from Sal knocking the phone off the hook so as not to be disturbed with some illicit lover, through to Sal on the phone to some other person (Sal's sister? Sal's mum? Someone I don't even know?), planning to leave me. I don't know what the hell Sal is playing at, but I'm not happy. I thought I had made the rules perfectly clear – if I call, Sal should answer. I spend every waking hour working my butt off to make sure I can provide for my family – I think the least Sal can do is answer the phone when I call. I smooth down my fair hair, sticking up at all angles where I've been pushing my hands through it in an attempt to calm myself while I concentrate on those bloody files Geoff dumped on me, grab my black jacket and head out the door. When I get home, Sal had better be there – and if Sal is there, I'll want to know why the bloody hell my calls this evening have gone unanswered. I'm not being ignored by anyone, least of all the person I chose to spend the rest of my life with.

ONE PLACE. MANY STORIES

Bold, innovative and
empowering publishing.

FOLLOW US ON:

@HQStories